One Small Life

A Novel By
Bernadette Chambers

authorHOUSE®

AuthorHouse™
1663 Liberty Drive, Suite 200
Bloomington, IN 47403
www.authorhouse.com
Phone: 1-800-839-8640

First published by AuthorHouse 2/6/2009

ISBN: 978-1-4389-3584-3 (sc)

Library of Congress Control Number: 2008912219

Printed in the United States of America
Bloomington, Indiana

This book is printed on acid-free paper.

Section 1: In The Beginning

The flowers and berries turn slowly and gracefully towards her as she walks among them in the strong noontime sun. They know her as the one who brings water when they're thirsty, shelters them from the cold with warm hay, and speaks softly of her gratitude for their beauty and their life-giving fruit. Today, she knows, they will gladly give of their abundance so she and Grandmother can stay strong and filled with life. Joy flows from her dancing fingers as she fills her dish with berries and the earth echoes that joy back to her. Absorbed in the bliss of her activity, she scarcely notices a cold breeze begin to sweep the landscape and the earth fearfully turn its attention outwards.

Mari looks up from the side garden as the men slowly and furtively approach her home, where Grandmother lies deep into her afternoon nap. Quickly and quietly she moves sideways into the rows of golden corn, becoming invisible in their protective arms. She watches as the two men, like ghostly invaders, silently approach the front door. A dark shadow moves with them, covering each of their footsteps, killing the plants they walk over and polluting the air around them, rolling slowly, slowly towards her in her hiding place. Swiftly, she scooches down in the corn rows – grateful for their presence and for their height and density. One of the men takes a knife from his belt and pierces the screen on the unlocked door, reaches through it, and slowly opens the door from the inside. She feels her breath quicken and the hair on the back of her neck lift as if it's been electrified.

She hears nothing from inside Grandmother's home. Nothing during the terrible days when she fears that even the arms of the corn won't be enough to protect her. Nothing during the nights when darkness closes around her, and she ventures to peek into the windows of her home where Grandmother lies still, and where the intruders sleep in their beds and eat their food.

Finally, they depart as abruptly as they'd come and she leaves the shelter of the cornfield and goes back inside. Grandmother lies still and quiet. The redness in her hair has turned brown and hard and she knows that grandmother will never again wake up.

Others come – this time, more men and women too. And this time, she doesn't hide. Nothing is left inside the little home that makes her want to stay, and she doesn't protest when these intruders lead her away. She is weak from hunger and lack of sleep, dirty and disheveled and grief stricken. The life that she knew is ended . . . .

Chapter 1

The sunlight pours through her body, bleaching her white, white, white as the driven snow. Mari longs for the rain, for shadows brought by the night, to hide, to shelter herself in darkness.

The sunlight is an enemy to her now, turning her world upside down and inside out. Only in the darkness does she feel safe, hidden - secure within herself. Her longings and her pain are her own, and from the depth of her soul, cry out to be fed, looked after, watered, cared for, until the darkness is all that matters, and her world becomes the solitary place that feels comfortable to her, puts her at ease, feels like home.

Few are bidden to come, and fewer still enter.

Ripping her out of her darkness becomes the cause of some, but they soon give up. It is where she belongs, and she despises their pulling and prodding up into the sunlight. How dare they! Caught in the web of their own ambition, their own ideas of right and wrong, they struggle for awhile, and finally need help themselves to come free of their own frustration. She is not to be redeemed. The darkness is a part of her and she needs it. Indeed, the darkness is all that holds her together and makes her life worth living.

She curls up inside herself, a fetus still inside its mother in the darkness of the womb, comfortable, not yet willing to be born!

She endures time in the light now simply because she has no choice. It's as necessary a part of her day as enduring the darkness is part of the lives of those who love light. Some can simply turn on the light and cancel the darkness out of their lives with the flip of a switch. She wishes she could do such a thing with the light that now invades her life, simply flip a switch and go back into the darkness that she needs.

She wants none of their redemption, only to be left alone. They find her in closets, in corners, by herself under the stairs, trying to block out the light. Always they bring her, forcibly if necessary, back to where they think she should be, back to the horrible, glaring brightness. Always, she seeks to be alone in the darkness.

No one cares what she seeks or what she thinks. Only their wishes matter. And they call her insane!

She knows that she's different from them. To her, they are the mad ones, always insisting on having their own way, never allowing someone like her just to be.

Their intrusions make her feel like a cockroach, searching for darkness, looking for a place where she can't be found.

She wants no part of the human race. To her, they're lost souls anyway; they just don't know it yet. She knows what they have yet to learn - that there is hope only in the darkness, in standing alone, in the safety of shadows. She is not mad. She *knows!*

Never, ever could she force herself upon someone like they force themselves on her. She feels raped, unclean, diminished by the light. It shrivels her, dries her up into nothingness. Let them pull and push at her. She knows that she alone can decide who she is and what she wants. She's here because others think she is mad, but she knows differently. If there is madness here, it isn't in her. It's in those who force their will on others without listening, without caring, without recognizing who they violate.

Chapter 2

"Looks like my dream job will just have to wait."

Cindy's bitter remark falls on deaf ears.

She hurries toward her nursing job on the night shift at Tillsboro Mental Hospital. She's already exhausted from a full day at home, and now this. It's a bitch trying to keep it all together with no man around and sole responsibility for everything on her shoulders. To hell with the bastard who left her with a mortgage and three kids to look after by herself. She's making it - that's all that matters. She can stand anything as long as the pay is good. She puts up with the screaming and the flying shit so her bills get paid on time and her kids eat regularly. That's all that matters to her right now. That's what needs to get done.

"One day at a time," she thinks. "Just take it one day at a time."

She would just as soon be like the rest of the world and forget that this place even exists. These are the dregs of society, people who can't be trusted to live even on the streets, who can't find something to eat and a place to sleep for the night, who can't pass another human being without causing some disruption in the person's life.

Some have families who care. Most have run out of caring - it's simply impossible for anyone to care too much or too long for these people. How can anyone live themselves if they are constantly caught up in this craziness? There's a necessary detachment, or the person who cares ends up in the same condition as the inmate. Their normal world ceases to exist and the insanity becomes their life too. No, it's never a good thing to care too much.

Cindy is very careful herself not to become attached, not to listen too closely, not to get too involved with the patients. She medicates them, she watches to see that they don't hurt themselves, each other, or another staff member, and she does her paperwork. That's it. That's what she's getting paid to do. She does it well and she does it efficiently and, when she goes home, she tries not to take any of it with her.

She knows some of it clings to her like cobwebs when you've been down in a musty cellar, but she does her best to stay detached. She needs this job for now, and she has to make sure she keeps it, much as she despises being here.

During the day, she's Mom - provider, nurturer, caring, loving person. During the night, she's what? Dispenser of medicine, provider of discipline, paper pusher - she does what she's paid to do. Survival - that's what matters in this job; survival of yourself, of the people who work with you and of the inmates.

Why the inmates, she doesn't know. What lives do they live anyway? What is the purpose of their existence, except to make everybody else's life miserable? Who decided the fate of these unfortunates? And why? Existence itself is so difficult for them. What sort of gods had cast them such an impossible lot?

The dreary gray building looms as she heads for the front doors and her evening shift. It casts a pall over the surrounding landscape, its façade indicative of what's inside. The building, like the inmates themselves, aren't wanted - not here - not in this community of freshly swept streets, hanging planters, mown lawns and prettily painted homes.

Actually, this particular building would have been unwanted anywhere, except maybe hell. Hopelessness, misery and despair seep out through the very mortar which holds the dirty, gray bricks together. It casts a shadow over the surrounding landscape, and especially over the town after which it is named.

There's a feeling in the town that they have done enough, suffered long enough under the stigma of having a mental hospital as part of their heritage. Every year or so there's a movement to shut it down and move the inmates elsewhere, anywhere, as long as it's out of this community. The movement is particularly strong when one or more of the inmates escape and the community lives in fear until he's caught and taken to a more secure facility. They ask if it isn't time to tear down the old building and disperse the patients elsewhere so the townsfolk can sleep at night, so they can forget that there are people such as these who don't fit into the world in a 'normal' way, who can't cope on their own, who need others to make sure they don't hurt themselves or someone else. What kind of life is that, anyway?

She feels the building sucking her in, depressing her, trying to get inside her and claim her too. She consciously raises a shield around herself.

"Just eight hours," she tells herself, "just eight hours and I'll be walking away from here and into the sunlight again. I'll be back in my normal world of light and caring and love and joy - the real world - the world of my children, my family."

Cindy has no intention of letting this horrible building and the people inside bring her down to their level. She knows who she is; she can never be one of them.

She opens the heavy front door and steps inside for her evening's work.

Chapter 3

Mari watches the night fall slowly down around her and rain pour into the crevices and cracks of the old, dark, worn-down building. She loves the rain, loves to listen to it thundering and pounding on the roof and the grounds. All she wants is an open window or door so she can hear it. The sound of the rain soothes her in some special way, as a friend come to let her know that, despite everything, life is worth living. It helps her make sense of things. It washes over the dryness of the day and makes her feel alive and whole again. Even in here, if only they would let the rain in or at least open a window so it could be heard she knows she could go on.

If they would just let her sit by the window and listen. She wants to - needs to - listen to the rain. She sneaks over beside the window and sends her mind adrift, letting in only the sounds of the rain pounding on the windows and the rooftop. She watches the drops fall into puddles and run down the walkways, bringing life to the sad, dried up lawn and whatever plantings have managed to survive the light and the heat of the past weeks.

It's dark and it's rainy. She pushes at the window and it opens a bit, just enough so she can hear the outside.

She can be in love now.

She can live.

She wants to be naked in the rain - to bloom, to blossom, to grow - like the grass and the plants. For now, she sits by the window and can only wish to be part of it. It's enough though; it brings her hope. Someday, she knows, she will live in the rain and the darkness, her outside world matching her inside world.

Mari's thoughts trail backward. Always, she loved the rain. Even as a child, she would dream of the days when the rain would pour down around her, invading every crevice of her body, washing her clean in a way nothing else could ever come close to doing.

She had once hoped that when she grew up, she would move to India. During the monsoon season, she could follow the rain as it poured into the villages and the cities, walking through it, swimming in it, living in the rain. And the darkness - the darkness - such a friend to her now. Sometimes they both come together, the rain and the darkness, and that is heaven. Sometimes she has to make do with one or the other. She prefers the rain, because it always brings at least some semblance of darkness with it, but the darkness doesn't necessarily bring the rain. So she prefers the rain. Darkness is necessary to her now, but the rain is a blessing.

In the darkness, she can feel her before life, before she had been imprisoned in this building with people who force their will on her, before someone decided that they didn't like who she is - that she is, in fact, a liability to them and needs to be changed or locked up. In the darkness, she can feel what life was like when she was a real person - when someone had looked at her and listened to her and cared about her.

She sees the gentle mist outside the home she shares with Grandmother. Dusk is announcing the beginning of nightfall. Knit, purl, knit, purl - she watches grandmother quietly knit as darkness falls around them. A gentle breeze caresses them and the fragrance of lilacs and Roses from their gardens floats in through the open doors and windows and tickles their noses. She tells Grandmother of her life and how she's feeling and what she intends. No one judges her, only listens and loves. The answers to her questions are suggestions, never orders; her decisions are always her own. She is growing into herself, and she likes that. She feels safe, secure and competent. Life is good.

Chapter 4

"Again tonight," thinks Cindy. "She's at that window again tonight."

"What's a girl like her doing in a place like this anyway?"

She looks to be about the same age as Cindy's oldest daughter, a pretty girl with long, golden brown hair flowing down her back. Her pale skin and strikingly bright green eyes framed by long, dark eyelashes give her an ethereal, almost angelic quality. She looks out of place, not frightened but uneasy, like she doesn't belong here really, like she doesn't belong anywhere on this earth.

"You'd expect - - what is it about her?" Cindy thinks. "She almost seems trapped here from another place, another time, another dimension - ghostly - unreal - like a sprite."

Cindy feels herself being drawn to the young girl. She realizes that she's treading in dangerous waters, and quickly pulls herself back.

"She certainly doesn't help herself seem any more real by the way she constantly hides in corners and in the darkness, like she's trying to make herself invisible."

She's no trouble to look after, never making any kind of fuss except when they try to take her away from the window and have her take the bedtime medications.

Cindy wonders what it is that she's seeing out that window.

Deliberately, Cindy looks away. She has too much to do; she can't be wondering and worrying about any particular patient. It always comes down to this - first you start wondering, then you find yourself involved in the patient's life in some unknown way. This young girl is dangerous to her because she reminds Cindy so much of her own children. If she wants to hang on to her own sanity, the only way to do so is to simply ignore the patients, pretend that they don't exist as people, only as things that need caring for, like plants, or inanimate objects that need to be dusted or weeded. Detach, detach, she needs to stay detached from them; no wondering. Get to the paperwork and ignore the girl at the window until it's time to medicate her and put her to bed. She always resists, but only a little. She seems to have no energy for much resistance.

Cindy knows that she needs to stay detached from the patients, not because she's inhuman or uncaring, but because she has nothing more to give. The truth is that she knows she's too vulnerable, that she could care too much, become too involved, and then, where would she be? Where would she and her family end up if she fell over the edge of sanity herself, down into the rabbit hole of mental illness? This is what terrifies her. This is what she's afraid can happen if she tries too hard to help, if she identifies too much with any one particular patient.

Every once in a while, she feels herself slipping over the edge. The realization that she is the only person who can or will look after her own children, that they need her desperately, helps her to stay detached. Her own struggles to survive have taken their toll, and she knows that her children need all her emotional energy if they're going to make it themselves. She needs to keep her own children from ending up in a place like this, or worse. She needs to keep herself sane for them.

There are times when she thinks how much easier it would all be to simply give up, to live in the corners like the girl at the window, to let someone else take care of her, to give her medications, tell her when to go to bed and when to get up in the morning, make her meals and structure her day for her - just give up the fight. She always manages to catch herself, though. How can she imagine herself a patient in a place like this? Here, there's no hope. At least she can envision her children rising above her own life. That's her reason to go on, to keep things together, to love and to care. Her children - she needs to keep things together for them.

Cindy refocuses her energy on the paperwork. Again, her eyes wander to the girl at the window - so still, so calm, so unseeing of everything around her except the night and the rain. She notices the window, open ever so slightly, perhaps to help the child feel more connected to the outside world. That's all right - whatever works for her. Whatever soothes her, works for Cindy too. It keeps the peace in here until it's time for medications. The girl always balks at taking her medications. It seems that she doesn't want to come away from the window even for sleep.

Where has she come from? Why is she in here? Cindy knows that, no matter how hard she tries to keep it from happening, this girl is going to stay with her. It certainly won't hurt, she tells herself, to check the files, to see how long she's been here and why. What could possibly have brought a young, beautiful girl like her to this living hell hole of misery and despair?

Chapter 5

It's medication time, time to leave the window and her backwards thoughts and sleep the drugged sleep of the insane. Mari knows that it does no good to resist, but she does so anyway. They always win. Sometimes, when the night shift changes and she has a new caretaker for awhile, she manages to get rid of the pills and stay awake into the night. Most times, she simply resists as much as she can, but they always manage to have their way.

She watches the night nurse approach. This one is kinder than the others - a thin woman, almost emaciated, her uniform never neatly starched or ironed. Her brown hair, flecked with wisps of blonde, sticks out at various unruly angles from the elastic that she uses to keep it in place. Her shoes are noticeably old and scuffed, her legs showing the beginnings of varicose veins. Mari feels safe when she's nearby, feels the energy of a kindred spirit who knows what it is to hurt, to suffer, to do without. Mari doesn't mind when this nurse approaches; her hard life has given her a warmth that soothes the cold edges of this prison and makes her coming welcome.

It always surprises Mari when the nurse insists that she take her pills and swallows them. It just doesn't feel right. It feels as if this person should be on her side. That's something that she will never get used to - the outside not matching what she knows is the inside truth.

Soon, the good night and the rain will be shut out and the nightmares will begin.

She shudders. Sometimes, she feels that she can tell this nurse what it's like when she takes the pills, why she resists, why she always pulls back. But no one has ever listened to her in this place, why should she think it's going to happen now?

They don't understand. If they did, they wouldn't force her into sleep, to dream these terrible dreams, to awaken so much worse than when she went to sleep. Sometimes she doesn't know if she's dreaming, or if it's actually happening over and over and over.

"Please," she silently begs, "Don't let it happen. Please don't make me sleep." But no one listens! The rain and the blessed darkness drift away and she cries softly, knowing what is waiting for her.

She's drugged and dragged into a place where the horrible brightness shines all night.

And once again, she is back at her home, creeping silently, silently up to the window. She needs to know what's happening. She peers through the bedroom window to see Grandmother lying on the bed with her life pouring, pouring out, until nothing is left of hope and caring and life and love.

When the evil men leave, she goes back inside and the rains begin. The parched earth drinks its fill and everything is washed clean and fresh. The sun goes down, nighttime comes, and the darkness and the rain bring safety. How she welcomes the night and the darkness. It becomes part of her. In the darkness, Grandmother is still with her.

But when it's light, other people come, and they drag her out of her home, out of the darkness, to this place where the light can't be turned off. It stays on, and her terrified screams only make it stronger . . . . .

They ask her questions – she doesn't know the answers. All she knows is that she is safe when she is alone in darkness. No one needs to bother her, no one needs to come. Why don't they just leave her alone, safe in the darkness . . . . . . waiting . . . . waiting for life to return to Grandmother . . . .

Morning arrives, and with it the bright light she hides from with her eyes open under the covers. Here, she can be safe. If she doesn't sleep, there will be no terror. If she stays under the covers, she can keep out the brightness.

They always make her come out. She tries to hide, to be alone, to stay in the darkness, but they always find her.

They lead her into the shower, where she closes her eyes and melds into the rain and the darkness once again. *Grandmother is reading to her now. The soft glow of the fireplace makes the shadows around her face dance and play, while the words flow from her lips into the evening air. It doesn't even matter so much what the story is about, it's the way she forms the words, the soothing sound of her voice mingling with the soft rain that patters on the windows and the rooftop. Each character comes alive; each place she reads about seems real, more real than life itself. Mari loves to hear Grandmother read.*

Grandmother's story is short today. A shrill voice keeps interrupting, getting louder and louder.

"Come on now, out. Time to come out of the shower, time for your meds and breakfast, time to face the day. Let's go."

Mari opens her eyes slowly to the blinding brightness. The stern looking nurse pulls at her, giving orders. Her crisp white uniform, the perfectly coifed hair, the tight, thin lips are a stark contrast to the kindly, frumpled evening nurse. It's useless to resist. A wave of nausea overwhelms her. Red is all she sees, bright, pulsating red, that same red she saw on the day that she had stopped being a person.

The gentle night nurse - where is she? Why does she come only in the night?

Doesn't she know that Mari needs her now, not just during the night? Now, in the daytime is when she needs her the most. Mari feels a connection, threads of silver flowing between them, invisible to everyone else but her.

She wonders, "Does the night nurse see them too?"

Mari knows the nurse feels them. She can tell by the way the nurse looks at her, by the way she acts when she thinks Mari isn't aware.

Where is she now? Why doesn't she help?

Chapter 6

Morning descends like a grey shroud. With her night shift finally over, Cindy leaves the hospital for home. Exhausted, she stumbles in through the front door and wakes the kids.

"Soon, I'll be able to get some sleep," Cindy thinks. "Soon as I get the three of them on the bus and off to school."

Usually, she's able to doze a bit at night while the ward is quiet but, for the past few days, that hasn't been happening. The young girl at the window bothers her a lot, more than she wants to admit to herself, probably because she reminds Cindy so much of her own daughters. She find herself, like it or not, obsessing over the girl.

It was quite a shock to go through the files and find out why she was locked up. She found it difficult to believe what she was reading.

"Why?" she asks herself, "And how could a child this young, who looks and seems so gentle and unassuming, do such terrible things?"

Cindy has tried to keep her distance, but she knows that it isn't going to be possible now. Against her better judgment, she's involved with a patient, and she knows she's being drawn further and further into Mari's life. She needs to find out more. What is it about this child? Could her impressions about her have been so wrong?

Usually, Cindy is very good at reading people. She has an instinct that tells her much more about them than they ever want to reveal to anyone. She knows that what she read in this child's file and what she's reading as she watches her each night don't make sense. There's something very wrong with the picture. She also knows that she's being drawn into it, and that she won't be able to keep her distance much longer. There's no way Cindy can believe that this child could have done what she is accused of doing. Someone has made a terrible mistake. How she knows this, Cindy can't imagine, but she does know it.

Cindy forces herself to stop thinking about Mari and the hospital and to focus on her children. She feeds them breakfast, kisses them goodbye and watches them board the school bus. Still in her nurse's uniform, she collapses onto the sofa.

A feeling of terror overwhelms her. She finds herself in an unfamiliar place, surrounded by a fog so thick that she can barely breathe. A low whimpering, crying, like the sound of someone who's despaired of life itself, draws her attention. She squints into the fog. It begins to give way. A large, grey mass moves deliberately, steadily towards the sound. Silently, carefully, Cindy moves closer and sees a large spider bearing down on a tiny figure stuck in the folds of a giant web. Slowly and confidently, it knows that its meal will still be there when it arrives. A small hand reaches out towards her, pleading. Cindy knows with certainty that any attempt to help will entangle her too, but to do nothing . . . . She glances around – there's no one else. Without further thought, she throws herself into the center of the web in the direction of the struggling child . . .

"Mom, Mom - are you OK?"

She startles, still in her dreamworld. *It's her child, her own child . . . .*

"Mom, what's wrong? Come on, wake up."

Slowly, she comes to, up out of the fog, and recognizes her own familiar living room. Sara, her oldest, is home from school and shaking her. She checks the clock on the wall.

She had put the kids on the bus at 7:30 and it's now 2:30. Did that horrible dream last that long? She must have been out for a full seven hours. That's unusual for her. Unfortunately, none if it was very peaceful, her haunted dreams calling her deep into some kind of minefield that she doesn't want to travel.

She looks at Sara's terrified face, and slowly lifts her arm to wipe the tears that run down her face. "It's okay honey. Mom just had a bad dream. I'm fine now. I'm glad you're home. How did your day go?"

Sara still looks frightened. "Mom, I thought something happened to you. I've been trying and trying to wake you."

"I guess I was really out of it, wasn't I?"

"You scared the life out of me." Sara starts to cry. She sits on the sofa and Cindy takes her in her arms and comforts her.

"It's all right, honey. I'm fine now."

Carefully and deliberately, she brings herself back to her own life. Forget the dream and trying to figure it out. What is important, she knows, is to look after those in front of her right now, sleep or no sleep, dream or no dream.

Cindy feels bad about scaring Sara like that. She knows she gives her oldest daughter too much responsibility, but she really has no choice. Someone has to look after the two little ones while she's at work, and she can't afford to pay anyone, not if they're going to live here in this nice community and eat decently. Her daughter doesn't complain much, just every once in a while. She would like to go out with her friends, have a little fun with other kids her age. Cindy feels bad that she has to be so grown up, with grown- up responsibilities so early in life, but she has no other choice. She tries to make it up to her daughter in other ways, but there are just so many demands on her time. What else can she do? Someday, life will be different. Someday, time and money won't be in such short supply and they will all be able to have some fun, to do the things they like.

But enough guilt. She's doing the best she can. And right now, she needs to clean up, make supper and get ready for work again. Sara helps her peel the potatoes and carrots, and they chat about her day as they work together.

She throws in some laundry. Thank God the old washer and dryer are still serviceable. Hopefully they'll hold together for awhile yet.

Get the mail - bills, bills, bills - which ones need to be paid first? It's always a balancing act to keep their world from falling apart.

All they need is one disaster and she doesn't know how they would cope.

Supper, then homework. She'll have to leave them when the dishes from supper are picked up and the two little ones are at the kitchen table doing their homework. She knows that Sara will make sure everyone has baths and clean pj's before she settles down to her own homework. Thank heavens for Sarah. What would she ever have done had she been a difficult child, or one who resented the work thrust upon her by her father's disappearance? Instead, Sara seems to want to make up to her mother for the additional work she has to do to keep things running. She acts like another adult in the house, even though she's only fifteen. Cindy wonders how she'd cope without her.

Sometimes, Cindy feels her resentment boiling over at the lot she has been cast, at having to be sole caretaker for her children, both emotionally and physically. It's so difficult. She tries to save herself from drowning in it by drawing into herself while she's at work, and by focusing completely on the kids when she is home. Even when the earth seems to keep breaking up under her feet, her kids are always a reason to keep going.

She kisses twelve-year-old Kelley and eight-year-old Julie good-bye and gives Sara a hug. She reminds the younger ones to listen to their sister and that she loves them, and walks out into the dusk. She is lucky that the hospital is only a few blocks away, just a nice walk, enough to give her a little exercise to get started on her evening.

She gives herself thirty-five minutes, and walks briskly enough to enjoy the night air, getting her mind together for the evening. She hates leaving the kids, especially at night, but it's necessary, and there's no point in dwelling on it. Soon enough, she will be at work and facing other problems. This is her time, so she focuses on enjoying her walk, which takes her through a wooded area and along the banks of the beautiful Midland River. The world seems to slow down for its evening rest, and she feels for the first time today that the universe is on her side. The daytime desperation and the nighttime hopelessness dissipate and she feels at peace.

The sounds and sight of the clear, cold waters of the river soothe her as she walks briskly along it towards the hospital and her evening's work. She feels a peace she never experiences while she's caught up in either of her jobs, that of looking after mental patients or that of looking after her children. The former is something she has to do in order to survive and the latter she does because her children are the light of her life and the only reason, some days, that she can go on.

But here, right now, the river speaks to her, mingles with the blood in her veins, fills her with peace and a feeling of timelessness. It tells her that she is where she's supposed to be at this time, in this moment of her life, and she needs to relax into it and enjoy it, if only for the present moment.

The river narrows, and she comes to the small bridge that leads over a culvert and into the parking lot of the mental hospital. Usually, this is the point in her walk where she can feel herself begin to spin down into a depression, but tonight is different. Tonight, she knows with certainty that she has a mission here, and that there is a reason she was led to this work. She doesn't know how she will accomplish it but somehow she needs to do something to save the child who sits by the window listening to the rain. Tonight, strangely, Cindy almost feels anxious to get to work.

Just before the river travels onward without her, out of the corner of her eye, she sees something caught on a pile of rocks. She turns her head, and it falls directly into her line of vision - a pile of what seems to be an unusual amount of rags and/or clothes sways back and forth in the current. Curious, she moves closer to check it out.

Cindy tries to scream, but the only thing that comes out of her mouth is the remains of her supper.

Chapter 7

A sudden shudder racks Mari's body! Something's happened - is happening - to the nurse she thinks of as her only friend. She can feel it, see it through her mind's eye.

She moves from her spot in the hallway towards the window, and scans the parking area that leads to the entranceway of her prison .... searching .... searching. A black crow, large and ominous in the evening dusk, enters her vision and she shakes her head to rid herself of the implications of its presence. She often watches the nurse as she appears from the direction of the woods, crosses over the small bridge and through the parking lot, heading towards the large, heavy front doors. The bright glow that surrounds her as she comes into Mari's sight diminishes as she comes closer and closer to the hospital.

This evening, she can't see the nurse, only the pandemonium of a group of people mingling, looking for .... looking for........

"*What?*" She wonders.

She knows that this has something to do with the nurse. Otherwise, why would they all be in the same place she walks each night - searching, searching? She feels it in her gut.

"What is it?" she wonders. "What are they looking for?" Her heart leaps. "A change? A change! But what?"

Through the barred window, the trees on the other side of the parking lot bow to her, their green and gold leaves glittering with dew and promise.

A dead frog, it's rotting, formless body floating jelly-like in a pool of brown and green scum, lies just below her window.

She watches, taking it all in, waiting . . . .

Suddenly, the group of people on the other side of the parking lot comes into focus. The nurse is in the middle of it all. She feels her presence, knows her anguish, cries silently for her.

Chapter 8

Cindy can feel herself losing it as she explains again and again to the police, to the detectives, together and individually, what happened. She explains how she had come along the pathway leading to the hospital and found this, with its' gaping mouth, empty eye sockets, dismembered body, this caricature of humanity swimming among the grasses and the reeds. She had once thought them so pure and so still. The river had once been her inspiration and her only salvation in her crazy, nothing-makes-sense nights and days.

Her head aches and her stomach heaves again and again, but the questions and the people asking them, are merciless. She feels she is not a person, feels invisible in this whole drama. Only the questions live, only the answers are important. No one notices her agony. No one cares that her only link to sanity has been ripped from her, viciously and without mercy. She feels herself falling . . . . falling . . . . . over the edge . . . . .of the world . . . . .

"Why?" she silently screams. "Why did this have to happen? What is it about me that causes me to be at the center of such horrible things? All I want is to look after my children, help them grow up to be happy. Nothing more. Is it too much to ask that life grant me a little peace and serenity on my way to work for a few minutes each day?"

Anger floods over her like white heat, waiting to erupt, boiling inside her heart and stomach. She can feel an explosion coming. She needs to get away. Away from the river that's betrayed her, away from the people who care only about the dead.

For the first time since she started working, all she wants is to open those heavy doors off in the distance and get inside them. At least, inside the building, she knows who she is and where she stands. Evil is evil. It doesn't come disguised as peace and serenity. It doesn't jump out suddenly, sickening and disgusting, just when she feels the most peaceful.

In the building, evil is omnipresent, her constant companion. It meets her and greets her at the door as she arrives. It follows her around in the night through the long corridors, into the kitchen where she goes to eat her measly lunch - or whatever you call it when you eat at midnight. Evil sits at the desk with her in the nurse's station and wraps its black arms around her, permeating every pore of her being, trying to get into her soul.

She expects it.

Suddenly, in the flash of a single instant, she knows . . . . .

And feels the struggle, a battle, for this one young girl. Now evil has attacked her on another front– just to let her know that there's no winning for her. Not even this one small battle. Especially not for this one small child.

Cindy feels tears coming. She wants to scream.

"I can't. I can't. - Why me? Leave me alone, leave me alone. I can't take on another fight. I can't - I won't. I've yet to win any of my own."

But she knows, as surely as she knows her own name, that the battle has just begun. And she knows that she's fighting, not only for the survival of this child, but for her own survival, and the survival of all those she loves. And she knows that she can't lose.

It's getting dark now and she asks to leave. "I have to get to my job." she explains. "The day nurse is waiting for me so she can go home."

They let her go and tell her that they may have more questions for her in the future.

"Fine," she replies in what she hopes is a straight forward, practical voice that doesn't betray her emotions. "You know where to find me.

I work right over there, and you have my home address. Just call if you need me."

Cindy finally heads to work, grateful that she's in familiar territory. Here, by keeping busy, she can manage her enemies and keep her demons at bay.

Chapter 9

Mari watches intently, her eyes focused on the group of people from which she feels the nurses' presence, fearful and anxious, then angry. She watches her bolt for the mental hospital, feels her relief as the huge doors swing open to admit her. The building swallows the nurse into the black pit of its interior once again but, this time, there's a difference. This time the nurse is anxious to be swallowed.

The building has won this round.

What could possibly have happened out there that would make the nurse so anxious to get back into this mire of darkness and despair?

Mari knows now that she and the nurse are linked. She feels the threads that bind them, knows that the only hope for her salvation lies with this one human being who cares for her, this person who feels life, this person who hurts like she does. Somehow, when the time is right, *she must tell the nurse what has happened to her*, ask for her help. If it's possible to get out of this hell, Mari knows that the nurse is her only hope. Somehow, she knows that they need to work together to overcome whatever it is that grips them and holds them captive in this horrible place - in this living hell.

A beetle lands suddenly on the windowpane just within her line of vision - a Japanese Beetle. This kind, Mari knows eats roses and hollyhocks from the gardens. The beetle folds its wings across its back, two light brown wings with just a hint of gold. Two darker, golden brown eyes stare at her. Its stick-like legs point upwards to feel the wind, while its other legs hold it firmly to the glass. It moves around, keeping its grip.

"Even with all its ugliness", she thinks, "it still shimmers with gold."

The beetle opens its wings, catches a breeze and disappears into the night.

Chapter 10

The familiar pandemonium of the evening ruckus is a comfort, as Cindy dispenses pills, checks charts and helps patients settle into the evening. Each patient responds to her only as he or she is able from the depths of their own world, from the pits of their own hell.

She breathes a sigh of relief when things have finally settled down enough so that she can go through Mari's file again.

Cindy is captivated.

"Despite all that has happened in the past few hours, despite the trauma of the evening, despite the realization that I'm too involved, I don't seem able to help myself. I still want to know about her. I still want, more than anything, to help her be free of this institution and its degradations."

Cindy again reaches over and pulls Mari's file towards her. After about fifteen minutes, she puts it down.

"I need more information," she thinks to herself. "What this file is telling me is so far beyond what this child seems capable of that it doesn't make any sense."

She needs to go back farther, dig farther.

"Ray", she calls to one of her nurses. "Ray, I need to get some additional information on a patient for Dr. Fitzsimmons. Could you just keep an eye on things for me awhile? I'll need to go down to the dungeon and dig through some back files. I only hope the file he's looking for is on top of the mess."

"Sure, Cindy. Be glad to do that for you." Ray is grateful that he's getting the easier job. The other nurses usually send him to the dirty, disorganized basement to find back files. He readily agrees to look after things until she comes back up.

Cindy trusts Ray. He's hardworking and respectful to the patients, a good guy. She is comfortable leaving him in charge of the floor while she does some digging for Mari's back files.

The old elevator rattles and creaks as it takes her down into the dungeon of a basement that holds evidence of all the horrors contained in the minds of the building's inmates. Her spirit sags as the doors open upon the massive mess in front of her. It smells bad, musty and damp. She can hear the drip, drip, drip of water someplace off in the distance. No one has bothered to look after things down here or arrange these files for many years and, as each successive box is brought down, they are stacked willy nilly in no apparent order. She's going to need a huge amount of luck and determination to find Mari's file, and, if there's more than one - well, who knows if all the files will ever be found.

"This place," she thinks, "is an indication of the state of the building in general. No one cares enough to straighten it out, as no one cares enough to straighten out the lives of the people who are sent here supposedly to be helped, but really just to be warehoused so they're out of sight of the community. Out of sight, out of mind, as they say." Cindy grins at her own unintended pun.

"Where to start?" She is almost tempted to give up before she even begins the search. Just take the elevator back upstairs and forget about all this nonsense. Why on earth does she have to take this upon herself? But she knows the answer to that. She knows that, unless she does something to help, indeed, anything she can to help, there will be no rest. Mari's plight will continue to haunt her.

"Guess I'll just have to start in one corner and work my way around the room" she tells herself. "Damn, what is dripping down here? That needs to be checked out."

Cindy knows that her time is limited. She can't leave Ray by himself up there for too long. She figures she's got about half an hour.

"When did Mari arrive here? About three years ago, they tell me."

She muses as she pulls out files to check their dates. "That would make her 12, maybe 13 years old when she came here. Would someone that young be capable of doing what she's accused of? Would it even be physically possible? If not, why would someone think she did? And why was she placed here instead of in a children's hospital?"

About half an hour into her search, Cindy finally hits pay dirt. There it is, sitting right on top of a large pile of boxes over in a corner under the dim glow of an unshaded light bulb. She's feeling such a level of anxiety and anticipation that she can barely contain herself. Surely something in these files will exonerate the child, cast at least some doubt on the wisdom of locking her up in this horrible place, maybe even get her out of here. She eagerly flips open the top file and scans its contents.

At the very back, on pages yellowed and torn from dampness and neglect, the bloody details leap off the page.

"No, this can't be true. It's impossible" Cindy hears her own voice echo off the walls. "So this is why they locked her up here . . . . I can't believe it . . . . This can't be true."

And that familiar feeling of nausea, of panic, of her life being out of control, jumps up and ambushes her once again.

Chapter 11

"Finally, darkness comes," thinks Mari gratefully. And with its arrival, she notices a subtle change take place in the asylum. Not just the shift from the cold, heartless nurse to the kinder, softer one, nor the shift from the glare of the light to the soft shadows of night, but another, subtler change.

Out of nowhere, the thought comes to her.

"The building is changing."

She moves closer to the window, watching a light mist fall with the coming of night. The walls around her become softer, flowing, as though she could step through them at any time, out into the mist and the darkness. This is not a backwards thought, but something real, something now. Feelings of her own power, feelings of relief take hold of her. Power because she feels herself part of them - part of the mist, part of the outdoors, part of the building itself, part of all - even the redness that feeds the parched earth in her dreams. Relief because the solid edges of the 'normal' world are finally giving way to the reality she knows is true. Something is finally happening that she recognizes . . . her own world, her before world, is returning to her. After such a long time, she's finally going home, back to a place she recognizes, back to being her own person.

She wonders what effect this will have on her, on the other inmates, on their caretakers. She trembles in anticipation. She stares out the window into the gathering darkness. Surely, this information was given to her for a reason. She needs to do something, but what?

No one listens to a fifteen-year-old inmate in an insane asylum. Even the crazy people have been told so often that their own reality is nonsense, and medicated for it, that they believe their jailers and have no respect for themselves or their own feelings or ideas. They truly are lost souls inside their own minds.

"Look at them," she thinks. "Look at the way their physical bodies answer to their mind's beliefs." They no longer walk without a shuffle, their shoulders slump; their eyes are glazed, their humanity gone.

"I could walk right through these walls and out into the darkness," thinks Mari.

"But the time just doesn't seem right." She knows that the power will be here when she needs it. *"But not yet, not quite yet!"*

She sees the man with the medication, the same man who brings it to her when the nurse is busy or doesn't want to have anything to do with her. She knows she bothers this nurse, some nights more than others.

"That's a good thing." she whispers, "To bother someone with your presence is a good thing. I'm becoming visible."

The medication man slowly and deliberately moves from one patient to another, dispensing sleep to the patients and peace to the staff. Mari knows that she no longer needs to resist him and his pills. There's no need to stay awake all night any more. The dreams that have haunted her nights aren't real, only a reflection of her inability to control her world. She doesn't feel the need to do that anymore, and so the dreams are moot, pointless, and should, like vapor, evaporate. She takes the medications, anxious to learn if she's right, if the dreams truly will disappear.

"Why am I here?" she asks, as she feels herself falling, falling into that in-between time before sleep. "What am I doing in this place?"

And through the fog and darkness, an answer comes to her - and the terror leaves her. She knows what she had known all the time - what she knew when she sat at Grandmother's feet and listened, and they talked about their day and the happenings in their lives.

She knows why she is here in this particular place at this particular time.

"Because this is the story of my life. It's who I am. It is where I'm supposed to be."

Mari watches a hornet walk up the side of the wall. It's cold and the hornet walks slowly, its movements impeded by its body's need to adapt to the changing temperature of the cooler night air.

Mari allows herself to be led to her bed and into her dreams.

She knows that she has been given a gift - *she is still aware. She knows the truth of herself and her feelings. All is as it should be. And yet, change is coming.*

Chapter 12

As Cindy clutches the file, a sudden chill takes hold of her. She feels like she's been plunged into a frozen lake. Her whole body shakes violently, and she realizes that she's been down here way too long.

She grips the file, not wanting to let it go. Along with the doctors' notes, it contains detailed interviews with people who knew Mari and her grandmother, as well as old newspaper clippings that are filled with gory and graphic details about the murder.

According to them, Mari lived with her grandmother a few miles outside of town. Each week, the two of them went into town to pick up groceries and pay bills and visit with friends. Grandmother was friendly and well liked by the townspeople, but the girl, the newspaper clippings implied, had always seemed a little odd. No one knew quite where she had come from. The old lady just showed up with her one day and told everyone that she was her granddaughter. After that, where ever the grandmother went, the kid went with her, always by her side, quiet, withdrawn. Didn't seem to mingle with other kids her age. The grandmother told everyone she was teaching her at home. This led people to wonder what the poor old lady had gotten herself into, taking in this kid who seemed a little different, to say the least.

When they didn't show up in town for a couple of weeks, someone got worried and went to check on them. Turns out that they found Mari living with the old lady's corpse. The poor woman had been bludgeoned to death, probably while she was sleeping. The girl wouldn't tell them what had happened, wouldn't tell them anything at all, as a matter of fact. Since she was the only one around, the only witness to what had gone on in the cottage, it seemed likely that there had been some kind of argument that the grandmother, being old and fragile, had lost. No weapon had ever been found, and there had been no reason to believe that anyone else had been involved.

The girl had been brought to the hospital to be evaluated, but that had proved to be impossible since she wouldn't communicate with anyone in any way. She just sat by herself and refused to speak or even look at anyone. She ate just enough to stay alive and only acknowledged the presence of other persons when she refused to take her prescribed medication. Of course, it was given to her anyway, by force if necessary, but that was it. That was all anyone knew about this patient. No attempts to help her had been successful, and she remained, three years after her arrival, in the same condition as she was when she had been admitted to the hospital. She was cleaner, much thinner, and that was it.

There is really no need to read any more. Cindy leaves the file behind on the top of the messy stack and takes the elevator back upstairs.

She checks for Ray and finds him busy dispensing meds and helping patients to their rooms. She works alongside, helping him.

"Sorry I took so long, Ray."

"It's okay - I'd rather be doing this than be down in that basement. That place is beyond help. Besides, I'm almost through here."

The din increases. Patients clamor for attention. Cindy grimaces - it feels as though everyone wants a piece of her tonight, and she can't deal with it. She needs to be alone, inside herself, wrapped up and isolated from the noise and the craziness, able to digest all that she's been through this evening.

But there's too much to do. After the patients are all settled in for the night, she gets to the paperwork that her employers insist must be done correctly at all times. That seems to be all they care about. But sometimes, it's simply not possible.

Even when the ward is quiet, she finds it difficult to focus on paperwork. The anguish and agony that goes on in these peoples' minds stays with her, seeps inside her despite herself, keeping her in turmoil. She feels the knot in the pit of her stomach, and wishes she could be like those to whom this is just a job, who don't care one way or the other about the patients, just about their paychecks. But she is finding that impossible, no matter how hard she tries.

She had always known that she shouldn't be working in a place like this. It just bothers her too much, but she had no choice. It was all she could find with a salary that enabled her to keep their heads above water financially. She needed to keep her own little family safe, sane, and on an even keel. So she took the job, figuring that she could keep the problems of the patients out of her mind and focus instead on the physical work that had to be done for them.

Why, she wonders, does she have such a difficult time with that?

Cindy knows that she has just opened the door that she made so much effort to keep closed, but she doesn't seem able to help herself. Like a wall of water pulling her along in its wake, the energy of the building insists on pulling her down the corridor to check up on the child who apparently murdered her grandmother three years ago.

"Why would she do these things she's accused of, it doesn't make sense." Another thought pierces the darkness of the evening. "And why does no one else seem to care?" At least now some of her questions have been answered about the girl at the window. What brought her to this place? Why does no one seem able to help her and send her home where she belongs? Why does no one come to visit?

Cindy thinks about her own children safe at home in their comfortable beds with their siblings safely tucked in beside them. She knows that the two little ones sleep together for comfort when she isn't there, and that her oldest waits until they are both asleep before going to bed herself. She knows that the troubles they've had to go through made her kids closer. It's also reassured them that their mother can and will provide for and always love them.

"What must it be like," she wonders, "for a child to know that she's been accused of murdering the person who loved her most in the world. How would it feel to know that no one else cares enough to visit, to call, to acknowledge her existence, or to find out the truth of what went on in that cottage.

"How," Cindy asks herself, "would any of my own children react if they knew that no one cared? Would they, perhaps, sit by a window in the darkness, hoping to see the face of someone who once loved them?"

Cindy tries to force herself not to look down the corridor, down to the door of the room where Mari drifts between waking and sleeping. She doesn't see, but only feels, eyes turn her way . . . . searching. They seem to be looking for nothing less than own soul.

Chapter 13

The medication no longer affects her, and Mari lies in her bed with her eyes closed, listening to the sounds of the night. Her body is completely within her control now; she no longer fears what may happen to it. She knows that she can't be touched in any real way by physical forces. She is without physical being, without boundaries, flowing into her surroundings, and they flowing into her. It's a good feeling, like floating on a warm body of water, just formed enough in her physical self to know herself separate from the water, and appreciate what it's doing to and for her. It's a feeling unlike any other, and she knows this is something she has been waiting for all her life.

Knit, purl, knit, purl. Listen! Listen to Grandmother's story. As stitches slip through her fingers, she tells Mari a story of a long ago time when the world was one. No one existed apart from each other, and the love of each one for themselves could only be found inside the others. Yet they were each separate beings.

Grandmother tells the truth.

"*I am,*" thinks Mari.

"*I am - and I am free.*"

Chapter 14

Cindy finally settles down, brings her evening back into focus, and begins to pour over her paperwork, anxious to get it done. She hates it, but it's a necessity. Filling out forms keeps everything in order and seems to be what keeps this place from falling apart.

And is that so important - that this place not fall apart?

"What," she thinks, "would be the difference?"

All that seems to matter to the powers that be is that the patients be confined, controlled, and kept out of sight.

No one ever sees them as people.

No one seems to wonder what it is that makes places like this necessary.

That is someone else's problem.

"We pay our taxes, and we expect a safe place to raise our kids".

"They're right on that count," Cindy thought. Everyone wants a safe place, for themselves, for their families - she knows that, she is one of them.

But what if they have it all wrong? Judging others as less than you, running scared instead of asking how to make life good for everyone, even the patients.

They're frightened, frightened of what might happen if they accept that even the inmates of a mental institution deserve to live a life with quality, a life they themselves chose, a happy life. Fear is a prison, more surely than any walls that confine these patients. Fear keeps people from seeing the humanity of the patients.

And she's one of them. She would just as soon not have to work at this place, would like to pretend, with the rest of the town and with society at large, that these people don't deserve the same quality of life that 'normal' people have.

"We work hard to have our quality of life. We deserve it."

"And what," Cindy asked herself, "is wrong with that?"

"Nothing," she thinks, "until one knows what I know, until one sees what I see."

Then they would know how very wrong it all is to treat people like these are treated - without dignity, without respect, with no control over their own lives. These are people who truly matter; these are the most vulnerable, because these are the ones who test our humanity.

Something isn't right. She doesn't know exactly what she's feeling. It's nothing she can get a grip on, put her finger on, put words to. Something she's feeling deep down in her heart, something coming from outside herself, and yet is a part of herself. That something is telling her that these people who are shut up in this mental institution are badly needed by the rest of us.

"What the heck am I thinking?" Cindy wonders. "I don't know. Finding that body in the river, and then discovering why Mari is here, it all gave me quite a jolt. Maybe coming face to face with death makes me realize how truly valuable life is - and here we have so many people, human beings, medicated beyond any level of reasonable existence. It just doesn't seem right. Surely there's a better way."

Chapter 15

Mari looks around in the darkness. Neither the medication, nor the fears of those who imprison her, nor the dark walls of the institution can confine her now. She rises slowly from her bed and drifts towards the open window. She feels herself become liquid, invisible. She slips through the walls and steps outside into the darkness, which envelopes her like a soft, velvety cloak.

The refreshing coolness of the evening is a wonderful contrast to the heavy gloom of the hospital.

"I had forgotten what it's like," she thinks. I'd forgotten how it feels to be one with the mist and the softness and the velvety darkness."

The farther she removes herself from the building and grounds, the more form her body takes until, fully formed once again, she moves gracefully across the miles, through fields and pathways. Like a homing bird, she finds her way back to the place where she had been so happy, back to the home she shared with Grandmother.

The beloved grounds - each flower, each tree, and each plant - she knows them all by name. She lingers over her greeting to each of them, finding strength in their quiet calm.

She moves towards the house where she and grandmother would sit in the evenings by the fire to read and knit and discuss the events of their day - the home where she felt safe and loved and warm - her home.

She flows through the door and inside to a neat, pretty, clean room, similar, yet different from the room she had shared with Grandmother.

"This will do, though," she thought. "This is good too. I have no problem here."

Her eyes scan the surroundings. The mess that had been left when they had taken her away has been cleaned up, and in its place are new furnishings. Different, yes, but nice. She stands in the center of the room, looking around, letting feelings wash over her.

Someone else lives here now. But how could that happen? This is our home, Grandmother's and mine. Who's living in our home? She notices shoes lined up at the door - two pairs of tiny ones, two larger pairs. Unfamiliar jackets hang by the back door. She doesn't recognize the dishes in a strainer at the sink.

This is her home, but she's a stranger here now. She knows how it feels to have a stranger in your home. Strangers had come to the house when it belonged to her and Grandmother and taken her away. She wonders if the people who live here now will fear her.

She can't stay, but she will visit for awhile and gain strength to get her through what awaits her. Just visit, get strong and then go back.

She feels Grandmother's love – feels her here – in this place where they were both so happy. But she knows now, she knows that it has to be like this. She no longer belongs in the little house, not without Grandmother, not anymore. And she knows that in leaving, she leaves nothing behind. Love will follow her, come with her, be by her side, surround her in all she does.

Her job, her purpose for being in the world lies back where she has come from, not here. She belongs back at the hospital. Only by coming here could she understand that she no longer belongs here. She needs to return, only this time of her own accord, through her own will.

Careful to leave no trace, she is gone before the family gets up.

Chapter 16

"Five a.m. - time to call it a night."

Cindy sighs deeply. She needs to make her final rounds to check on the patients, some of whom are stirring already. The day nurse, her supervisor, won't be happy with that.

"Up their meds for tomorrow evening so they'll sleep longer," she'll say.

It's been a difficult night. Cindy spent some of it crying silently when no one was looking, sometimes making a supreme effort to concentrate in order to do the paperwork that the supervisor will expect when she begins her day shift. She hasn't even begun to process what she's been through and what she's learned about Mari. It's been tough enough just to get through the night. She needs someone, anyone to talk to so she can try and make sense of it all.

"Ray's a friend. She thinks. "I could talk to him."But she quickly dismisses the thought.

"Why the heck would he want to hear my problems? No doubt he has enough of his own to tangle with. I need to get myself together."

Cindy puts the paperwork away and gets ready to go home. A walk should clear her mind somewhat, but she knows she simply can't walk by that river today. She'll call a cab. It's a luxury, but she figures it's a necessary one, considering the circumstances. She will need some energy left so she can pay attention to the kids as they get ready for school. Hopefully, she will be able to get some sleep before they all come trooping back this afternoon, but she doubts it. She knows that, with what she's just gone through - the body in the river, the horrible information she's just discovered about Mari - how could she sleep?

One last check on the patients before she leaves. She starts her final rounds.

Mari is missing.

Cindy's puzzled. How on earth could she get up and wander around the hospital this early, considering the medication she's on? She must have one awfully strong constitution.

She can't be too far away, maybe just in the bathroom.

"I'll make sure she's okay before I leave."

Cindy carries on, popping into the bathroom on her way down the corridor. But there's no sign of Mari. "How could I have missed her?" She thinks. She hurries back to the room. No one is there. Cindy feels herself begin to panic. She has no idea what to do next. She's never lost a patient before. "Ray, Ray," she calls to the only other person who comes to her mind. "Have you seen the patient from room 204?"

Ray comes around the corner and stares at her in disbelief, "you mean the one who's sitting right there on the windowsill?"

Cindy turns around. Mari is indeed sitting on the windowsill, her eyes fixed on the sun as it comes up over the horizon.

"That's odd," she mutters to herself. "It's the first time I've ever seen her up so early. She usually fights us to stay in bed and hates to get up and into the shower in the morning. The window sitting is usually reserved for the nighttime when the sun is going down. What is she doing here this morning? And why didn't I notice her when I made rounds just a few minutes ago? She almost looks as if she's waiting for someone or something."

She moves towards the girl at the window and stops. The child looks directly into her eyes, a far-off, misty look that reminds Cindy of the dawn itself. She finds herself tongue-tied, not quite knowing what to say or where to go from here. She knows that Mari waits there for her.

She says nothing, but reaches out and touches the child with her hand. The current that runs between them cannot be expressed in words, but Cindy knows without a shadow of a doubt that this child did not kill anyone, let alone her beloved Grandmother. Nothing but love flows from Mari, and Cindy finds herself caught up in a rapture beyond language, beyond imagination, beyond anything she's ever experienced. All she wants is to stay forever with this child.

Chapter 17

Mari looks into the nurse's eyes. She sees not only goodness, caring and compassion, but also the pain of a life that carries the past like a cross that needs to be borne. Mari feels the strength that's now inside her go out to the woman and will her to be healed.

"Everything will be all right," she whispers softly. "You needn't worry anymore."

Cindy has no idea what is happening. She only knows that she feels a huge burden being lifted from her shoulders. She feels light, lighter than she has ever dreamed possible. She feels almost as if she can fly.

"Thank you" she says softly.

Nothing more is necessary. She takes her hand off the child and makes her way back to the desk, goes over some paperwork with the morning staff, puts on her coat and says good morning to the supervisor who has just arrived. She goes out the front door of the hospital, and heads home on foot. She has no fear now - no fear of the river and its contents, no fear of her own reaction to it, no fear of other people invading the privacy of her mind. No fear.

With her mind clearer than it has ever been, Cindy gently directs her thoughts. "What," she wonders, "is the next step in her life? What should she do next for Mari, for my children, for myself?"

Before she is even aware of it, she is coming around a corner, and into sight of the decrepit little home she shares with her children.

It needs a coat of paint, but the flowers that she planted with the kids in the spring bloom along the pathway up to the front door. Someone has been watering them while she's at work. Amazing! She hadn't realized that anyone would care enough about the flowers to go through the extra trouble of watering them and keeping them alive. Why had she never noticed them before? Yellow and deep pink roses, blue bachelor's buttons, white Queen Ann's lace all bow to her as she comes up the walkway. They're simply beautiful . . . . Beyond beautiful.

Are they truly bowing to her? Why not? Why would they not acknowledge her, as she acknowledges them?

Cindy opens the front door and steps inside to the hubbub of the kids starting their day - grabbing what they can to eat, yelling that someone has been in the bathroom too long, madly trying to find a missing sock or shoe or hairbrush.

She smiles.

Someone has already put on the coffee, and she gratefully takes a cracked cup out of the well-worn cupboard, fills it and goes to the fridge to get some coffee cream. As she sits down at the tired, old table, she takes in the scene around her.

For the first time, she sees with thankful eyes all that she has.

Three happy, healthy kids who love and argue, hug and fight. Three very independent young women making their way by helping their mom get through each day just by being themselves- looking after everything that comes up in their lives without all that much help from her, only her advice every now and then. Three young girls very sure of themselves and their own abilities. Three happy kids.

She has never seen this before, just as she has never taken notice of the flowers that grow so gloriously, lining the walkway up to the front door of her home.

The kids continue with their own activities as she watches, astonished at what she is seeing for the first time.

Finally, fed, dressed, bossing and reminding each other as they see fit, they begin to roll out the front door.

Cindy calls after them.

"Sara, do you have track today. What time will you be home?"

Cindy hears Sarah's anxious voice coxing her sisters to hurry up. "Let's go, you guys. We'll be late. Hurry up. I'll be home around four. Mom will be here when you get home. Do you have a key to let yourself in so you don't have to wake her up if she's still sleeping?"

"Leave it to Sarah to worry about me getting enough sleep," thinks Cindy, "Sarah the worrier."

She watches as they climb the steps up to the open door of the school bus.

"And they're off," thinks Cindy. Off to their own worlds of teachers and lessons and friends and sports. I've been so worried about making a living and looking after them that I never realized how independent and self sufficient they are. They have lives apart from me and what I can provide for them. All my worrying doesn't change a thing. It just makes me miserable and sick and tired. Now there's a revelation!"

It's still only seven o'clock in the morning as Cindy starts to tidy the place up. Orange juice and milk back in the fridge, cereal back in the cupboard, dishes and silverware in the sink with nice, warm, sudsy water. She's not tired like she usually is when she gets home from work, and she has no desire to sleep. She'll need her energy for all that she intends to do today.

Chapter 18

"Is it truly just a coincidence that I find a body in the river on the same day that I discover that Mari has been branded as a murderer?" Cindy asks herself, amazed at her own thoughts.

She feels such a connection, like Mari is still with her. Not like a shadow, but a force that pulls her along, encourages her, directs her and guides her into an understanding of what she has to do next.

On fire now, she decides to call to the police station. No one is willing to speak to her over the phone, so she calmly gets dressed in street clothes. Carefully, making sure to wear something that says,

"I'm determined to do what I came here to do, and I don't intend to leave until you tell me everything you know about the body I found in the river."

As she dresses, Cindy goes over the questions that she wants answered,

"Was this body that of a man or that of a woman? How did he or she die? Did no one miss this person? Why was there no fuss, no mention of it in the papers, no gossip, no one looking or wondering or searching when he or she went missing?

Obviously, the body had been in the river for some time before Cindy had come along and noticed it floating there like a pile of rags. What kind of a life is it if no one misses you or looks for you after you're gone?

For the first time in her life, Cindy doesn't stop to think of consequences, of how her actions might affect herself and her kids. She doesn't care what the police think of her, she doesn't care if they contact her work to ask about her, she just doesn't care. She has to know why that body was in the river.

Is it an escaped mental patient? Is it someone from town who had a disastrous accident? Is it a stranger? The body must have been there for a long time in order for it to look like it did. Why was there nothing in the news about anyone missing?

Her mind spins with questions. At least one person, herself, cares about the owner of the body she's dragged out of its watery grave.

Before she realizes what's happening, almost as if she is on autopilot, she is dressed, out the door and heading toward the center of town. Step by step, she approaches the grim doors that separate the police station from the rest of the downtown. Quickly and quietly, she opens them and finds herself in a small lobby. Several well-placed burgundy and grey chairs line a wall. Opposite them is a thick glass pane. She supposes its bulletproof glass. She approaches, and a partition slides open, reminding her of the sliding door of a confessional when she had been forced to confess her childish sins a long time ago. She didn't like the sound then and she hates it now.

Pushing her anxiety deep down inside her gut, she explains to the officer behind the glass why she's here. He's sympathetic, but doesn't give her anything. It may be days, but more than likely weeks and maybe even months before they discover the identity of the body, he tells her. "Go home. When we find out anything, we'll give you a call." Cindy knows that's a lot of bunk. She'll never hear from anyone, and will only find out anything secondhand, from the papers. And it'll have some spin on it. She becomes more insistent.

She refuses to leave, she tells him, until she can talk to someone who knows about the case.

Finally, he tells her to "wait here."

She's still waiting an hour later . . . .

"They're ignoring me, hoping I will just give up and go home. It isn't going to happen. I'm staying for as long as this takes." She thinks to herself, "If they won't see me today, I'll be back tomorrow."

Finally, after more than an hour, her persistence pays off. A young man in a suit approaches and tells her to follow him. He leads her to a room and asks her why she is so insistent on learning more about the dead body from the previous night.

Cindy tries to explain - a near impossible task, but at least he listens. She tells him how she was the person who first noticed the body in the river, and that she feels an obligation to whoever this person was. Everyone needs someone who cares enough about them to mourn them if they are missing, or to at least care about what's happened to them.

The young detective looks at her strangely.

"Surely," she tells him, "surely you've felt this way about some of the people you've worked with".

He silently agrees. There have been those cases that mattered more than others to him. For no other reason than that no one else cared, he felt he had to care. Someone needed to.

"Yeah, I understand," he tells her. "But there's nothing about this person that gives us any clue as to who he is or what might have happened to him. It could be just a derelict who decided life wasn't worth living, or who simply drowned by accident. Odds are that the reason no one seemed to care for this person is that his or her life had very little meaning to anyone. I strongly doubt that, after all this time, and considering the condition of the corpse, we're going to be able to find an identity anytime soon, let alone a reason why this individual died."

"You have to," Cindy tells him. "This was a person. If this life was of no value - well, I can't help but wonder - if this life was of no value, then of what value are any of our lives?"

She knows that probably sounds a little strange, but it's exactly how she feels, so she says it anyway.

Again the detective looks at her strangely. "If we find out who this person was, and what happened, I will call you. How does that sound?"

"If that's the best you can do today, I guess I'll have to be okay with it," Cindy tells him. "I will be calling you, detective what is it?" She tries to read the name on the desk - detective . . . .

"Oh, that's not me. This isn't my desk. I'm Larone, Detective Jim Larone."

"Oh, great," Cindy thinks. "This guy is so new here he doesn't even have his own desk. Oh yeah," she tells herself facetiously, "I guess this mystery should be solved any time now."

She tries not to let her feelings show. Maybe his lack of skills mask a caring concern for others that an older, more jaded officer might not have.

"Thank you for listening, Detective Larone," she says. "I'll be in touch."

With that, she takes her leave, not too convinced that she's made any difference in how the case is being handled, but at least someone knows that what was pulled from the river last night isn't just a nameless, faceless dead body. Someone cares.

Now if she can just get herself home and get the house organized before the kids come home from school and get ready for her shift at the hospital. Maybe she can even catch a few winks of sleep, something that's been in very short supply lately.

"It's still early; I'll walk home and think things over. I can always take a cab to work if I don't feel up to the walk later tonight."

Cindy can't really afford a cab, but taking one once in awhile won't tax the budget too badly. Sometimes a person has to treat themselves a bit.

"And if I ever needed to give myself a bit of a treat," she thinks, "tonight is the night."

Jim Larone watches Cindy leave the police station and walk back up the main street of the town.

"This lady has no idea of the shit she's getting herself mired in." he thinks to himself. "I only hope she can keep her curiosity about that body in the river under control. Too bad it had to be her that found it and not one of us. I really don't need some civilian digging into things and interfering with my work here."

Cindy arrives home from the police station and tries to get some sleep, or at least a rest. Before she knows it, the kids are home from school, it's past supper time, and she's heading out for work again.

She called for the cab at least half an hour ago. "Where the heck is it?" She's starting to get antsy. She can't be late, particularly tonight, not after her late arrival last night. The day nurse doesn't really care what it is that makes her late. By the time Cindy arrives, she's tired and cranky and she just wants to get home. Cindy understands that feeling. All she needs is to come in late another night. Finally, she sees the cab slowly round the corner onto her street and stop in front of the driveway.

"Come on, come on," she urges, "come to the door. I don't want to have to trot down the walk and up the driveway. I've walked too far already today. If I wanted to walk, I'd be doing it now."

She waits. The taxi turns slowly into her driveway and approaches her door. She tells the kids goodbye, reminds them no TV until they finish their homework and bedtime is at ten. She leaves the house, quickly heads down the front stairs, and opens the door to the cab.

"I don't believe this. This can't be happening!"

She feels a presence - something evil - pulling her into the cab. What on earth is happening? Something inside her tells her to move quickly away, but she stands - paralyzed - her hand still on the door, her body halfway inside.

Chapter 19

"And many are the dead men ....too silent to be real."

Line from a song by Gordon Lightfoot

The line, playing over and over, like tickertape, echoes through her mind.

Cindy trembles. With great effort, she removes her leg from the cab.

"I've . . . . forgotten . . . . something," she tells the driver, trying to keep the panic out of her voice. "I need to go back - back inside."

She feels his eyes locked on her as she races into the house and slams the door closed behind her.

"What! What now! I have to get to work! I can't go in this cab!"

A great, paralyzing fear overwhelms her! What the hell is she supposed to do now?

"Panic - don't panic," she tells herself. "Breath, breath deeply now."

She makes a decision. She opens the front door and goes back out to the cab.

"I can't leave right now, sorry. We have an emergency I need to take care of. I'll pay you for coming, though." She reaches for her purse.

"S'awright lady. You look like you just seen a ghost. Just pay me the basic for the trip over and it'll be OK. You don't need me to take one of the kids to the hospital or anything, do ya?"

Cindy tells him no. With shaking hands, she holds the first bill she finds in her purse out to him, thanks him, and watches as the cab slowly leaves the driveway and heads down the street. As it recedes farther and farther into the distance, her mind clears and her panic subsides.

She thinks to herself. "Now what the hell was that all about? Like I can afford to let my imagination take over like that. I might as well have just flushed that money down the toilet. I still have to get to work, and now I'm going to be late............ Man, am I good at making life difficult for myself."

She picks up the phone. "I need to call the hospital, tell them that I'm going to be late again tonight," she thinks.

Suddenly, she stops, the phone still in midair.

"The cabbie - what was it he said?"

"You don't need me to take one of the kids to the hospital, do ya?"

"How could he know?" she asks herself. "How did he know that more than one child lives here? How does he know that any children live here?" She racks her brain. There's no possible way!

Icicles work their way up and down her spine!

"I can't, I can't leave them alone!"

Panic once more closes over her like a cold, wet blanket, threatening to overwhelm. Her mind races.

"I need to get to work, but I can't leave the kids. Who can I call to stay here tonight while I'm at work? I don't know anyone well enough - I've been too busy working to make friends. The only reason I'm living in this stupid, snobby town is because I got a job that pays well enough for me to support myself and the kids, not because I know anyone. My social life consists of having cake with the staff at the hospital when it's someone's birthday. That's about it! So who can

I ask for help - the police? I don't think so. They already think I'm nuts."

The one person she trusts in this town is Ray - from the hospital. Sad to say, he's about the only person she's gotten to know. He's a good guy, but she can't call him for help. He works the night shift too; he can't watch her kids for her.

Maybe she should call the police - and tell them what? That she has a weird feeling about a taxi driver? Yeah, right. That should do it.

The phone rings. It's the day supervisor from the hospital. "Where are you? You're late. I need to get home."

Cindy starts to tell her what's going on, how she is afraid to leave her children after what's happened during the last twenty-four hours.

She's interrupted by an angry response.

"I just need to know, are you coming in or not?"

Cindy realizes that her fears sound ridiculous, even to herself.

"I'll be there shortly," she tells the supervisor. It's after eight, time for her to be hanging up her coat at work. Cindy makes a quick decision. There is one neighbor she greets on occasion.

"I can call her and ask if she will just keep an eye on the kids and the house while I'm at work tonight. What's her name - Alice, I think."

Cindy calls Alice and explains some of what's gone on - about finding the body in the river; and that she's a little skittish about leaving the kids at home tonight, considering what has happened. The neighbor is great. She's one of those people who absolutely love drama (one of the main reasons Cindy doesn't like to ask her for help too often).

"Oh my God, I don't believe it. In this little town? A body in the river? Who do you think it is? One of the mental patients from the hospital, I'll bet. Did you hear of any missing persons? You know, what a shame that no one would even miss a person who's gone and drowned in the river. What a shock it must have been for you to find that........blah.....blah....blah...."

She even offers Cindy a ride to work, can't miss any of the juicy details. Cindy doesn't care. She's just grateful for the ride, and for someone to be looking in on her kids while she's at work.

She calls upstairs to Sara and tells her to keep the doors firmly locked and that Alice will look in on them tonight and make sure they're OK. She explains that she had a frightening experience last night and she's a bit nervous about leaving them alone. She doesn't want to frighten her, just wants to make sure she's careful.

Chapter 20

Night falls again, and Mari is at her favorite spot - her window - looking out, enjoying the coming of dusk, yet aware of frantic activity in the institution from the direction of the nurse's station. The night nurse hasn't arrived yet, and she feels the unhappiness and agitation of the day nurse. It surrounds her and moves outwards toward the rest of the staff and from them, to the patients. She raises a barrier around herself, bathes herself in light, and consciously asks that only good things happen for the agitated nurse.

Immediately, she feels a change, a soft glow begins to move outward from herself to challenge the grimness that comes from and surrounds the day nurse. The nurse's voice softens, her actions become smoother, replacing the jerky, frantic movements of moments ago.

In gratitude, Mari utters a thank you.

"If only people knew," she thinks, *"if they only knew. . . . They see the power that evil has every day. If only they knew the power that love has - and that it wants only to be acknowledged."*

Mari looks back out the window. She sees the night nurse get out of a car, walk up the steps and enter the institution through the heavy front doors.

"Something's wrong!" Mari feels a tightness in the pit of her stomach.

Cindy removes her overcoat and stores her empty purse in a drawer. She listens to the nurse/supervisor explain what has gone on during the day, who has done what, and what needs to be done this evening and throughout the night. Surprisingly, she doesn't seem as agitated as she did when she spoke to Cindy on the phone earlier. Mostly, she's annoyed that all the paperwork from last night wasn't completed and filed properly. Cindy assures her that she will try her best to get it done tonight.

Paperwork is absolutely the last thing on Cindy's mind right now. She is trying to make some sense of the events of the past few hours and her own reaction to them. Her supervisor's voice drones on. Cindy's mind wanders.

"Of course I'm especially antsy tonight considering what happened just last night," She thinks to herself, "Who wouldn't be shaken up after coming across that rotting, bloated carcass that was once a human being. As far as the taxi driver is concerned, he was probably just being kind and guessing that I have kids and might need some help. How could I have made that into a crisis?"

All the rationalizing in the world doesn't still the turmoil that's taking place in the pit of her stomach.

"Please, please keep them safe," she begs anyone out there who might be listening. She'll be grateful when this night is over!

The supervisor is finished giving instructions for the evening. She doesn't seem to have noticed that Cindy isn't listening to a word she's saying. "Please," Cindy thinks, "just go home and let me do what needs to be done around here."

She looks down the hallway at Mari, sitting at her window, stuck here probably for life, if no one does anything to help her.

"They need me. Mari, my kids, they need me. I can't let fear, negativity, and, yes, evil, determine where I go and what I do, determine our lives."

Her neighbor calls. "I just wanted to let you know that I checked on the kids when I got back, and they're fine. I'll keep a close eye out this evening. Don't worry."

Cindy thanks her profusely. She knows Alice's type. Anything unusual, and she'll be right on top of it. Cindy will probably never hear the end of it but, nevertheless, she's glad she asked for help.

"Might as well take advantage of her need to be at the center of things, at least for tonight," she thinks. "I have to keep my wits about me, and I can't do that if I'm worried about the kids."

As soon as the supervisor leaves, the tension on the ward dissipates. A gentle silence softly descends over staff and patients. Cindy, Ray, and several orderlies move up and down the corridors, settling everyone into their nighttime routines.

As soon as she can manage it, Cindy once more slips quietly down to the basement, grabs Mari's file from the top of the messy pile where she had left it, and quickly takes the stairs up to the nurse's station once more. She'll go over it again to see if she can find anything in it that sheds more light on what happened to Mari's grandmother. It's unimaginable to her that Mari could have had anything to do with her death. Did no one check the facts? Did no one make sure that this is what actually happened? Did anyone even care that they were about to lock up a twelve-year-old for something she might not have done? Was it just easier to lock up the child so that they wouldn't have to deal with her anymore? There has to be something more to this than the information contained in these files?

So many questions. Bit by bit, she takes the file apart, trying to find something, anything, that might have any chance of explaining things. Finally, hours later, she finishes. She takes the files back down to the basement.

"I can't believe it. Nothing. There's nothing to even suggest the possibility that someone else could have murdered the grandmother. Tomorrow, I spend the day at the library and see if I can get any more information from the newspapers than I got from the file."

Cindy didn't get much sleep today, and it sure looks like she won't get much again tomorrow. No matter. It seems as soon as she closes her eyes, nightmares take over anyway. If she doesn't figure out what has happened, what <u>is</u> happening, she may never get a decent sleep again.

"I have no idea what it is I'm looking for," she mumbles to herself. "I just know that there has got to be a way to make some sense out of this, and I need to find it. I have to help her. This could be my child."

Slowly, Mari pulls her attention away from the outside, away from the velvety darkness and the clear, full moon, away from the stars twinkling like candles lit by some grand hand of the universe. She pulls herself back inside the building, back to the night nurse and her anxiety that mingles with the musty smell and the swollen dampness permeating the place.

The telephone rings. The nurse speaks for a few minutes. She seems much more at ease when she hangs up. Mari can tell that she's feeling pulled, that she's here and wants to be somewhere else, probably at home. She probably has her own children at home.

"What must it be like," she thinks, "for someone to care? What must it be like to live in a home instead of here in this institution?" She can barely remember. For just a minute, she feels more than sad as she realizes that her home, the home where she was so happy, will never again be available to her.

Mari watches the evening nurse dole out the medications that will incapacitate the patients for the night. The nurse carefully prepares each little cup, one per patient. "Mine won't be necessary tonight," she thinks. Tonight is the night I will finally tell the nurse about the before time, before I was brought here . . . . . and about the unfinished business I have with the people who brought me here. It's time. I need to, want to, bring her, bring someone, into my life.

But the kind nurse doesn't come to give her medications to her. It's the man, the one who tries to be her friend - Ray. She begins to speak, but he's in a hurry to get all the medications into all the patients and he has no time to spend begging her to take her medications or listening to her. She opens her mouth, then closes it again. He wouldn't understand. Mari takes the pills like he asks and puts them in her mouth. She opens it so he can check that she's swallowed, just as he is supposed to do.

"Well," he says, "that was easy tonight. "Thank you Mari."

"*You're welcome,*" she whispers, as he moves off down the hallway.

His head jerks around. "Did you just say something?"

As he turns, just for an instant, he catches a glimpse of a long, silver thread flowing between them, connecting them - the child and himself.

Then, just as quickly, it disappears from his sight.

He stares at her. Mari's eyes look directly into his. He feels her compassion and her caring concern for him, her gratitude for his kindness to her. Suddenly, his job doesn't seem so mundane, so difficult, or so ordinary. It takes on meaning and purpose that he's never before realized. He gazes at Mari. The change in her delights and intrigues him.

"Mari? Did you just speak to me?" He whispers softly.

He feels, rather than hears a response.

"*Thank you for caring.*"

Ray feels a lightness to his step as he makes the rest of his rounds. He finds himself grateful for his job, for his ability to help these people about whom no one else cares. "Just being near her," Ray thinks, "makes me feel good about myself, my job, and my world."

He turns around and looks back at her from down the long corridor. She sits as she always has, quietly, facing the window, a slight smile on her lips, her eyes looking outwards into the darkness and stillness of the soft, velvety night.

And he wonders, "Who is this child? Why does she have such an effect on me? Does she affect others like this or is it just me?"

He moves down to the nurse's station, standing in front of Cindy. She's reading a file.

"There's something I want to ask you," he begins. Then, realizing how foolish he'll sound, he hesitates.

Cindy looks up. "Oh, hi Ray. What can I do for you tonight?"

"I don't know how to say this, but have you noticed something strange about that patient, the girl who sits by the window?" Ray figures this is the best way to approach it. The child really is quite strange, especially compared to the other inmates. If Cindy has no idea what he's talking about, at least she won't think he should be locked up too.

"Do you mean that one?" Cindy nods her head in Mari's direction.

"Yes."

"What do you mean by 'strange'?" Cindy asks him.

"Well, I find it hard to describe, really," he answers. "She seems almost like she doesn't belong here, like she's from another realm. I know it sounds a bit odd, but . . ."

Cindy makes a quick decision. She has always trusted Ray.

"As a matter of fact, I've been so taken with her myself that I've been reading up on why she's here. That's why I asked you to cover for me last night when I went down to the basement to see if I could get some information. It wasn't because of any doctor's orders. It was to find out more about her." Once again, Cindy nods in Mari's direction.

"And have you found anything?"

"Sit down here with me Ray. Let's talk."

Cindy tells him what she found. She explains how Mari's grandmother was murdered, and that she thinks the easiest way to solve the murder was simply to blame it on Mari since she was the only one there. She wouldn't speak to them, wouldn't explain what had gone on. They said that was evidence of her guilt. Cindy thinks that the poor child was so traumatized by everything that she was in shock and couldn't speak.

"Tomorrow," she tells him, "I'm going to the library to find out more about what happened to her grandmother and why she's here. I'll let you know what I find."

Ray looks at her, then he looks down the hallway to the window where Mari sits. They're right, he knows. The child doesn't belong here. And he knows that he will do anything Cindy asks to help right the wrong that he feels sure was done.

"What can I do?" he asks. "What can I do to help?"

Cindy looks at him. "Ray, you've already done so much, just by being here. Thank you. Oh, and I heard something dripping when I was downstairs. It should be checked out. Maybe that's the reason we never have enough hot water for showers in the morning."

"Probably."

"I need to figure out how to get someone to fix it without letting on that I left the floor."

"Just tell them that you were concerned about a patient and needed more information on her. I can't see how anyone could object to that."

"You're right. Now, these patients look like they need to get ready for bed. Let's get them organized."

Cindy and Ray work together quietly, settling the patients in for the night, talking softly to them, consoling them, letting them know that someone cares. It goes well, and they relax into the job, happy to be able to help those who need them so much.

The anxiety of the night fades away, and Cindy realizes how very long it's been since she has had anyone in whom she can confide.

"Yes," she thinks. "Things are finally beginning to feel right."

Chapter 21

Morning comes quickly, and, once again, Cindy breathes in the crisp fall air as she makes her way home. She can't bring herself to walk along the river, although it would be quicker, so she takes the back streets. She's anxious to get the kids off to school and disappear into the library to find out what she can about the story that brought Mari to live in the mental hospital.

Soon enough, she finds herself on its steps. Strangely, the heavy doors remind her somewhat of the doors at the hospital. They seem to be made out of the same dark, dingy oak or mahogany.

"Probably built around the same time," she thinks.

She pulls them open and is surprised to find the inside of the library eerily similar to the inside of the hospital - desk by the front door, imposing librarian instead of head nurse on duty, stacks of books lined up along aisles that look very much like the corridors in the hospital. It strikes her as a little strange, but she refuses to let it put her off. She heads over to ask the librarian how she can go about looking up clippings of something that happened three years ago. She gives the approximate dates to the librarian and gets a quick lesson on using the microfilm library.

A little research brings her to the time in question.

The local paper had dedicated quite a lot of press to the murder of Mari's grandmother. The police finding was that the granddaughter was the only logical person who could have committed the murder.

The paper went on at considerable length about how the poor old woman had taken in the child several years earlier when her parents had been killed in some kind of an accident, and yet this was what she got for all her efforts and kindness. It also made several references to how easy it would have been for the granddaughter to kill the old woman. Seemed the screen door had been cut, probably by a pair of scissors that were lying on the floor. The scissors had the granddaughter's prints on them; although why she had cut it was never questioned. There was some speculation that the grandmother had been afraid of her or wanted to discipline her, and locked her out for some reason. Then, exhausted from the effort, she lay down and went to sleep, never to wake up. Mari was the only one who had been with the grandmother when she was murdered. There was no evidence whatsoever that anyone else had ever been in the house. In addition, the girl refused to speak to anyone. The only recourse, it seemed, was to put her in a mental hospital and see if someone there could figure out what had happened or what was wrong with her. Letters to the paper from that time indicated that more than one person in the community thought that punishment was too lenient, and that they should try her in court and jail her for life. The paper had tried her, found her guilty, and convinced the people in town that she was a danger to them all. Fear is a powerful motivator.

"And nobody even considered any other scenario," Cindy thinks. She feels anger rise up in her like bile, red hot anger that she knows she will have no control over if she allows it to surface so she swallows it.

"How could they not realize that there's no way this child could possibly have done this? I can't believe the police took her guilt for granted and made no other effort to find the real killer or killers. How damned lazy can you be?"

But at least now she knows what Mari is doing in the hospital. And she knows, just as surely as she knows her own name, that someone else murdered Mari's grandmother, that Mari knows who it is, and that it traumatized her so much that she isn't able to tell any of them what really happened on that tragic day.

Cindy also knows that she will have no peace until she helps this child.

"And just how," she wonders, "am I going to do that?"

The only thing she has to go on is her knowledge and belief in Mari's goodness, and her determination to do right by her.

And that, she guesses, is just going to have to be enough.

She checks the time. It's already noon. She will have to get at least a few hours of rest before the kids arrive home from school. She walks slowly back to the house and lies down on the sofa. Half an hour after the library door closes behind her, Cindy is deep into a refreshing sleep. The kids arrive home and tiptoe around until it's time to wake her and send her off to work.

"They're amazing," she thinks. "They're still just kids and yet they know how tired I am and try to make life easier for me."

Cindy is still a bit worried about leaving them alone tonight. Maybe she should call Alice again. It hasn't been that long since she found the body in the river. She realizes that she's still a bit jumpy from that, probably without reason, but she can't get it out of her mind that her kids are in danger.

She makes the call. "Alice, would you mind just keeping an eye on my house again tonight? I'm still feeling a little antsy about leaving the kids at home alone, considering what happened."

"Sure, Cindy, be glad to. I know how hard it is to work with kids and all. I'll check up on them tonight for you. No problem."

Cindy hangs up. Three sets of eyes glare at her.

"Mommmmm. You didn't tell her to check on us again tonight, did you? She calls like every fifteen minutes. It's really annoying."

"Mom had some things happen to her recently that just make her a bit nervous about leaving you kids alone all night. I'd like to be able to stay home with you, but you know that's impossible. It just makes me feel better to know someone is checking to make sure you're all right."

"But why her, Mom? You know how annoying she is."

"Because she's the only one I know around here who is willing to help me out. Try to see her positive side. She offered me a ride to work when I was late last night, and she's good about checking on you guys when I ask her to. I can't do my work properly if I'm worried about you.

"All right mom. We don't mean to be a pain." Sarah answers for the three of them, even though the other two still look upset at the idea of Alice's calls and what they consider to be her interference. "We don't want you going to work and worrying about us all night. We'll put up with her."

"Great. That's settled. Love you. Get all your homework done and to bed on time."

"Sure Mom. Love you too"

And with that, Cindy is out the door and off to work. Seems like she has walked miles today, but she doesn't mind. She's anxious to let Ray know what she found out at the library. Maybe he will have some ideas on where they can go from here

Chapter 22

Mari watches from her window as the night nurse comes briskly up the walk.

"She looks different tonight," she thinks.

Mari feels the energy of the hospital change as Cindy opens the front door and steps inside.

A light glow surrounds and fills the air around the nurse.

"This is the night that I talk to her. She needs to know what happened to Grandmother. It's been such a long time since the men came to our home. I remember Grandmother in bed with dried brown stuff on her face. I was so young. I thought she was sleeping and just needed her face washed. But she never moved. After they left, I tried and tried to wake her up. I remember people coming to take me away. I don't remember much after that, only the loneliness of living without Grandmother. My caretakers seemed to despise me, to consider me nothing but a nuisance, until this nurse came. She cares, I know it. And it makes me feel . . . . real."

Mari waits until the day supervisor leaves and Cindy is sitting at the desk sorting out the nighttime medications for the patients. Slowly, she leaves the window and approaches the desk. Cindy looks up. Mari waits.

"Hello, Mari. How are you this evening?"

She says it so matter of fact, like there's nothing unusual about it and she's been expecting Mari to approach her all along.

Softly, so softly, Mari answers her. "Hello. Who are you?"

"I'm Cindy, the nurse who looks after you at night."

"I know you look after us at night."

"Can I do something for you, Mari?"

"Yes, do you know me, why I'm here?"

"Well. . ." Cindy doesn't really know what it is that Mari is asking her, so she simply asks her. "How much do you know about why you're here?"

Cindy notices Ray watching and motions for him to come closer. As he does, Mari shuts up immediately, like someone put a clamp on her lips.

"It's OK Mari," Cindy says softly. "I just want him to look after things while you and I go somewhere so we can talk."

"Don't worry about the patients. I'll see to it that they get their meds and everyone behaves. Why don't you and Mari just pop into the office down there."

"God bless Ray," Cindy thinks. "This evening is going better than I could have ever planned. How ironic that Mari would pick this time to speak for the first time since she's come to the hospital."

Cindy takes Mari's hand and leads her down the corridor to the office at the other end of the long hallway. She opens the door with her key and locks it after them.

"Now no one can interrupt us," she tells Mari.

Mari's eyes are skittish. She almost reminds Cindy of a deer or a fairy creature that has finally come close to her after she's tried again and again to earn its trust.

As gently as she can, she asks her.

"How much do you know, Mari? Do you know where you lived before you came here?"

Mari's voice surprises Cindy. She expected it to be weak and timid, but it's not at all. It flows from her like an extension of her being, light and mellow, yet strong.

"Yes, I lived with grandmother in a little house with a garden that had plants and flowers and a friendly bunny. The house is still there, you know. I visited it the other day while you thought I was in bed. Some other family lives there now. What happened to

Grandmother? I know she was hurt. Did she die? She must have or she wouldn't have left me here so long; she would have come and taken me out of here."

Cindy doesn't quite know what to make of this revelation. There is no possible way that Mari could have left the hospital. Perhaps she was hallucinating or dreaming. Maybe she truly is mentally ill.

"Yes, Mari, I'm sorry, but your grandmother did die." Mari's eyes turn dark and fill with anger, a response Cindy didn't expect. "You're angry. Can you tell me why?"

A knock on the door interrupts them. Cindy answers it.

"Telephone for you," says Ray, "some lady named Alice."

"Oh my God," Cindy leaves on the run, heads for the front desk and the telephone. "My kids."

Mari turns towards Ray. Her eyes are dark pools of sadness, as she walks past him and slowly leaves the room. She goes back to her seat in front of the window, staring out into the night.

Ray hears Cindy's frantic voice in the distance calling him. "Ray, Ray! I have to go - my kids - I have to leave. I need your car."

Ray asks no questions. He reaches into his pocket and tosses his keys in her direction.

"I'll look after things here. You go."

She flies out the front doors and races towards Ray's old, battered car in the parking lot.

"Shit, it's a standard," she almost screams into the night.

She sticks the key in the ignition and manages to drive it out of the parking lot. She hasn't driven a standard in years and the car lurches and bucks, but at least it moves. She has to get home. Alice called to tell her that someone is moving around the grounds outside her house, peering into her windows. She needs to get to her kids before something happens to them.

"This is ridiculous," she thinks. "I should have told Alice to call the police immediately."

She knows why she didn't. She's worried they will report her to social services for leaving three kids alone at night. None of them seem to care that, without her salary from working the night shift, they wouldn't eat properly or have a roof over their heads. "Damn them all. If anything happens to my kids . . . ."

Ray's old car grinds up the hill leading to her house.

"If anyone is around, they'll know I'm coming." she whispers to herself.

Finally, she's pulls into her driveway. At the house, she struggles with the door. It's locked, and the deadbolt is hard to turn. It takes awhile to get herself inside. She sees nothing but the kids' books on the kitchen table where they had been studying and left everything out. Quickly, she thinks, "That's not like them. They usually put their books away so they won't have to run around so much in the morning."

She races upstairs to the bedroom, only to find it locked.

She hears her own voice, frantic, yelling through the door. "Kids, it's me, Mom. Are you in there? Why do you have the door locked?" Her heart thumps violently in her chest!

"Oh my God, Mom. You scared us to death." Sara's voice answers her from out of the darkness. "What are you doing home?" Sara opens the bedroom door. "I thought you were an intruder. We were so scared. We locked the bedroom door and called 911.

"You're OK" . . . . Cindy's whole body goes limp with relief. "You called 911?"

"Yes! Of course. That's what you always tell us to do in an emergency. Should I call them back and tell them not to come?"

"No, that's all right. They are probably on their way now anyway." She can hear sirens in the distance.

"So there," Cindy thinks to herself. "The police are coming after all. That's good. Maybe they can tell me if there are any signs of someone outside my house tonight."

"Well, at least I can't say I haven't had any excitement this week," she mutters to herself.

"What, mom? What did you say?" Sarah asks "Oh my God, the police car has just pulled into the driveway. What a racket. The neighbors will be wondering what the heck is going on."

"Don't worry about it," Cindy replies, "I'm sure Alice has them all on notice by this time."

"What are you talking about Mom? I can't hear you over all this noise."

Cindy notices the two little ones cowering in a corner of the room, still terrified. She starts over to comfort them, but hears the police calling through the door.

"Is anyone home? Are you all right?"

"Well," thinks Cindy, " if we had an intruder, he's certainly long gone by this time. No one would stick around with all this racket."

"We're fine," Cindy calls to the officer. She quickly races down the stairs and opens the front door.

"I was out and the kids got a little startled, thought they heard an intruder."

It's true, even though the intruder they thought they heard was her, Cindy thinks.

"Could you just check around the outside of the house and see if there's any sign of anyone being around here in the last few hours?"

"Sure, ma'am. Be glad to."

"Thank you, officer."

Cindy goes back upstairs to see what she can do about the kids, but Sarah, good big sister that she is, has gotten them all calmed down and back into bed. "It's just Mom," she's telling them. "Mom decided to come home early and scared us all to death. The police are checking outside just in case. No, there's really no need to worry, no one is out there. You can go back to sleep now."

"Can Mom stay home with us now? We don't want her to leave." The little one starts to cry.

"You'll be fine with me," Sarah answers. "Didn't I know just what to do when we got frightened and thought someone was trying to break into the house?" She shoots Cindy quite the look. "You're perfectly safe with me."

"There's no way I'm going back to work tonight, so don't worry kids, I'll be right here," Cindy tells them.

"I'll call Ray and let him know," she thinks as she heads back downstairs. "He'll understand. He'll just have to look after things by himself tonight."

The police return. Cindy steps outside to talk to them so the kids won't hear anything.

"Yeah, looks like someone was out there all right. We found fresh footprints right outside the window that looks into the kitchen. Looks like someone tried to jimmy it open. We're going to leave an officer outside your house for the rest of the night so you should be safe. Anyone you know would want to hurt you or the kids?"

Cindy can feel panic rising in her throat. "Not that I can think of. You're sure the officer will be right outside? I have three kids here."

"I can see that, ma'am. You and the kids will be safe tonight with Officer Navaro."

The officer at the door leaves and Cindy goes back inside. She hears a car pulling away. She checks outside. A police car is still there.

She has to make some calls. First, she calls Alice to thank her for being on guard and to tell her what's happening.

Alice is happy that she's been such a help, and terrified that there may be an intruder in the neighborhood. Cindy knows that before the night is out, every neighbor within five blocks will have learned what happened. It's just as well. The more people on guard, the less chance of someone prowling around.

Next Cindy calls the hospital. Ray picks up and relief floods over her at the sound of his familiar voice.

"Cindy? Are you all right? Are the kids OK?

Bloodcurdling screams pierce the air.

Cindy listens, horrified . . . . unable to put the phone down. What the hell . . . and then it hits her - **the terrified screams are coming from her own throat** . . . .

Through the kitchen window, she sees the face of her nightmares . . . .Cindy drops the phone.

Chapter 23

And then it's gone. But she's very sure what she saw. And now she knows that she can never go back to the hospital tonight. Her children aren't safe. She doesn't know if they are any safer with her here, but she can't leave. She can't believe that the cop on duty right outside hasn't moved from his car, despite her screams.

The terrified kids come to the top of the stairs.

"Mom, Mom, what's wrong?"

She puts her still shaking arms around them and leads them back to their bedrooms.

"It's all right. Mom just thought she saw something. I guess my imagination is getting the best of me tonight." Cindy tries to make her voice sound calm.

She thinks, "Thank God this is a two story house and they are upstairs. Anyone would have had to go past me to get to them."

She settles them down once again; checks to make sure all the doors and windows are still locked, and returns to the kitchen.

Ray, she needs to call Ray back and let him know what's going on. She can't come back to the hospital but she has his car. He'll need it when he goes to leave in the morning. She'll have to get it back to him. But how? She is not leaving this house with her kids in it and someone stalking them - or her - or all of them.

Cindy looks frantically out the window towards the police car. The darkness makes it impossible for her to see anything. She needs to call Ray and let him know what happened. She needs to call the police about the face in the window. She picks up the phone with her still-shaking hands.

It's dead. There's no dial tone.

All the horror movies she's ever seen replay in her head. .

Someone has cut the phone lines. She is sure of it.

Never has she felt such panic.

She races back upstairs to the kids' room, shuts the door behind her and locks it, puts a chair against it and whispers to Sarah, "Don't ask any questions. Just help me push the desk against the door, quickly."

With all their might, they slide the desk across the room and against the door.

"Now give me your cell phone."

"Mom, it's in the other room. I'm charging it. What the heck is going on?"

"I need your cell phone. Come on, we've got to move the desk again - away from the door so I can get out. Where's the phone?"

"In my room. On my bureau. Ma, we can't move this again, it's heavy."

"Listen to me Sarah. Stay here with the kids. As soon as I'm out, push the desk as hard as you can so it's back against the door. Don't open it until you're sure it's me. Someone is in the house."

"Ma," Sarah starts to cry. "Don't go. Stay here."

"I have to get your phone to call the police. This is no time to panic, Sarah. Stop crying. Help me."

They struggle with the desk again and open the door.

"Now, quick, shut the door behind me and . . . ."

The door shuts. Cindy can hear Sarah pushing desperately on the heavy desk, trying to move it against the door again.

She moves along the hallway, against the wall, as silently as possible. She comes to the entrance of Sarah's room and, in the reflection of the mirror, she sees someone or something on the bed.

Cindy's heart feels like it's about to pound right out of her chest.

He's seen her. There is no retreat. She has no choice. She grabs the nearest object, raises it over her head and steps towards him into the bedroom, screaming at the top of her lungs, loud enough that the cop who's stationed outside can hear.

"Who are you and what are you doing in my house? Get out! Get out!"

Icicles spread up and down her spine, as she hears a familiar, smoothly saccharin voice.

"Why, Cindy, what a way to greet your husband."

Chapter 24

Her shock quickly transforms into white-hot anger.

"You bastard, what are you doing in my house? How dare you come in here like this?"

"You already asked me that, darling. I came to see you and my kids. Anything wrong with a man wanting to visit his family?"

Pounding on the front door pulls her attention away for a minute from her anger and terror.

"That's the police," she tells him.

"Why don't you answer it then?" he asks

"No problem. I'm sure they will have the same questions I have when they find you here."

"I'm only visiting my kids, Cindy. I'm sure the officer will understand. I'm not the one who's hysterical and screaming all over the place. I'm not the one telling the kids to barricade themselves in their room against their own father. I'm not the one pulling dead bodies out of the river, and I'm not the one who works in a mental institution. Looks to me like you belong there more than some of the patients, if you ask me. Go ahead, open the door for the officer."

Cindy stares at her ex in amazement. "What the hell?"

She can hear the banging on the door growing ever more frantic.

"Just a minute," she yells. "I'm coming."

But shock slows her movements, and Andrew quickly rushes past her and opens the front door for the officer.

"Sir, may I ask what you're doing here?"

"I'm so sorry, officer. It seems that I startled my wife here by showing up unexpectedly to see the kids. I just let myself in the back door with my key. I thought she was at work, and I would surprise them."

"Ma'am?" He addresses Cindy, who has managed to get herself downstairs and to the front door. She feels like she's speaking from underwater, every movement slowing, her speech incoherent.

"Ma'am, could you please tell me what your relationship to this man is? I wasn't aware that anyone but you and the children were in the house."

"Unfortunately, Officer neither was I. This is my ex-husband. How ironic that he should pick this evening to break into my house and scare the children and me to death. And I would like to know how he got that key. I never gave it to him."

"What? You don't remember giving it to me? Of course, you did. How else would I have gotten it? I visit the kids all the time when you're working. You know how I feel about you leaving them all alone at night, Cindy, so I check up on them and make sure they're all right - while you're working, that is. I've told you a million times that I don't think it's a good idea to leave three underage kids alone all night."

Cindy's mind races. What on earth is going on? Why has Andrew suddenly shown up, and like this? What benefit is it to him to scare her like this? He had always been a bit of a sleeze, but if he wanted something from her, why didn't he just ask? What on earth is he doing here in the middle of the night, scaring her and the kids and making up stories? And why is he making her out to be an unfit mother? This doesn't make any sense.

"Sir, I'm afraid you will have to come with me. We have some questions for you down at the station."

The officer takes Andrew by the arm and Cindy closes the door behind them.

Puzzled by this turn of events, but nonetheless relieved that it was only Andrew stalking her and the children, Cindy slowly ascends the stairs and knocks softly on the bedroom door where the terrified kids are still hunkered down. They have no idea what's going on and she doesn't know how much she should tell them. Their father is an ass, but she's certainly not afraid of him and she knows he would never hurt the kids. Desert them and leave them to starve, maybe, but he never raised a hand to any of them, herself included, and she has no reason to think he would do so now.

What on earth could have caused him to act so strangely? When she had last seen him, he declared his intention to live without the restrictions that bringing up children placed on him, and then he disappeared out of their lives. This was the first she'd seen of him since then. And how odd was it that he showed up now and in this way. She wanted a chance to talk to him, to ask him what was going on. She hoped that the police would keep an eye on his whereabouts, at least for tonight. Tomorrow, she would go down to the station and see if she could get some answers.

Quickly, as emotionlessly as possible, Cindy gives the kids an overview of all that's gone on that night. She thinks it best not to keep too much from them, let them draw their own conclusions about their father's strange behavior. Just when she thought they were doing so well, despite all that they had been through, this has to happen. They're strangely silent, but the look in their eyes speaks of their confusion. Aren't fathers supposed to love and care for their children? She knows how they feel. She was deserted too. And the agony of her own experience mingles with this one and threatens to overwhelm her, a luxury she can't afford.

As gently as she can, she assures the children that their father's erratic behavior is in no way their fault, and that the danger is past. They will not sleep tonight, that she knows, and there will be no school for them tomorrow. She'll have to stay with them.

From Sarah's cell phone, she calls the hospital. Ray picks up.

"Thank God, it's you! I tried to get back to you, but your phone is out and I had no idea what to do when I heard you scream like that, so I called the police. I figured 'better safe than sorry'," he tells her.

As briefly as she can, she explains to Ray what's happened.

"I think he did something to the phones. What was on his mind, I have no idea, but it couldn't have been good. Maybe he just wanted to scare me, for some reason. I'll have to get the phone company out here tomorrow and have it fixed. I can't leave the kids right now, but as soon as they are settled down, I'll get your car back to you."

"Don't worry about the car. Why don't you wait until morning? That way, I can drive you home when you bring it back."

Cindy thanks Ray and asks him to call her when he's about to leave the hospital.

"Just in case I doze off or something," she gives him the number for the cell.

"Sure, Cindy, take care. Try to get some rest. I'll see you in the morning."

At a time like this, it's good to know that at least someone cares what happens to her and the kids.

Cindy goes back upstairs, throws off her sweater and slacks, and crawls into bed with the kids. Despite all she's been through that evening, she falls asleep almost immediately. Her dreams are filled with images of small, helpless creatures in her care, and an unnamed, unseen stalker who picks them off one by one, despite her best efforts to protect them.

An overwhelming feeling of sadness and despair fills her, and she clutches her children tightly in her arms.

Chapter 25

A noise from the other bedroom startles her awake, and it's several seconds before she realizes that Sarah's cell phone is ringing.

It's Ray. "Thought I'd better call before it's time to leave. Did you get any sleep?"

"Actually, yes. I'm just waking up. I have your car. I'm sorry. I'll throw something on and be there in a few minutes."

"You know, Cindy, why don't you just go back to sleep. I'll just walk home. I can come by your place later and pick up the car. You don't want the kids waking up and you not being there. It'll scare them, and they've gone through enough already."

"No, it's fine. I'll just wake Sarah and let her know where I'm going. Besides, things seem a lot different now that it's light out. Morning puts a whole new perspective on things, don't you think?"

"You're sure they'll be OK?"

"I'm sure. See you in five. I'll be waiting for you right outside the front door."

Cindy hears the uncertainty in Ray's voice.

"All right. See you in five then."

Quickly, Cindy grabs last night's clothes up off the floor and throws them on. Then she nudges Sarah awake and tells her that she's taking Ray's car back to him and she'll be right back. Sarah grunts her OK, turns over, and goes back to sleep.

Ten minutes later, she's pulling up in front of the hospital doors.

She waits. . . . . and waits. Where the heck is Ray?

Ten, then fifteen minutes pass. She can feel her anxiety begin to get the better of her. This isn't like him. It's way past time for his shift to end. He knew she was coming and that she would be anxious to get back home. He should have been watching for her.

"What on earth is keeping him?"

Cindy makes a decision. She pulls quickly into the parking lot. As she's about to get out of the car, she sees Ray heading in her direction.

"Sorry, didn't mean to keep you waiting like that," he tells her. "Just as I was about to leave, Jean motioned me into her office. She was in a particularly vile mood, even for her. Said someone has been messing around with the files down in the basement and did I know anything about it. Can you believe that? No one ever goes down there, and the one time you do, she's on to it."

"Damn. How the hell did she find out about me going down there? What did you tell her?"

"I told her you had been looking up some information on a patient that might help in her treatment. She wasn't happy. I hope I didn't say anything to get you in trouble. I can't see how trying to get more information on a patient could possibly be something negative."

"Don't worry about it, Ray, but you're right. I wasn't aware that anyone cared in the least about what was in that basement. They're just old files, and the mess they're in - you just wouldn't believe. Did you tell her why I wasn't at work last night?"

"She didn't ask. I figured it wasn't my business to tell her. You can tonight if you want to. Do you think you'll be able to work tonight? Let me tell you, it is nuts around there without you."

"I'm flattered, Ray, but I'm sure you made out just fine without me."

"Not really. For one thing, Mari is acting strange again. I try to talk to her, but she turns away. She won't take her meds anymore either. I didn't have the energy or the will to force her to take them last night, so she just sat by the window most of the night. Guess

I should have done something about it, but what the heck. She'll probably sleep today, and I'm sure that will make Jean happy. She'll have one less patient to deal with. I just hope Mari is OK today while we're not there. I don't know how the day staff will react to her if she gives them any problem."

"I'm sure she'll be OK. I don't know why but, for some reason, I'm glad you didn't force her to take the meds. Try not to worry too much about her. Tonight will come fast enough."

Ray stays quiet for awhile. Then, as if measuring his words carefully, he says, "Yeah, that's the way I feel too. I hope you're able to come back tonight. I need to bounce some things off you. Here we are."

He pulls in to Cindy's driveway. She starts to open the door, then hesitates.

"Ray, do you want to come in for coffee? The kids are still sleeping and we could talk. I really want to hear what you think about Mari. I know she's a strange girl, but did you know . . . ."

Cindy goes on to tell him a little of what she learned from her trip to the library: how Mari came to be at the hospital, how she doesn't believe what she's read about her, that she couldn't possibly have had anything to do with her grandmother's death.

Ray interrupts her, "You're right. Let's have that coffee."

He parks in the driveway and gets out, then stands back so Cindy can unlock the front door of the house and go in ahead of him.

The house is silent, except for an old black cat that keeps rubbing against him. Strange how its tail is down between its legs. It follows them into the kitchen.

"That's odd", he thinks "I've never seen a cat carry its tail between its legs like that."

Cindy gets out the coffee, puts a filter into the pot, and starts measuring.

"How do you like your coffee, Ray - weak, medium, strong, extra strong?"

"Better make it strong. Hey, Cindy, look at the way your cat holds his tail. I've never seen a cat do that before."

"I don't have a cat, Ray. It must have followed us into the house. Just a minute, I'll put him out. He's got to belong to someone and they'll probably be looking for him. Don't look at me like that. He won't go hungry. If his owners don't claim him, you can be sure that my girls will adopt him."

"Cindy, that cat was in the house when we got here. What's he doing in the house if he's not yours? How did he get in? Maybe the kids are up and let him in."

"The kids are not up. This place is too quiet."

Cindy can feel her heart pounding. She drops the coffee filters and points towards the stairs. Quicker than she can think, Ray is up them and opening the bedroom doors.

"Cindy, which room are they in? Where are they?"

She's right behind him. "Sarah? Kids? Where are you?" They're not in their room. She checks the closet, under the bed. She can hear herself, louder now,

"Kids, where are you? It's Mom. Don't hide from me, you're scaring me."

But there's no answer. **Her children are gone**!

Ray is on the phone calling 911. "Cindy, there's no dial tone. What the heck went on here last night?"

"I told you the phones were out. Sarah has a cell phone. It's on my dresser."

She races into her room, finds Sarah's phone, and calls 911.

"It's Cindy Murphy. My kids are missing." She hears the hysteria in her own voice, but she can't control it.

A calm female voice answers from the other end of the phone. "Yes, ma'am, you say your kids are missing? Can you give me some details?"

Cindy tries to keep it together as she explains what has happened. Suddenly, something occurs to her -

"The police picked up my ex-husband, Andrew Murphy, from here last night. Could you tell me if he's still in custody?"

"Yes, ma'am, he is." Cindy can tell from the tone of her voice that she knows exactly who Andrew Murphy is and why he's there. She detects no note of sympathy for him in the voice on the other end of the line.

"We'll send someone out immediately, ma'am. Check with your neighbors. Maybe the kids got frightened and went next door."

Right. Alice. They've got to be with Alice. But they would have left a note or something, wouldn't they?

"Thank you, I'll check." Cindy can feel the tears start as she begs.

"Tell them to hurry, please."

There's no way Sarah would have gone anywhere willingly without her cell phone. She would have called. She's too responsible. She knows I'd be frantic. She calls Alice anyway and asks her if she's seen the kids. Before she can hang up the phone, she sees Alice coming through the yard heading for her house. She slams the front door behind her and takes Cindy firmly in her arms. "It'll be all right." She tells her. "The police will find them. I'm sure of it."

Cindy looks at Ray and sees her own fear mirrored in his eyes.

The now familiar sound of sirens splits the air again.

Chapter 26

The police have left. The kids weren't found. They noted that the same window someone had tried to jimmy last night is now wide open. Other than that, there's no clue as to what happened to them.

Cindy sits on the bed where she last saw them, clutching a small teddy bear, silently crying. It's all she can do. She knows for a fact that it is, indeed, possible to die from a broken heart.

Two detectives are still there, asking questions, trying to figure out anything they can about how and why three kids could or would have vanished in the early morning hours. Why are they here? Why aren't they out searching?

It's 7:30. The kids should be heading out the door for school now. Cindy suddenly feels very calm.

"Ray, you need to go home and get some sleep."

"I know. Are you sure you'll be OK?"

"I'll stay with her. Why don't you try to go and get some sleep?" They had forgotten all about Alice, but she's still here, anxious to be of some help.

"She's right, Ray. You do need to get some sleep. One of us needs to be able to work tonight."

They both knew that it certainly wouldn't be her. Even if the kids were found, she wouldn't be able to leave them. What was going on and why on earth were these things happening to her? He was sure that the disappearance of the kids had something to do with her ex's visit last night, but what? He was in police custody when the kids disappeared. Why did he arrive on the scene so suddenly when neither she nor the kids had heard from him for more than two years? At least as far as Cindy had told him, she hadn't heard from him in that long. And why would she lie about something like that? She wouldn't. It doesn't make sense. None of this makes any sense.

Out loud, he says,

"You're right. I'll be no good to anybody if I don't get some sleep. I'll be back in a little while. If you need me, just call. Here's my number."

He writes something on a piece of paper and places it on the bedside table. He looks back at a devastated Cindy as he leaves the room. His heart breaks for her, for the kids who are God knows where. But he's got to get home and get some rest. The way things are going, who knows what is going to be needed of him later today, or this evening, or tomorrow. He can't afford to let himself get too exhausted.

"They will find them, Cindy," he tells her just before he goes out the door. "They'll be back before you know it."

Her tearful face turns away.

"Odd," he thinks. "I barely know her beyond work. Yet I feel like her tears are mine too, like they're burning me from the inside out."

Chapter 27

Out of the immediate vicinity of the crisis taking place in Cindy's home, Ray is able to clear his mind a bit as he drives the short distance to his home. "This all doesn't make any sense. There's something we're not seeing here. There is something we're missing that'll pull it all together. What? What is it? Where's the missing piece?"

Cindy is being targeted. There's no doubt in his mind. How the hell did Jean know that she had been in the basement? Someone has been watching her, maybe even stalking her, and it's not just her ex-husband. He was in jail when the kids disappeared. These aren't coincidences. Whoever is doing this must have known that the police would be involved, and has decided it's worth the risk. She's in danger, and, wherever the kids are, they are definitely in danger. The only piece of the puzzle that's available to him is Andrew Murphy. He needs to find out what Cindy's ex is doing back here and exactly what his involvement is in all this. He turns the car around and heads back to the house.

The cars are gone from the driveway. So, the detectives who were questioning her are probably back at the station.

"And that's just where I'm going," he thinks. "I want to know what's going on with this guy, why he suddenly showed up and why he found it necessary to frighten the crap out of Cindy and the kids. He's got to have at least some of the answers."

As he pulls into the police station, he thinks to himself, "Well, this isn't exactly what I had planned for this morning." He takes the stairs two at a time and pulls open the heavy doors. He asks for the detectives who are looking for the Murphy kids. Immediately, one of the detectives, Brown, he thinks his name is, appears in front of him.

"Aren't you Mrs. Murphy's friend? Come in here. I want to talk to you." He leads Ray down a narrow hallway into a small room, and points to a chair. Brown stands over him. "Now, do you want to tell me why you're here?"

"I just wanted to ask if you found out anything about Andrew Murphy, the ex-husband, who, I believe, is here. He's got to be involved in this in some way. She doesn't see him in two years and then he just shows up and scares the devil out of her and the kids. Then they disappear. What's that all about?"

"Mr. Murphy is here and he's denying any involvement in his kids' disappearance. Swears he would never harm them and that he just showed up wanting to see them, and knew the ex-wife would never let it happen, so he took matters into his own hands, found a way to get into the house when he thought she'd be at work. He claims he never intended to scare them or her or anyone. Just wanted to see his kids. And that he has no idea where they are now."

"OK. Well, that's all I wanted to know. Do you think it would be possible for me to see him?"

Ray is certain that, if he can just get near the guy, maybe talk to him a bit, he can figure out for himself what kind of a person he is - dumb and stupid, or smart and callous. That would make all the difference in his next move toward finding the kids. If he's dumb, then maybe he's telling the truth about just wanting to see the kids, and he's not involved in the kidnapping. If he's smart and callous, maybe he got someone else to take them for him. But what the heck would he want with three kids anyway, other than to make Cindy miserable? The reason he left in the first place was because he didn't want them and the responsibility that went with caring for them. It's looking more and more like this guy is probably just stupid, and someone has asked him to scare Cindy for some reason; maybe even paid him to do it. There's no other reason a guy like him would do something like this. Someone must have told him what to say when he got caught, too. The question is why?

"Can I talk to the guy?" he asks again.

"Nope, he's in custody. We're still questioning him."

"I hope you let him know that, if those kids are hurt and he's had anything to do with it . . . ." Ray can't finish. He can feel himself losing it.

The detective motions to the door of the room.

"Sir, I think we can handle it. You can leave now. That way."

Ray takes his time leaving. He's wondering how long they will hold Andrew Murphy, and whether it would be worth his while to wait for him until he's far enough away from the police station. Then maybe he can get his hands on him and get some information from him. Ray's a big guy. Years of wrestling with unruly mental patients has given him a sense of what he can do to make someone give him information without actually hurting them.

He sits in his clunky, old car for a few minutes before changing his mind. Cindy's right. The best thing he can do for all of them is to go home and get some rest. Surely the cops know how to get any information they need that her ex might have.

Ray heads for home the long way, past Cindy's place once again. All seems calm. No one would ever guess the horrible agony that clutches at the heart of the sole occupant of this dumpy little house with the white clapboards and the dark green shutters. No one would ever guess that, inside, a desperate woman is waiting beside a phone, hoping beyond hope for a call that will tell her that her children are OK.

"Didn't know she lived so close. Maybe after all this is over and the kids are safely home . . . ." He can't believe this, what he's thinking.

"Forget it," he tells himself.

Cindy is a good friend. She's been real kind to me at work. I owe her. I'd do the same for anyone if they had to deal with all this shit."

But he knows, deep down in his heart, that it's not true. He's known since the very first day she came to work at the hospital that there's no one like Cindy. There never has been, nor will there ever be anyone else like her in his life.

Ray's thoughts are beginning to scare him. He needs to focus on the present - what's in front of him right now. He pulls into his driveway, puts the old car in park and heads for his back door. He throws himself on his sofa and turns on the TV. Before he can change the channel, he's deep asleep.

Ray doesn't see the face pressed against his window, its nose flat, its eyes wild and frantic, its unkempt hair sticking out from its head in all directions. He doesn't hear the scraping as someone tries to open his closed window. He doesn't see the window slowly lift up, up so someone can crawl in through it, into the room where he lies sleeping. He doesn't realize that, whatever his feelings for Cindy, their lives are about to intermingle in a way that they will never again be able to untangle.

Chapter 28

Someone is in the room with him. Ray is awake, but stays very still, keeping his eyes closed. He feels someone there, staring at him, watching him sleep. Whoever or whatever isn't moving, is barely breathing, but he knows it's there...

Slowly, he opens his eyes. To his shock and great relief, staring back at him is a young girl. At first, he's positive it's Mari, but then he realizes there's no way it could be her. Slowly, so as not to startle her, he sits up on the sofa.

"Who are you," he softly asks, "and what are you doing here? How did you get into my house?"

Tears start to wend their way down her cheeks. He sees her lips move. She softly tells him, "He said 'go in through the window'."

Ray leans closer. He asks, "Who? Who said that? Who told you to go in through the window?"

"He did - the man who drove me here." The child speaks so softly he can barely hear her.

"My sisters. He has my sisters."

Ray whispers softly, trying not to scare her anymore than she already is.

"You're Cindy's kid. Oh hell, that's who you are. You're Cindy's kid."

Ray can barely believe what he's saying, that she's nodding her head. He picks up the phone. It occurs to him that he doesn't have the cell phone number that Cindy gave him. "What's your cell phone number?" he asks.

He dials as she tells him. Cindy picks up. "I have one of your kids, Cindy. She's here, in my house." He turns towards the child. "Which one are you? Here, speak to your mother."

"Who is this?" Cindy asks from the other end of the phone. Ray passes the phone to the child. "Speak to your mother." he tells her. "Let her know that you're OK."

"Mom, it's Sarah. I'm all right. But I don't' know where Julie and Kelly are. We were sleeping and a man came in and he said to come with him. He had a gun. Then he took me here and told me to go in through the window. He told me to tell you to leave town or he would hurt my sisters. Mom, what's going on? Why does he want us to leave?"

Cindy can barely believe her ears. Sarah is safe. Thank God. But what has happened? What's happening to the other kids? Who took them and why? She needs to get to Sarah right away, talk to her, ask her what happened, and try to figure out what's going on.

"Where are you now Sarah?" she asks her

"I don't know."

Ray motions for Sarah to give him the phone, and tells Cindy that she's with him. "Don't move, Cindy. I'm bringing her right home. We'll be there in less than five minutes."

Ray bundles her into his old car and heads for Cindy's home.

What the heck is going on? Why was she dropped off at my house, and why only her? Where are the other two?" His mind races.

Cindy is watching for them. She runs out to meet the car and takes Sarah into her arms. Quickly, all three go back inside, locking the door behind them. They sit at the kitchen table.

"Sarah, what do you know? Do you have any idea where your sisters are? Did he say anything about why he dropped only you off at Ray's home? Are Julie and Kelly safe? Did he say how we get them back?"

"Yes Mom. Before he dropped me off, he said that if you told the police to back off, that we had just gone to a friend's house, he would deliver them to our front door as soon as he saw a moving van out front. He wants us to move away from this town and away from your job right away. He said that, if you don't do what he says, then we will never see Julie and Kelly again."

Big tears pour from Sarah's eyes.

Cindy can't believe her ears. "I'm calling the moving van now. If all I need to do to get my children back is to quit my job and move, it's done."

"I think you should let the police know what's going on, Cindy. There's a good probability that whoever is behind this could still hurt the kids even if you do everything he says. You have no guarantees they will be safe. You can't trust whoever is doing this. The best way to make sure they're safe is to keep the police involved. Besides, it doesn't make any sense. Why would someone want you out of here so badly? Why go to such an effort? And how on earth would anyone know enough to put your kid through my window? How did they know I'd get her to you immediately without contacting the police?"

Cindy knows Ray is right, but the thought of getting all her kids back safe and sound is a powerful motivator. She doesn't care who wants her out of this town. All she cares about is the safety of her kids. She picks up the phone.

"Who are you calling, Cindy?"

"Ray, I'm calling the police to tell them the kids are OK. Then I'm calling some moving companies. I intend to hire the one who can get to my house the fastest."

"And what do you expect to do after they have arrived. You have no place to go, and no one is going to hire you if you leave your job with no notice. Think about it, Cindy. You want to do what's right for your kids. Whoever is pulling these stunts on you is hoping you will react without thinking. I'm just telling you to think, that's all. Give the police a chance to do their job. It's the best chance for you and for your kids. Don't run. That's just what he expects you to do."

"Cindy, listen to me." Ray's voice is showing signs of desperation. "If you don't tell the police what's happening, you're liable to find your kids bodies somewhere after all this is over."

That gets her attention. "All right, all right, Ray, I'm listening." Her voice rises. She's on the verge of hysteria, complete panic.

"What do you suggest? How can we tell the police anything without letting on to anyone who may be watching us? We don't know. Maybe whoever is doing this has ties to the police. We don't know who it is. We don't know anything except that my kids are in danger and I want them back here, with me and Sarah."

This isn't good. She's about to lose it. Besides that, she's right. How do they know just who's involved in this? How do they know anything?

"You know what, Cindy, get a phone book. Call a moving van. See if you can get one here today if possible, or tomorrow. I'll help you. Start packing. If anyone is watching, we want them to see that you are doing what they want, that they've got you on the run. I'm heading for the hardware store for a 'home for sale by owner' sign for your front yard. Meanwhile, go to your neighbor's house, the one who helped you out before, borrow some newspapers from her to wrap your pictures and things in. Do you think you can trust her?"

"Who, Alice? Yes, I trust her. She's the one who called me about the stalker in the first place."

"OK, that's good because we can use her help. I think we're going to have to risk letting the police know what's going on, and Alice needs to contact them. Make sure she understands how important it is that she does it immediately, that no one else knows, and that she's as sneaky as she can be about it. We're just going to have to trust her to be our go-between."

Ray heads toward the door before she has a chance to argue.

"We'll never be able to find them by ourselves, Cindy. This is the only way. Right now, you can start taking pictures off the walls. We want anyone who's watching to think that you're actually going to move. First things first, we've got to get your kids back. Oh, by the way, when you go to Alice's to get the newspapers, take Sarah with you and leave her with Alice. The police might be able to get some information from her that could help them find her sisters."

Chapter 29

The pictures are down from Cindy's walls and packed into boxes. Cindy hated to let Sarah out of her sight, but she has to agree with Ray that she will be safer with Alice than with her, and may be of use to the police.

Alice is horrified when Cindy tells her what has been happening, but Cindy knows she loves the intrigue, too, loves being involved in it. She'll put Sarah in the car and pretend she's going grocery shopping. She can call a cab from the store and head for the police station with Sarah, fill them in on what's happened and why Sarah is with her. Then they go back to the store, pick up her own car and head back to her house. That way, anyone watching her car will just think she's shopping and not catch on that she's talking to the police. It's the best she can do. She only hopes it's enough.

Cindy makes a call to the hospital and speaks to Jean, the nurse supervisor. She explains that, due to personal problems, she needs to take some time off. Jean is furious. She has no idea what's going on in Cindy's life, nor does she care, she tells her. All she knows is that she's already short-staffed due to budget cuts and now she will have to find someone to cover for Cindy.

Cindy suddenly realizes that the reason Jean is so angry is because she knows that she will never get anyone to take the night shift at that hospital for what they're paying Cindy. Maybe she is more valuable to the hospital than she had thought.

"Sorry, Jean. I am taking some time off, starting right now, at least a couple of weeks. I'll have to let you know when I can come back to work. You're just going to have to figure something out."

She can sense Jean's astonishment on the other end of the phone. Meek, compliant Cindy has never before spoken to her like this.

When Ray comes back with the sign, she tells him, "Maybe you should tell Jean what's going on. I know she's a bit caustic, but I think we can trust her. Maybe she will be able to help. At the very least, it'd be good to know that I have a job when all this is over."

"I'll do that tonight. I've put the sign out front. Now, I'm heading home, this time for some sleep, I hope. You can start packing."

"Thanks, Ray. The van will be here tomorrow, first thing in the morning. I don't know where to tell them to take my stuff, but we'll figure it out."

Ray can't believe the sudden strength in Cindy's voice. He thinks, "She's determined to get those kids back safely, and she is convinced she can make it happen. I guess she just can't afford to imagine anything else."

He leaves a worried and frightened - but determined - Cindy and heads off for his own house.

This time, as Ray drifts off to sleep on his couch, there are no interruptions. He wakes at five p.m.

"Oh wow, I actually got five hours of uninterrupted sleep." he thinks. He's anxious to speak to Jean and explain to her what's happening. She's nasty to work for but she is trustworthy. They will just have to take their chances with her. Besides, he really needs to get another opinion about what's going on, talk to someone outside of this mess. Maybe she will be able to add some pieces to the puzzle.

Ray showers and dresses rapidly. He'll stop to see Cindy before heading to the hospital. It suddenly occurs to him that she has probably not eaten all day, so he makes sandwiches from the only thing he has in the fridge - eggs - and takes a can of soup with him. It's not much, but it's better than nothing.

As he pulls into the driveway, he notices that the front door is wide open and he can see her working steadily inside the house. All ornaments, including paintings, pictures of the kids, everything, is off the walls and wrapped in newspaper. There are boxes everywhere.

"Man, she's sure going at it," he mutters under his breath.

He pulls open the screen door and makes himself known. "Cindy, it's Ray. I've brought something to eat."

"Hi Ray." He hears the tension and tiredness in her voice. "Man, am I happy to see you." She crosses the room and hugs him. "Did you get some sleep?"

"Yes, as a matter of fact, I did. Can I use your kitchen? I've got egg salad sandwiches, and I need to heat up some chicken soup to go with them. Have you eaten?"

"No. I'm not particularly hungry." She follows him into the kitchen.

"How's it going?" He asks this under his breath. It occurs to him that the place may have ears. Who knows what Cindy's husband was able to do when he was in here without any of them knowing about it. He looks around. "Could be that I'm just getting paranoid now," he mutters to himself.

Cindy picks up on his cue. It never occurred to her that someone might even be listening inside her house, but anything is possible.

"I'm pretty much packed. The van will be here at nine tomorrow morning. I'll just work most of the night and I should be ready for them."

"Where did you get all the packing material?" Ray is hoping she will let him in on whether or not Alice was able to contact the police.

"My neighbor is helping. She found the newspaper and got these boxes for me."

Now Ray knows that she's been back and forth between the neighbor and her house a couple of times at least. In case anyone's listening, he asks her,

"What did you tell the neighbor about why you are moving on such short notice?"

Cindy has a ready answer.

"I told her my mother had a stroke and needed us with her immediately. She's been good about it. Told me she would do anything she could to help. She even said she knew someone who might want to rent the house for a couple of weeks or even a month while we're gone and save me some money."

Cindy is talking loudly now. Ray hopes it's not too loud.

"Do you find it a little hot in here?" he asks her.

Ray goes over to the light switch and turns on the fan. He takes a writing pad out of his pocket and writes on it. "Do the police know what's going on?" He smiles.

Cindy nods, smiles back.

"She catches on fast," he thinks.

They finish their soup and sandwiches in a silence broken only by the swish, swish, swish of the fan. He's relieved. He feels better now that he knows the police are involved. He's hoping Sarah can give them some information that might let them know where her sisters have been taken. Meanwhile, Cindy has to appear to be doing what the kidnapper or kidnappers want.

By six-thirty that evening, he leaves the little house and it's sad but busy occupant and heads for the hospital. He wants a chance to speak to Jean before she heads home and he gets busy with his shift.

Chapter 30

It's a good thing he's early. Jean is on the warpath. He can't help but feel irritated at her wrath, considering all that Cindy has been through. Jean couldn't handle half of what Cindy goes through on a daily basis. She's only got herself to look after, and she thinks she knows how everyone's life should be run - according to her rules, of course. Well, it's time for her to come down off her high horse.

Ray takes his supervisor firmly by the arm. "Come with me," he tells her. "You need to be made aware of some things."

Surprisingly, she doesn't resist. He leads her into the office and closes the door. As succinctly as he can, he tells her what's going on with Cindy. He can tell by her reaction that she's trying hard to digest the information. It's a lot, he knows.

"My God, why didn't she say something to me about this?"

"She couldn't. We don't know who has the kids and why. We decided to trust you and thought maybe you might know something, anything that could help us get more information on where her kids are."

"Surely neither of you would think that I'd have anything to do with taking her children . . . . how could you ever believe . . . .?"

"Of course we didn't. I just thought . . . We thought . . . . Maybe you knew someone in town who was capable of this, not that you would have anything to do with it. Now listen, Jean. We don't want anyone to inadvertently say anything about this. Who knows who might be listening? Two lives are at stake. We can't be too careful."

Jean, the consummate professional, takes charge.

"What we need to do right now is to go over everything that's happened in the last few days and see if we can't come up with anything. Do you have any ideas where the police are on this?"

"No, they won't tell me anything. All they say is that they're handling it," Ray tells her.

"It figures. This is a small town. They've probably never had to deal with anything like this before. I'll bet they're sitting on their asses hoping that the kids have simply run away or gone somewhere with friends and they will show up eventually. Meanwhile, look at the risk they're taking that something dreadful could be happening to them at this very moment."

Ray had never thought of the police as being inadequate bunglers. He truly believed they were more prepared than any of them to look after the situation, especially considering the information that Alice had given them, along with what Sarah would tell them. Surely they would be able to find those children.

"Damn, I hear sirens again." He mutters, mostly to himself. "What the heck is going on? I've heard them maybe once in all the time I've lived here and now, suddenly, I'm hearing them constantly."

Jean is looking out the window.

"You're hearing them because they just arrived in our parking lot," she tells him dryly. "Didn't you say that you sent word to them by a neighbor that whoever took the kids told Cindy not to contact any police? And that it was especially important for the kids safety that they not be too obvious in their search?"

Ray can't believe his ears or eyes. In the parking lot, two cop cars pull to a screeching halt and four officers step out and come tearing into the building. So much for secrecy.

"We're looking for Ray LeBrun. We understand he works here."

"Yes, that's me. What's the problem, officers?"

"Sir, I'm afraid you'll have to come with us."

Jean rolls her eyes towards the ceiling. She was right - these people are bungling idiots.

"Could you tell me what this is about?"

"We have some questions about the disappearance of two young girls. Their mother works here with you, I believe, and you have a relationship with her."

"Yes, their mother works here, and we're friends. We have no other relationship, although I am concerned about the welfare of the kids."

"Well, sir, please come with us. We need to speak with you."

Ray is thankful that Jean is aware of what's happening. Thank God he decided to let her in on this. He leaves with the officers and climbs into the back of the police car. They arrive at the station and, this time, they're more than happy to talk to him.

Apparently, the fact that Sarah was left at his house makes it obvious to them that he's involved in the disappearance of the other two children, even though she told them that it was someone else who took her and her sisters and made her climb in through Ray's windows. He tells his story again and again, and asks them to please keep their investigation and their sirens quiet as the kids lives may depend on it.

"My God," he thinks, "do any of them have a brain in their head? Why don't they listen to the kid? Why don't they listen to me? They're so caught up in their own importance that they're risking two kids' lives. They won't admit that anyone outside of themselves can know anything about what's going on and they insist that they're going to do things their way, no matter what. They don't really care if the kids are in danger, as long as they look important. Cindy was right not to want to get them involved. Their stupidity is going to get her kids killed."

Finally, after they have convinced themselves either that he knows nothing or that he's never going to tell them what he does know, he is able to leave the police station. His car is back at the hospital, and he'll be damned if he's going to ask any of them for a ride. Cindy was right. These guys are useless, and the kids would probably be safer if they weren't involved at all. He manages to grab a cab and makes it back to the hospital for the rest of his shift. It's after ten, but Jean is still here. She can't leave until he's back.

"You know," he tells himself, as he buzzes the front door to be let in, "I'm glad I told Jean. She is probably going to be more help than the cops."

"Thank God, you're back. I need to get home and get some sleep," she tells him as soon as she catches sight of him. "Did you get any information on whether they have a clue as to where the kids might be, or did they just hassle you?"

"They're useless," he answers. The worried look on her face surprises him. She's the last person in the world that he would expect to be concerned about Cindy or her kids.

"I'm going to sleep on it. I'll come in first shift - don't leave till I get here. We'll put our heads together and see if there's anything we can come up with. Can you handle things here tonight by yourself or should I try to call in someone to help? Most of the patients are asleep for the night. The two orderlies are John and Elmer. You should be okay."

"Thanks, Jean. I'll be here when you get in. Someone has got to find those kids soon. I have a feeling that the longer they're missing, the more danger they're in."

"Yes, same here. I'll be in early."

Ray watches her head towards the front doors. The clomp, clomp, clomp of her matronly shoes on the tiles, her rigid posture, the severe bun that holds her hair at the back of her neck all belie the fact that a caring heart beats underneath it all. Who would have thought it?

Aimlessly, he wanders over to the window that looks out onto the parking lot. Through the darkness, he sees someone in the shadows, off to the side, watching as Jean gets into her car and drives away. The figure then heads over to another car in the lot, gets in and leaves in the same direction that Jean just took. Ray notes the plate number, silently thanking whatever Gods there be for the recent onset of his far-sightedness.

"Odd," he thinks, "that someone other than our staff is in our parking lot. I wonder . . . .?"

Too bad he can't call the cops with the information, but he's not too certain now that he can trust them. Something about the way they were grilling him made him think that they were more than a little anxious to pin this on him. Hmmmm . . . . I wonder . . . .

Ray sits down at the computer.

"I wonder if I can get anything off this, if it's even on-line." Ray has never used the darn thing. It is ancient compared to the nice new one that he has at home. He may live in a dump, drive an old car, and wear old, outdated clothes, but his computer, well, that's something else.

He pokes around a bit and discovers that it is on-line, and that he can get into the website for the Registry of Motor Vehicles. He clicks on 'replace plates' and punches in the plate number of the car license that just followed Jean out of the parking lot. After a little more tweaking, he manages to come up with a name. He calls directory assistance and asks for a phone number for the person whose name and address he's located on-line.

"They're right when they say you can get just about anything off the web," he thinks to himself. He dials the number.

A male voice comes on the line. "Hello"

"Sir, I apologize for calling so late, but this is Security from Tillsboro Mental Hospital. Were you aware, sir, that your car was recently seen leaving our staff parking lot? I was wondering if there was any particular reason why it was there, and if you would be so kind as to find another place to park it in the future. This is private property, sir. We wouldn't want to be responsible for any damage to your car while it's on our property."

An angry voice answers him. "First of all, it's almost midnight. Furthermore, my car was stolen last week and I have no idea why it would be in your parking lot, or anywhere else, for that matter. Who did you say this is?"

"This is Security at The Tillsboro Hospital," Ray answers.

"You mean the mental place? Call the cops in the morning and let them know that you saw my car in your parking lot. Now, I'm going back to sleep."

"I'm sorry to have disturbed you sir," Ray tells him.

That's about what he thought would happen. Whoever was following Jean didn't want anyone to know who he was, so he used a stolen car.

Ray searches the Rolodex for Jean's number. He needs to make sure she made it home OK and that she locks her doors and her windows. He calls her number. Silently, he waits and counts - Five rings - six - seven . . . . . No one answers.

Chapter 31

"They are all right."

Ray hears a soft voice. He looks up to see Mari standing beside him.

Strangely, he's not surprised. Why does he feel in his gut that, somehow, all this has to do with her and the reason she's here? If he can just figure out how and why, the pieces of this puzzle should fall into place.

It was when Cindy started caring about Mari, checking her files, looking up information on her in the library – that was when her own kids began to be in danger. It is like someone's telling her not to reach out, not to stir things up, to leave Mari and any information about her buried. But that's just plain foolish. Why on earth should anyone care if she tries to find out more about Mari? It seems like a normal thing to him that Cindy would want to help, since Mari is about the same age as Cindy's daughters and seems so out of place here.

The sound of Mari's quiet breathing beside him brings him out of his reverie.

"What do you mean, Mari?" he asks.

"The children - they're all right," she whispers softly, so softly that he can barely hear her.

"How do you know that?"

"I know."

Mari turns slowly and makes her way back to her place by the window. In her long robe, she seems to Ray not to be walking, but floating on air. She sits, her face turned outward toward the night.

"She seems almost unreal," he thinks. Whatever Cindy is going through now, she's right to try to help her. We have to find out what's up with this child and get her out of here."

Something tells him that Mari does know that Cindy's kids are all right. How she knows is a mystery to him, but he has to believe it. He has to. He can't even begin to imagine what life would be like for Cindy if they're not.

Ray gets up from his desk and walks down the long corridor to where Mari is sitting at the window. He sits beside her on the window sill.

"Mari, you need to tell me. How do you know the kids are ok?"

"*I know.*"

"I need more than that. I want to help. What do you know? Who's got them? Where are they?"

"*I don't know that, but they're OK.*"

Mari's voice is so soft that Ray doesn't even know if he's hearing her right.

"Are you sure, Mari? Are you sure you can't tell me anything else about them?"

"*It's dark, and they're alone. They're scared. They don't know where he took their sister who looks after them.*"

Ray can't believe he's actually having this conversation.

"Their sister is home. He left her at my house. She's fine."

"*It's big and it's dark and they're alone and frightened. It's not good. We need to help them get back to the light.*"

"Yes Mari, that's exactly what we need to do", he tells her. "And I have no idea how."

Mari looks directly at him. Her beautiful green eyes speak volumes through the silence. *Ray feels himself falling, falling into the gentle emptiness, and he listens to the softness of the night for just a moment – just for a moment . . . .*

Chapter 32

"Yes, of course," he whispers, "of course. What we need to do is get them back home. But just how are we going to do that?"

Ray gives his head a slight shake, trying to clear it.

This isn't a world of magic and mystery. This is reality. Do something - he needs to do something. He feels strangled, like his hands are tied. A sense of desperation swells upwards from his gut, into his chest. He hears his heart, beating rapidly. He struggles not to let it overwhelm him.

So many things are running through his mind. He can't leave the hospital and check that Jean is OK. He can't call Cindy to go check on her; she's home waiting by the phone in case there's any word on her two daughters. And he can't call the police. What would he tell them? That he can't reach his supervisor? That he thinks he saw someone trail her from the parking lot? They've done nothing to help so far, except imply that he is involved in the kids' disappearance. Best to just leave them out of it. All he can do is hope that Jean has the good sense to lock herself tightly in her house.

He checks the time. It's after midnight already. He's just going to have to keep busy, bite the bullet, and hope that Jean shows up for work in the morning. He feels like he needs to do something, anything. His anxiety mounts as the night wears on, a huge black lump of crap rising from his gut up through his middle and into his throat.

"Everything I know leads me down another trail of questions," he mutters angrily, frustrated at his own inability to somehow move things forward, to reach some kind of conclusion.

"Why on earth would anyone cause such pain for a person like Cindy? Why would anyone want her out of the way so badly that they would go to all this effort? And why the hell is someone trailing Jean?"

He draws a blank. He's got nothing. He sits at the front desk and puts his head into his arms. Something, there has got to be something he can do.

At six a.m. Ray startles from his dreamy half-sleep to the whoosh of the front door as it opens and closes. He is so exhausted that he can barely raise his head.

It takes just a moment for it to sink in that Jean is here, alive and well.

"When she says she'll be here early, she's here early," Ray thinks.

He tries to recover his balance, his thoughts still surrounded by the fog that folded over him in his dreams.

"Jean, thank God you're here." His voice seems to come from a place far, far away, deep down inside of him. "I tried to reach you by phone last night. I was worried. There was a strange car in the parking lot and I thought I saw it follow you when you left."

"Well, I'm here now so whoever it was didn't do me any harm." Jean seems not to have noticed anything different about him or his speech. "Are you sure they were following me? Maybe it was just a coincidence that they were in the parking lot and happened to leave when I left. We're both jumpy - not surprising, considering what has happened to Cindy."

"That's what I thought, too. But it worried me, considering what's gone on the past few days." Ray can feel his thoughts clearing - coming back to him in some semblance of order. "I tried to call you to let you know, but you didn't answer and I didn't know what else to do. I couldn't leave here to check on you, and I didn't know who to call for help."

"You couldn't get me? That's odd." She thinks for a moment. "I was probably in the shower or asleep when you were trying to reach me. I didn't sleep for long, though. I spent most of the night going over and over what you told me, and all I came up with was questions. Like - who the heck would be so invested in trying to get rid of Cindy that they would take such extreme measures as kidnapping her kids? And that strange thing with her husband . . . . I take it the police don't think he had anything to do with it - the kidnapping, I mean."

"He was in their custody when the kids disappeared." Ray's thoughts are clearer now.

"Yes. Quite the alibi."

"I guess the first question we have to ask ourselves is why. You know, Jean, I may be way off base here, but it seems to me that Cindy's life was quite unexceptional until she started taking an interest in that young girl who sits by the window, Mari. She felt a certain empathy towards her, probably because she's about the same age as her own kids. She had started to do some digging. Do you remember her checking the files in the basement?"

"Yes, I remember." Jean looks pensive. Ray gives her some thinking time.

"You know, I remember now. I got a call from one of the higher-ups, someone on the Board of Directors. Told me he'd had complaints of nurses leaving the floor during the night shift, leaving patients unattended. He said that I'd better make sure it never happened again or my job was in jeopardy."

Ray looks at her, astonished. "How would anyone know that Cindy wasn't on the floor for such a short time? I never said anything. She left me in charge, so the patients were perfectly well looked after anytime she was down there."

Jean and Ray look at each other. The question hits them both at the same time,

"Who made that call?"

"You don't have any idea who the caller might have been?" he asks her.

"I don't remember his name. The only thing I can recall is how upset I was by it."

Ray's mind is in full gear now. "He probably didn't give his own name anyway, so don't feel bad. Whoever this is, he's using whatever is dear to us. For you, it was your job; for Cindy, it's her kids. He's using them to control you, get you emotional so you'll just react and not be reasonable or practical."

"Yes, you're right. We have to keep our wits about us if we're going to get any answers. "

"You're right, Jean." Ray knows now that he can trust her, so he's not holding anything back.

"Cindy did some research at the library." He tells her. "She was checking to see when and why Mari turned up here. Thought if she could find some answers, maybe it'd be possible to help the kid somehow."

"And did she find anything that could help?" Jean asks him.

"How much do you know about why Mari is here?"

"Not much. Her file says that she's dangerous to herself and to others and that she needs to be here for intensive therapy.

"Well, Cindy found out that before she came here, she was living with her grandmother who mysteriously wound up dead. It was thought that Mari killed her, even though there didn't seem to be much proof of it other than the fact that she wouldn't talk to anyone and tell them what happened. No relatives showed up to claim her, so she's been here for almost three years now."

"And wasn't there anyone who objected? No one looking out for the child?" Jean finds it hard to believe what she's hearing.

"I really don't think they took it that far. They just put her here and left her, hoping that no one would ask any questions. And no one did, until Cindy came along. We all just went along doing our jobs. No one ever bothered to wonder about Mari and what she was doing here, and she obviously wasn't in any position to help herself."

"Well, isn't that interesting." Jean slowly mutters, as much to herself as to anyone else. "Looks like Cindy has touched on something that's making someone very anxious to get rid of her. And that something could very possibly be about Mari and why she's here."

Ray can't believe that Jean has come to the same conclusion that he has. He had thought maybe his imagination was working overtime, and that Cindy's stupid husband had simply had someone take the kids while he was locked up because he wanted vengeance on Cindy for some reason. That really didn't make a lot of sense to him, since the husband hadn't wanted the kids in the first place. Nonetheless, he decided to ask Jean what she thought about that scenario.

"You don't think . . . . the husband might have had anything to do with it? That he hired someone to do it while he was being held by the police so he wouldn't be a suspect?"

"Absolutely not. Not from what you've told me about him and his relationship with the kids. He didn't want them in the first place. No, there's something far more sinister going on here."

"I just wish we could figure it all out. I don't think we're going to get much help from the police, but I'm grateful to have you on our side. If you'll take over for me here, I'm anxious to touch base with Cindy and see if she's got anything new to add to this."

"Great, you go do that." Jean is distracted, her mind like a machine, checking every possibility she can imagine. "See if you can make her understand how important it is for her to rack her brain for any details, no matter how insignificant they may seem. This guy, or whoever is behind it, is keeping her off balance emotionally, and he's hoping she will be so focused on her kids that attention will be drawn away from Mari's problems and away from the truth of why she's here. You know, Ray, we probably know the person who's doing this. We just have to put the pieces together."

"Yes, OK. So we've got to keep calm and try to make some sense out of all this. And we need to get Mari to talk, to tell us exactly what happened to her grandmother three years ago. We need her account of it."

Jean agrees. "You're right, Ray. That's definitely my first step. I'll work on it today and see if she can tell me anything. You go check on Cindy. Let me know immediately if you find out anything."

Ray had always felt kind of resentful when Jean issued commands before. Now, however, he is more than happy to have her take charge.

It feels good to know that he's leaving things in her capable hands. What a difference a change in attitude can make. The day shift should be in soon. She'll have some help and be able to relax a bit. Maybe she can work some magic and get Mari to fill in some blanks on what happened to her grandmother and why she ended up here. Ray guesses she's got as good a chance as anybody at getting some information out of the kid.

Meanwhile, he's heading for Cindy's house to see if there have been any new developments on her kids whereabouts. Maybe Cindy can give him something that might be of help. Ray heads for his car. He doesn't see the small, young face at the window watching him. He doesn't hear her speak silently to herself . . .

Help me. Help all of us.

Ray feels eyes burning into his back, following him, and he turns around, looking upwards. He sees only a ghostly shadow, but he knows that Mari is in the window, watching. Her brilliant, piercing, green eyes focus on him through the darkness, and he wonders, "What does she know? Does she have the answers to our questions? Can she help us save the children?"

Chapter 33

Ray unlocks his car, gets in, puts the key into the ignition, and turns it. He looks up as the car starts and sees something stuck under his wipers - something white. He hopes against hope that it's a joke, an advertisement, or something equally inane.

With slow and deliberate movements, he gets back out of the car. He lifts the wiper off the paper. His heart falls as he reads the scribbled letters.

"I've got the kids, moron. Stay away or they're dead. Soon."

Ray stares at the messy writing for a moment, then crumbles it and tosses it inside the car. Stay away from what or who - from Cindy? From the hospital? From the police? What the hell does it mean? He feels himself losing it. He can barely see straight. Who the hell do these people think they are, that they can screw with him and the people he cares about, and then tell him to stay away? A white hot anger threatens to consume him.

He can't help but think, "Too bad this isn't CSI. Then we'd just have to dust for fingerprints on that napkin, and we'd find the culprit in an hour. Unfortunately, real life doesn't work like that." But he can't help the thought, "I'd sure love to be the hero here. I'd sure love to see someone catch this jackass, and see the kids safe at home with their mother."

If the point of the message is to keep him off balance, to make him angry, by God, it's working. He's angry, all right.

Ray barrels out of the parking lot and down the main street. His face burns, his arms ache from the pressure of his hands on the steering wheel. Even as he's fuming, he's thinking, "This is ridiculous. What the heck is wrong with me? Why am I letting this asshole get to me like this? I can't help anyone when I'm so out of control."

It's a little after six a.m. when Ray pulls into Cindy's driveway. The lights are on and he can see through the window shades that she's still working, wrapping and packing everything in boxes. He knocks at the front door and tries the knob. It's not locked. He pokes his head in as she looks up, exhausted.

"Ray, it's you. Come in. I'm just about finished."

"Have you heard from anyone? From the kids? From the police?" he asks her.

"No. I haven't heard anything. I'm just doing what I was told, and I'm hoping that whoever has the kids will keep his end of the bargain. The movers are coming at nine this morning. He said that he would give the kids back to me when the movers came."

"Yeah, here, let me help you. Give me some of that paper and tell me what you still want packed." Ray needs to keep busy. He's not at all sure that those kids are going to appear when the movers do. As he packs, he tells Cindy about the note he found under his windshield. She obviously hasn't had a wink of sleep, and he can tell she's barely listening to him. He keeps up the chatter, just as a way of staying connected to her. He can tell that it wouldn't take much to send her over the edge into hysteria, that she's struggling to maintain her composure. He's hoping that his presence there might make it easier for her in case the van arrives and leaves with no sign of her kids.

"Cindy, just tell me what you want done and I'll have it finished for the movers when they arrive. Why don't you try to get a little rest?"

"You know I can't do that. I have to keep busy."

"Yeah, OK. Where's Sarah? She still with your friend?"

"She's with Alice. The police gave her a hard time about her sisters. They told her that they were probably with friends or had run away. They claimed that she was making up stories because she didn't want to be punished because she didn't take good care of them."

"Sounds like they're a real help. Has Sarah ever made up stories before?"

"No, never. It's just not something she would do."

"Well, I guess the only thing we can do right now is to keep packing and wait and hope that the kids will show up when the moving van arrives, or shortly afterwards."

It strikes Ray as a little bizarre that he and Cindy both have more trust in the word of the kidnappers than they do in the police.

Finally, with things as organized as humanly possible, considering the circumstances, Cindy and Ray stand in the middle of the chaos and check the time. They're close. It's a little past 8:45. Ray's feels his anxiety level rising.

"Come on, hurry up with the van," he implores. "One way or the other, this needs to be over."

They wait.

Chapter 34

Ray stands beside Cindy at the open front door. Both stare wordlessly down the street. Nine o'clock comes and goes, with no sign of any moving van. Each moment that passes rips at his heart. He can only imagine what it's doing to Cindy. By 9:30, the tension in the little house is almost unbearable. Ray takes a phone number from Cindy's shaking hand and calls the moving company. The van heading for Cindy's address left half an hour before it was due to arrive, about 8:30. It should have been there by nine. Ray checks with the dispatcher to make sure it was heading for the right address. He asks him to please contact the van driver and check his location.

The dispatcher's patient voice interrupts him. He's obviously used to dealing with unreasonable clients.

"Sir, sometimes our drivers get caught in traffic or have to make an unexpected stop for some reason. They're all very dependable. I'm sure he will arrive shortly."

Ray tells Cindy that the van is probably just caught in traffic. She doesn't answer, just continues to stare down the street. Ten o'clock finds them still standing at the open front door.

Ray tries to get her to come inside. It's raining and cold, and it's doing no good for her to be standing half outside in this kind of weather. She doesn't move.

At 10:45, they see the moving van slowly make its way up Cindy's street and stop in front of the house. Cindy turns back inside. She's

118

on to the next step, getting her things into the van. She's convinced that the only way to get her kids back home is to move out of here, quickly.

Ray heads for the van, intent on giving the driver a piece of his mind. He whips open the door closest to him, the passenger side, and finds himself staring right into the eyes of two terrified kids.

He can't take his eyes off them, afraid they'll disappear again. He gently lifts them down from the van, takes their hands, and heads for the house. Cindy is on her way out the front door, boxes in her arms. She hesitates for a moment not quite realizing what she's seeing, then drops everything and runs to wrap them in her arms. Tears stream down her face.

The kids are quiet, too quiet. Cindy leads them inside the house.

Ray heads back to the van. He has questions for the driver. What happened to him? Why is he so late? How did he end up with the kids?

The driver has barely moved. He's still standing just below the van door. He's looking pretty shaky himself. Ray figures he's not having such a good day.

"What the hell happened? How did you end up with the kids in your van?"

"Yeah, OK. I wuz stopped at a sign on Rogers Street, and some guy stepped in front of the van. He didn't move, so I yelled at the idiot to get out of my way or I'd move him myself. Then another guy came round to my door and stuck a gun in my face. The first guy, the one who stopped me, opened the passenger side door, threw the kids in, and told me to take this route - along the river, up the highway and they'd follow me. If I went any other way, they would shoot out my tires and kill me and the kids. And don't use my two-way. They said when I got here to tell you guys that you had better keep moving or they would take the kids again. Only this time, they would kill 'em for sure. They said you should remember that they keep their word. And then they told me to keep my trap shut too."

"Did you see the car, get a license? What did they look like?"

"I didn't see nothing - just did what they told me. Those freaking guys are maniacs. I'm not taking any chances on my life."

"Can't say I blame you," Ray tells him. "Want to help me get this thing loaded up so we can get out of here?"

"Hang on a minute, I gotta check in." With that, he climbs back into the cab and picks up his radio. "Yeah, I know I'm late. Had to take a different route - detour."

He turns back to Ray.

"Where're you headed? They didn't tell me back at headquarters. Just told me to be here at nine this morning and that it would take the whole day."

Ray figures the guy sure looks like he's telling the truth, but maybe not. He's not about to give him a whole lot of information.

"I don't know where she's going. I'm just helping her out here. I'll ask." He heads for the house.

"The guy wants to know where you're headed once we get all this loaded up."

"Ray, I don't know. I don't care. My kids are back. That's all I care about."

Ray takes her by the arm and moves her away so the kids can't overhear them. He speaks as softly as possible, but makes sure she hears him clearly.

"Cindy, you've got to do what they told you. They left a message with the driver that they will take the kids again if you don't. And the next time they're not fooling around, they will kill them. These are nasty people. We won't be able to protect the kids, and the cops are either too lazy or they're mixed up in this. You know we can't depend on any help from them."

"I don't know where to go."

"Don't you have any relatives or friends away from this town that you can move in with until you find a place?"

"No one I can think of who I can ask to take me and three kids on the spur of the moment. No one who would want to get involved if they knew what was going on."

"Well, just where were you headed?"

"I hadn't thought about it. All I wanted was to do what they said and get my kids back. I guess I figured I could just check into a motel."

"I have a place up north. I'll give you the address and you can stay there until we can come up with something else. It's just a cabin on a lake, but there's room for all of you. We'll take this stuff to a storage company. I've got a friend who owes me a favor and who works at one. I'll give him a call and tell him he's got to make room for all this crap. I'll have to go with the driver and help him unload. I can't believe they sent only one person to load and unload. Didn't you tell them that you needed help?"

"Ray, I don't know what I told them. All I remember is telling them to be here as soon as they could. I guess they assumed I would have people to help me."

"Probably. Just put the kids in the car and head for this address." He quickly writes something on a piece of paper he takes from the kitchen table. "When you get there, the key is under the rock that's beside the drainage pipe. You and the kids stay there until I get in touch."

Cindy is looking at him strangely. "Thank you Ray," she says in an odd voice.

"Cindy, you have to trust me," he tells her. "I'm going to see what I can dig up here. I'll be up to see you as soon as I can. Stay there. Don't come back. I don't care what the circumstances are."

"I'm picking up Sarah on my way. I'm not leaving without her."

"That's fine. I'll do my best to figure out what's going on here and sort out this mess. If I can't, at least you and the kids will be OK."

"Do you really think so, Ray? What's to stop these people from following us up to your cabin and killing us all while we're sleeping?"

"You're doing what they want. I'm hoping that will keep you safe. Somehow, you have managed to stumble onto something that these people want locked up for good. The only thing I can think of is that it's got to do with Mari and why she's in the hospital these past three years. They don't want you here digging up dirt and getting all emotionally involved with her. It's dangerous to them for some reason."

Cindy is stunned. She hasn't thought about Mari since this crisis with her kids started. It never occurred to her that this might have anything to do with Cindy's interest in her.

"Ray, do you really think there's any connection between Mari and what happened to my kids?"

"It's about the only thing that makes any sense. Didn't all this mess start right about the time you started poking into her files and investigating why she was in the hospital?"

Yes, you're right. It's got to be about Mari. "Looks like my kids lives aren't the only ones at stake here, Ray. We've got one more life to save."

"Well, you're not going to be the one doing the saving this time, Cindy. You've got too much at stake. You need to get out of here. Here," he hands her another piece of paper with directions scribbled on it. "I want you to go straight to Alice's house, pick up Sarah, and head north. It will take you about two hours and forty-five minutes to get there. Call me right away when you get there so I know you made it all right. OK? I can't concentrate on helping Mari if I'm worried about you and the kids."

"Ray," Cindy can feel the tears start, "this is way beyond the bounds of friendship. Thank you."

"Just get going. You have the cell phone?"

"Yes, it's right here. We're going to be OK Ray."

"I know that. You'll be fine, Cindy."

"And so will Mari," he whispers to himself as he watches her pull out of the driveway and turn up the road. "I'll make sure of it."

Ray heads back into the house and puts in a call to Jean. "Cindy's gone, headed north," he tells her. "She's got the kids." He hears the swift intake of Jean's breath. "They arrived this morning with the moving van, as promised," he tells her curtly. "I've got to make sure her furniture and stuff gets safely to a storage place. It will probably take the rest of the day. I'll be in to work later on. Will you still be there?"

"Yes, I'm staying for the second shift. I'll leave when you get here." She's obviously as anxious to talk to him as he is to her.

"We'd better solve this thing soon or we'll all be dead from exhaustion." He thinks. "I don't think any of us has slept since this nightmare began."

Now that Cindy and the kids are on their way to safety, Ray gives in to the luxury of feeling overwhelmed.

It seems like Cindy's investigation into Mari's problems has stirred up some vile muck from the bottom of a vast river. The muck is not settling, won't settle, just drifts along on the top, polluting everything it touches. Someone needs to skim it off the surface so the water will be clear and clean again. Ray knows that he and Jean are the ones who'll have to do the skimming.

His next job is to call the telephone company and tell them to shut off service to this number, just in case anyone is wondering if Cindy is serious about moving away from here for good. He figures it will make sense to leave the gas and electricity on since she's selling the house, but no one leaves their telephone connected when they move. That's always the first thing people think to disconnect.

Ray finally finishes emptying the little house. It really doesn't take all that long once Cindy is out of the way. She had pretty well packed everything up. The furniture isn't anything that he has to be particularly careful with. Even the kids mattresses are worn and hardly worth saving, but the men pack them into the truck and he padlocks the front door of the little house. At least if she wants to keep anything, it will be safe for awhile. Ray gives the driver a check and the address of the storage place, puts in a call to his friend who runs it, and asks that he help unload and look after Cindy's things. No problem. The guy owes him a favor.

He has a few hours left before he heads in to work.

Anxious as he is to see Jean and go over the day's activities with her, he takes the time to go home and lay down for a few hours. Then he showers and changes before heading back to the hospital.

"Man, I didn't realize how good a shower can feel," he thinks.

Refreshed, and in a much better state of mind, Ray locks up his house and heads for work, his mind already running ahead, anticipating what waits for him in the hospital. Now that Cindy and her kids are OK, at least for now, he's anxious to get back to solving the mystery that seems to be at the center of all this. What exactly is going on with Mari, and what can they do to prove what they all know is true. There's no way this child could have done what she's been accused of doing. Perhaps they can even find and hold responsible those who put her in this institution and right the wrong that's been done to her.

"This has been going on long enough," he mutters to himself. "It's more than time that someone cared enough to help her."

Chapter 35

Jean feels her energy rapidly fading. She's been a good twenty hours without sleep, and the sleep she did get last night was fitful and filled with nightmares. She knows she can't leave till Ray gets here and fills her in on the happenings of the day. She will never be able to get any rest again tonight if she doesn't find out what happened. From her talk with him earlier, she knows that the kids are back with Cindy, and that they are on their way north to his cabin and safety. Miracles happen.

All day long, Mari, the other unknown in this whole drama, has been sitting silently, her face turned outwards as if looking for something through that window. All Jean's attempts to speak with her have led to nothing. Mari will hold her hand, even look directly at her - something that she's never done before. It does seem like she's trying to communicate with her, but without words. It's almost like she feels that words aren't necessary. Strange. Ironically, when Jean sits with her like that, and feels Mari's eyes look directly into hers, she feels a peace that words would only disturb. She could stay there forever, just being with Mari, in her presence.

It sounds ridiculous now that she thinks about it, for a practical woman like Jean. But she doesn't doubt the reality of it, and all she wants is to get back to it - to feel it again, to be with Mari. Nothing matters more to her now than helping her, than finding out why she's here, in this hospital.

Jean feels chosen, like it's a privilege to be one of the people trying to help this child.

Her thoughts move outward again, and she wonders what's become of Ray.

She's eager for him to arrive so they can begin their search into Mari's life: how she ended up here, what they can do to help her, and who these people are who go to such great lengths to keep anyone from discovering the secrets of her past. What is it to them? What stake do they have in this?

He's here! She notices Mari's attention change focus and knows it's because Ray has just entered the parking lot.

"Now why would I know that?" she asks herself.

She watches the big front doors whoosh open and close behind him. She's impatient to be filled in on what happened today regarding Cindy and the kids, and to share her own information with him.

Jean calls one of the nurses and tells her that she needs to confer with Ray about a patient. The nurse nods her OK; she will watch things on the floor for her. Jean motions for him to meet her in her office. It occurs to Ray that the place may be bugged. (He may be paranoid, but better safe than sorry.) So he asks Jean if she will just walk outside with him for awhile. There's a small garden where the patients can go for walks and smokes. They tell the nurse on duty there that they will watch the patients for her, so she heads back inside. Ray fills Jean in on the details of the day's events.

"And the kids were sent back with the moving van driver, just as the kidnappers had promised?" she asks incredulously.

"Yes, but for some reason, it seemed important that they arrive late, really late. They made them take a long, roundabout route to the house. I don't know why - what the purpose of that would be."

"Maybe to create more anxiety in you guys, make you more grateful when they did arrive, more willing to do what they wanted?"

"You mean, maybe they were just stacking their cards . . . ?"

"Yeah, I guess you could say 'stacking their cards', in case, for some reason, Cindy decided to stay once her kids were back."

"I never thought of that - it makes sense."

Ray is amazed. "Two heads really are better than one," he thinks. "This lady is smart, and cares . . . . I have never given her credit for any of that. Here I thought . . . well, forget that now."

"Ray, where are the papers or files that Cindy got from the library or the basement? Did she say where she put any of it?"

"I don't know if she actually took any papers. She just told me what she had read."

"We know that someone is watching those files. If we go searching like she did, we're liable to put someone else in jeopardy, most likely ourselves, or even Mari. Did Cindy tell you what she found in them?"

Ray tells Jean about Cindy's findings.

"Something is missing. What you're telling me doesn't make sense. We can't figure anything out from what we know now," she tells him. "We need to find out more. We need to get our hands on those papers ourselves. We need to be able to read between the lines. I'm going to the basement tonight and take a look at the files myself. And most importantly, we've got to get Mari to open up to one of us. We have got to find out if she knows anything about what happened to her grandmother, who killed her. She must have seen something."

"Well, looks like that's my job for the night, trying to find out what Mari saw and experienced when her grandmother was murdered," Ray says. "Let's go back inside. How about you go home now and get some rest. We don't want a repeat of what happened to Cindy. If someone in here is reporting our activities to anyone, it's important that no one know you're down in the basement looking at the files. So how about this. Later on tonight, about midnight - no one should be awake by then - I'll open the side door and let you back in. I'll be the only one who knows you're here. I hope! You can go down to the basement and check the files for any ideas of what happened - any indication of who handled the case, what they found -- anything."

"OK, let's get these patients back inside and I'll leave with the rest of the shift, so you can start getting things ready for the night. Don't give any meds to Mari."

"No, of course not. She doesn't need them anyway . . . . Remember, midnight, the exit door on the left side of the building as you face it."

"What about the alarm?"

"I can shut it off. I'll do that as soon as you leave."

Ray is more than happy now that he's been able to confide in Jean. She was definitely the right one to help with this. She might be able to figure out more than Cindy was able to put together from the files. After all, Cindy only had a few minutes, whereas Jean can take her time tonight. No one will even know she's down there, not if he can help it. And Jean is obviously smart enough to put two and two together, given the chance. Finally, he feels like things might be moving in the right direction.

Ray can feel a difference as he steps back inside the hospital. The ever pervasive feelings of gloom and despair have been replaced by feelings of hope and lightness.

"Is it just me, my imagination, that's causing me to feel this way?" He wonders.

He looks over in Mari's direction and sees the brief glimpse of a smile in the corners of her mouth.

"She knows," he thinks. "She knows what we're doing, that we're trying to help her. But how?"

Chapter 36

Jean's behavior after her midnight foray into the depths of the dungeon that they call the basement strikes Ray as strange, at least for her. She is not a woman who shows much emotion, but Ray can't help but notice her demeanor as she approaches him. She's quite obviously upset. She should have gone right out the side door to her car, which she parked on a side street since they're doing their best to keep anyone from noticing her presence in the hospital tonight. Obviously, something has gotten her so worked up that she doesn't want to wait. She needs to speak to him right away. He leaves his desk and heads in her direction. She goes straight to where Mari sits at the window, looking outward into the night, that same pensive smile still on her lips. Ray sits also. It feels to him like the three of them are enclosed in a capsule. Jean's agitation over her discoveries mingles with Ray's sense of anticipation and Mari's calm presence.

"So, Ray," Jean asks softly, as she places one knee on the floor, bringing herself to the same level as Mari, "Have you and Mari spoken? Was she able to tell you anything about why she's here or about her grandmother?" Ray knows that her words are intended not just for his ears, but for Mari's also.

He thinks, "Jean wants Mari to be involved in solving the mystery of why she's here." he thinks.

"No, we haven't spoken yet," he answers. "What did you find down there tonight?"

"Besides a mess, you mean? The files are gone, Ray."

"What do you mean, the files are gone?"

"I looked. There are no sign of any files on Mari. Are you sure Cindy didn't take them with her. Are you certain that she put them back down there?"

"I'm sure, I saw her put them back myself. How the heck could they just disappear? One of us has been here constantly since - it must have been done right after Cindy saw them . . . .That means it's got to be someone from inside here. You know, I bet someone took those files even before Cindy's kids were taken."

"Ray, are you sure there was anything worth noting in the files? Perhaps this fuss is all about nothing. Perhaps we're just spinning our wheels, maybe we're on the wrong track altogether."

Ray can tell that Jean's words are for Mari, perhaps to get her to tell them something, anything, that she knows about why she's here.

Mari moves her eyes from the windows and looks directly at her.

"What is it, what should we know about why you're here? What do you know about the people who brought you here?" Jean asks her.

Mari moves her mouth as if to speak, but it's her eyes that move slowly back and forth, from one to the other - bright, brilliant, and piercing. Words have no meaning or purpose here, only her eyes speak in a language Ray has never before heard or experienced, the language of their souls.

"The reason I'm here has nothing to do with files. It's to help you know your own goodness. It's to help you help the others. "

Ray is incredulous. He looks over at Jean. Did she hear? No, she seems oblivious. She's on to her own agenda.

"But I did find out something interesting. Just as I was about to come back upstairs, it occurred to me that maybe I ought to check and see if anything pertinent had happened here around the time that Mari arrived. I found some reference to the fact that two inmates had escaped from here just about that time. Ray, when did you come to work here? Do you remember any of this?"

Ray pulls himself back into the world of spoken words. He smiles at Mari, acknowledging that he understands what she is telling him. He rises and begins to walk down the corridor towards the front desk. Jean follows him. He thinks back . . .

"That was before my time. I only came here two and a half years ago. I understand that Mari's been here about three."

"That's what I thought, that she was about twelve or thirteen years old when she was admitted. But why take her here? Weren't there any other places that would have been more suitable for such a young patient? I don't remember any of it either. I must have been hired just after you were. No one seems to remember too much about Mari being brought here. We've all heard bits and pieces of her story, we've all speculated about her and why she's here. No one ever bothered to look up her files and try to actually learn something about her and her situation until Cindy came."

Ray looks at Jean strangely. "Yeah, Cindy seemed to have felt some kind of a connection to her. I thought it was just because she had kids the same age."

"That could be it, but I think there's more to it."

Jean's eyes take on a faraway look. *She remembers the peace that surrounded her when she took the time just to sit with the child, to just be there with her.*

She considers telling Ray about the experience, but decides against it. He brought her into this because she's a practical, logical, person, someone who can help him unravel the mystery behind all this crap that's been happening to them. Surely, what he doesn't need or want is someone who's intrigued by or caught up in unseen, ethereal happenings.

And there's another thing she doesn't want to tell him - how truly spooked she was down in that basement - how the hair on her arms and the back of her neck stood straight up on end all the while she was down there.

It's almost like there was another presence there, watching her, anxious for her to leave, not sure what to make of her. . . . .

She shakes her head, forcing herself back to reality. She needs to help him solve this mystery. She wants to do it for Mari, for Ray, for

Cindy. But most of all, she wants to do it for herself. It's impossible for her to put into words just what her relationships with each of them have become, how important they are to her. All she knows is that she no longer wants to live the sterile, busy, scheduled life she's made for herself.

There's something more in her life now, and that 'more' is her relationship with these very special people that she's only now coming to know.

"These changes that are coming over me, they're wonderful. I never knew that such a world existed. I was so unaware. I feel like I'm just waking up from a very bad dream."

Jean remains silent for several minutes, then turns back to Ray.

"You know what? It's time for one of us, or both of us for that matter, to take another trip to the library and check out the newspapers from three years ago. Fortunately, they're on microfilm, so it would be a bitch of a problem for anyone who decided to do away with them. We've got to find out what else went on then if we're to find anything about Mari's situation."

"Jean, you really need to get some rest. You've been going all day and now tonight too. When I get off work tomorrow, I'll head down there and see if there's anything interesting."

"I want to come with you. Two heads are better than one. I've got someone else scheduled for today so I can take it off. Why don't you pick me up about noon and we can go together. I'll be waiting."

Jean knows exactly what she wants to find out, and she's afraid Ray might miss it. There's an idea percolating in the back of her mind that she wants to check on. If she's right, it could answer a lot of their questions.

Ray suddenly realizes that he's not too fussy about both of them being at the library. If anyone is watching, wondering what they're up to . . . . no need to make things easy for him - or them.

"You know, Jean, why don't you just go to the library yourself. I think I'll do a little research myself."

"Sure, what are you up to?"

"I'm going to check that Cindy and the kids made it to the cabin all right. Then I'll see if she can give me any more information about how Mari came to be here. And I'm going to do it from a pay phone in another town, just in case anyone is watching."

"OK, let's do it then. I've put Becky in charge of the day shift for tomorrow, so I can come in with you tomorrow night. We can compare notes then."

This delegation of jobs appeals to Jean's sense of order, but now she doesn't feel like a bossy, anal retentive supervisor. Instead, she feels powerful and decisive. There's a sense of purpose to her actions, like she's working for something larger than herself.

"It feels good," she quietly tells herself. "It just feels right."

Chapter 37

Jean allows herself little time to rest when she gets home. By ten o'clock that morning, she is already at the library. It's open, but the front desk is strangely empty.

"It's only ten o'clock," she thinks. "The librarian can't be at lunch yet. Strange there's no one looking after things here."

A large note on the counter directs anyone returning books to put them in a certain place, and the librarian will look after them when she gets back.

"Must be break time. Lucky thing I know where I'm going."

Jean has been here before and knows the layout. She heads straight for the records room. It takes about an hour and a half for her to get what she wants. The most important thing - the reason she's here in the first place - is to find out some dates. Something is percolating in the back of her mind. Those inmates that escaped from the hospital - when was that? Were they dangerous? Were they ever caught? How soon after their escape was Mari's grandmother murdered? And who were they? If she could just put some kind of a timeline together, maybe things would start to make sense.

"Could the two escaped mental patients have had anything to do with the murder of Mari's grandmother? Maybe I'm completely off base, but it would fit in with what I'm thinking, and it's worth doing some research on it."

She finds that there's a little less than a two-week interval between the time of the escape and the time that Mari was discovered living with her grandmother's body. But just why would no one else suspect what she suspects? And if what she's thinking is a possibility, where was Mari while her grandmother was being murdered and why was she unharmed?

Jean can find no evidence in the records of any recapture of the two mental patients. She is, however, able to find out their names. Her next stop is the police station. She's going to have a little talk with the detective who was in charge of the case, and was instrumental in getting Mari admitted to the hospital. She has some pointed questions for him.

Jean got what she came for. She leaves the records room and quickly heads for the door, passing right by the librarian, who is back behind the large front desk and now seems to be busy filing. She looks up, startled.

"Excuse me. I wasn't aware anyone was in the library. Do you need help? Would you like to check anything out?"

"No," Jean tells her, "I was just in the records room doing some research."

"Oh, OK. Well, have a nice day."

"Thank you."

As Jean opens the door, she takes a quick glance back into the library. She sees the librarian pick up a phone.

"She's calling someone," she thinks. "That phone never rang."

She shivers, a sudden chill gripping her. "What secrets does the library hold? And to what lengths will someone go to make sure they stay hidden?"More questions, nothing but questions. How far," she wonders, "will Ray and I be willing to go in our search for answers? How far will we be able to go before someone tries to stop us?"

Chapter 38

Ray, meanwhile, is up early himself, considering that he worked the night shift. It's about eleven o'clock and he can't sleep any longer. His dreams of darkness and demons and despair frighten and infuriate him at the same time. They drain his energy rather than refresh him so he might as well be up. He's sure that worries about Cindy, her kids and Mari are the cause of his anxiety. The only way to exorcize these demons is to solve this mystery and put his mind at ease.

So he's about to do some investigating of his own. As he promised Jean, he intends to call Cindy, check on her and the kids. He will also find out if there's any information she can give them that might help solve even a small piece of this very large puzzle that he and Jean are trying to piece together. Sometimes, he knows, just the smallest bit of information can make a very large difference.

Ray gets himself ready and heads over to the closest town. He wants to get away from Tillsboro to makes his call.

"Just in case anyone is watching, it never hurts to take every precaution, since we have no idea what or who we're dealing with here."

"Or," he thinks, "maybe I'm just paranoid or still dreaming, I certainly don't feel very awake yet."

No matter. It's such a lift to his spirits to hear Cindy's voice on the other end of the phone. She and the kids arrived exhausted but safe at his cabin. No problem with the directions. She picked up groceries and is all settled in. The kids have their school books with them and she's having them keep up with homework until she decides what her next step will be. That will depend a lot on what Jean and he find out about Mari and/or if the police ever find out and let her know who took her kids and why.

"Not much chance of that," thinks Ray.

He doesn't tell Cindy this, however. He's anxious to hear anything she can tell him about Mari and what she found out from the files. He doesn't feel comfortable asking her over the phone, but he's got no choice. Other than taking the time to go up there personally, he doesn't see any other way for him to find out what was in those files that someone was so anxious to hide. So here goes.

"Cindy, the files on Mari that were in the basement of the hospital are gone. Did you take them or put them somewhere?"

"I left them right on top of the cabinet at the bottom of the stairs. You couldn't find them?"

"No, and Jean spent nearly half an hour down there looking for them. They are nowhere to be found. Did you see anything in them that might tell us more than we already know about Mari or why she's in the hospital?"

"Ray, I really didn't have much time. I just took a quick look over the papers and saw that, number one, when she was admitted, she couldn't or wouldn't speak to anyone. Two, that it was recommended that she stay in the hospital until she made some progress and could tell someone what happened to her grandmother. Number three, what I found most unbelievable, the doctor said in his notes that there was a very good probability that Mari herself had killed her grandmother while she was sleeping, and the shock of what she had done caused her to be unable to communicate with anyone."

"Cindy, this is important. Can you remember who signed those papers? What doctor examined her and dictated these opinions?"

"Yes, I remember distinctly that it was a Doctor Simon, Ray. I was surprised because I can't remember anyone by that name working at the hospital, so I assume he either left for another position or retired before I came."

"I don't remember him either. I'll ask Jean; maybe she's heard of him. It would be a help if we could find him and ask him a few questions."

"You're right. That would be a big help. Listen, why don't you start with Dr. Fitzsimmons, the guy who's there now. Maybe he replaced the other doctor - Simon, is it? Maybe he can tell you something about him or where to find him."

"Good idea, I'll try to find him."

Ray knows how that will be. Fitzsimmons comes once a week to check on the patients. He signs whatever the nurses tell him to sign and he leaves. He is, to say the least, as ineffective as he can possibly be. Ray suspects he only comes to the hospital to collect his paycheck.

"Well, I'm glad you and the kids are doing well. I'll let you know what develops on this end. In the meantime, if anything happens that I should know about, you have my phone number."

"Ray, did I ever thank you for all that you've done? I really appreciate it."

"It's nothing, Cindy. Glad to be able to help. Take care now."

"I'll be careful, Ray." She says softly into the phone. "You take care too. I don't know what we'd do if anything happened to you."

"You know I've got your back, Cindy." Ray tries to say, but the words catch in his throat and come out as a sort of croak.

"Bye now." He hears the click of the phone as she hangs up.

"Good bye, Cindy," he says. He holds the phone in his hand, staring at it for a long time before he hangs up and focuses his thoughts again on the business at hand.

He had hoped that Cindy would know where the files were so he and Jean could go over them with a fine-toothed comb. At least the phone call confirmed that Cindy and the kids are all still safe - that's a big thing.

Maybe Jean has made out better with her investigation at the library. After speaking with Cindy, he feels an urgency to solve this mystery and bring her and the kids back home where they belong. They should be living a life of work and school and normal, everyday routine, not hiding from some weirdos in a cabin in the woods.

As he steps out of the phone booth, Ray can't help but notice a man in a grey suit watching him from across the street. Now where did he come from? Ray takes note that he's about average height, short brown hair, a bit stocky with a ruddy complexion. He seems not the least bit concerned that Ray sees him, and makes no pretense of reading the paper or looking away.

"He wants me to know I'm being watched." The hairs on the back of Ray's neck stand straight up on end. He feels like he's being stalked by someone who is very sure that its prey is already in its grasp and has no need of hiding.

"Nothing to do but call his bluff," Ray thinks. He begins to stride purposefully over to the man on the corner who's obviously staring at him.

As he approaches, the man removes his hand from his pocket. The movement causes Ray to notice that he's got a weapon - a gun. Ray stops in his tracks, and the stalker turns and walks down an alley, disappearing out of sight.

Chapter 39

Wow, these guys aren't fooling around. Ray's attempt to confront the guy was, he now realizes, foolish. He should have just pretended that he didn't notice him. There's a possibility that this was one of the thugs who stopped the moving van when it was headed for Cindy's house. No doubt he took or helped take Cindy's children. This is not a nice guy.

The knot in Ray's stomach slowly loosens. His non-meeting with the stalker/thug leaves him anxious and more than a little bit curious. He needs to hear what, if anything, Jean has found out on her visit to the library, so he checks her address in the phone book and heads across town. Her place is up a lovely, tree-lined street. Carefully tended flowers and plants dot the median, which separates the coming and going traffic. Each lawn is mowed to a perfect length that keeps it nice and green and well manicured.

"How do they do that?" He wonders. "What an incredible amount of energy it would take to keep your yard like that. You'd have to be at it every single day."

He pulls into Jean's driveway. There's no car in the driveway, so either she hasn't come back from the library yet, or she's parked in the garage. He parks, gets out of his car, and walks over to the garage, intending to check and see if her car is there before he knocks on the door. A reflection from the garage window catches his attention.

Someone is parking on the other side of the street, just across from Jean's house. It's a woman with a bag of groceries in her arms.

On instinct, Ray hurries over to her and asks if he can help her carry in her groceries. She looks at him oddly. "I've never seen you around here before," she tells him. "Who are you?"

"Oh, I'm just visiting across the street. You look like you could use a little help here."

"No, that's OK, I'll manage. Thank you."

"No problem." Ray heads back to Jean's house and knocks on the door. He knows she isn't here, her car isn't in the garage, but he figures that he has to knock now. That neighbor obviously thought he was a kook. He still wonders, though, why she didn't park in her own driveway. There's no car there, and wouldn't she want to be as close as possible since she was carrying in groceries?

His questions are answered when the door to the garage starts to open and a man drives out. She obviously parked on the street because she knew he would be coming out and didn't want to block him in. The man, probably her husband, stops the car to speak to the woman. She glances towards Jean's house, telling him about Ray, he guesses. She looks like she's uncomfortable with his presence. Ray waves at them, gets back in his car and drives away. So much for that. All he's done is made the neighbors suspicious of him. He had better remember to mention this to Jean or they'll be telling her that some hoodlum was here today casing her house. They're both anxious enough. She certainly doesn't need something else to worry about.

Should he go to the library and try to catch Jean there, or what? No, best to cool his jets and just go home. They had agreed to meet tonight at the hospital, and he should stick to the plan. Obviously, someone is keeping close tabs on him, as evidenced by the guy in the grey suit with the gun. No need to put Jean in jeopardy if they don't know yet that she's involved. He might as well take a break and consider what he's learned so far.

The section of town where he and Cindy live is closer to the hospital, and thus not in as desirable a part of town as the place where Jean lives. Nonetheless, it's good to be on his own familiar street once again. Ray gladly pulls into his own driveway - at least no one questions who he is and what he's doing here. His place isn't fancy, certainly not as well manicured as where he's just come from, but it's snug and comfortable and makes him happy. He gets himself a cup of tea and makes a quick sandwich. It's past lunch time and he didn't realize how hungry he is. It's been a while since he's had anything to eat, caught up as he's been with all that's been going on.

About half an hour later, he's snuggled up in his old recliner and dozing, not quite asleep, not quite awake, trying to clear his mind. If he can just stop the racing, maybe something will come to him. He's feeling more and more like there are some elusive pieces that need to be found, some pieces to this mystery that all the research in the world won't reveal to either he or Jean. Ray dozes off . . . .

. . . . *and finds himself in a large field searching . . . . searching for what? For treasure of some kind. The field is filled with lush, green grass and beautiful flowers. Shade trees overhang pools of inviting, clear blue waters. He begins to strip off his clothes. He feels so tired. He wants to refresh himself with a swim in one of the pools. As he comes closer, about to dive in, he notices dark shadows swirling beneath the surface, and he draws back, afraid. The earth moves under his feet and he looks down to see that the lush grasses mask a dark muck that slowly, inch by inch, draws him down into it.. An overwhelming terror takes hold of his soul, deep inside him, and works its way outward until his very extremities tremble with fear. Then, from outside himself, from outside his dream, a soft, comforting voice tells him, 'you can do it, Ray. It's all inside of you. Know who you are and feel your power.' The voice is warm, caring and loving. It fills him with confidence and peace beyond words. His terror dissipates. The shadows in the pool disappear and the earth is once again firm under his feet . . . .*

Brrr....iiiing, brrr....iiing, brrr....iiing - the insistent ring of the telephone jars him out of his dream, and he grabs at it, anxious to make it stop.

"Go away" he mutters into the receiver.

The voice on the other end jolts him awake - it's Cindy.

"Ray, I'm sorry, but I thought you should know. I got a telephone call at the cabin, on your line. Someone on the other end told me not to get too cozy, that I needed to go farther away. He suggested a little town up on the Canadian border that has a hospital that needs nurses. Told me to call and set up an interview for next Monday. He even rented me a place to stay with my kids. I thought I should call and let you know. What do you think? Should I go or what?"

"Where are you now?"

"I'm still at the cabin. I don't want to leave the kids. I'm afraid something might happen to them. I'm calling you on the cell phone."

"OK, well, I guess you'd better call the hospital like you were told and set up the interview. Did he give you specifics? The name of the hospital, maybe a phone number? How far away is this place, anyway?"

"I really don't know, about a seven or eight hour drive, I think. I'll have to check on it."

"Well, try not to worry too much, Cindy. I think whoever is doing this just wants to make sure you're far enough away and settled somewhere else so he doesn't have to worry about you returning. Do what he says and I think you and the kids will be safe enough. Do you really want to return to Tillsboro anyway? I wasn't aware that you had any fond feelings for it."

"I just don't like the idea of having to relocate again. The kids were doing so well at school, I was starting to make some friends, like yourself and Alice, and my connection with Mari is still there, Ray. I need to help her. It's like I've left one of my children behind. This just doesn't feel right. Not to mention that the kids will have a fit at having to make another move, after what they've been through. This is all they need right now."

"Well, Cindy, you really don't have any choice."

"Ray, I'm sick of having no choices, of always doing things because I *have* to do them."

Something about the misery and despair he hears in her voice brings his dream/vision back to him. He tells her, "Don't worry, Cindy, it won't be much longer."

The confidence in his voice is a new thing to her,

"Ray, I hope you know how much you mean to me. I don't know how I'd get through this without you."

"You mean a lot to me too, Cindy, and we'll get through it together."

"Thank you, Ray." she softly answers. He finally hears some hopefulness in her voice. "Tell me you'll call me when it's safe to come home."

"Let's just take this one step at a time, OK? You make the call and set up an appointment," he hesitates for just a second, "and yes, I will let you know when it's safe to come home."

Cindy slowly hangs up the phone. "It's odd, she thinks, "if anyone had told me two weeks ago that I would be longing to be back in Tillsboro, I'd have thought they were out of their minds. Now . . . . What a difference a couple of weeks make. What a difference having someone who cares about me makes."

Ray hangs up also.

What's happening to him? He had sworn after his last devastating relationship, one that left him so bereft that he couldn't even dream of ever caring for anyone in that way again – he had sworn that he would never get emotionally involved with anyone ever again - and now this. Damn it, he did care for Cindy. He couldn't deny it. Cared more than he had ever intended to care. Why did he do these things to himself? Why didn't he look after his emotions better? Why couldn't he close himself off, for heaven's sake? Just do his job and enjoy keeping to himself - no involvements, no heartbreak, no problems.

Now, he's got big problems, lots of them. Now, he's being stalked, and didn't that guy look like a peace-loving individual. What's worse, Ray sees no end to this. He's running on gut instinct now. All he knows is, for all their sakes, his gut had better be right.

He needs to talk to Jean.

Chapter 40

Ray places a couple of calls to Jean's house, but there's no answer. He's beginning to get worried about her. That thug who was following him had certainly made it clear that he was watching and willing to take action, if need be. Jean would be just as easy a target.

He's about to head out to try to find her when there's a knock on his door. He opens it.

"Jean, thank God. Come in. I stopped by your house but you weren't home. We need to talk."

Jean says not a word, but crosses the kitchen and seats herself at his small, beat-up table. Ray clears a spot in front of her. She looks exhausted, but then, that's the way they have both looked for the past few days. Too little sleep and too much worry will do that to a person. She clears her throat. "Haauuuhhh."

She does it again, "Haauuuhhh"

"So, what's going on, Jean? Did you find anything in the library that we didn't already know about? Anything that could help us figure out why Cindy had to move away?"

Her eyes move about the kitchen, never once landing on him. She's trying to tell him something. Out loud she says, "Ray, from what I've seen, everything I've looked at, there's really nothing to worry about. We're just spinning our wheels. Cindy and her kids - what's best for them is probably to get away from Tillsboro and the hospital here. Her attachment to that kid on our ward wasn't healthy either for her or for her own kids. She has enough to look after. She doesn't need another kid to worry about, especially a nutty one who, we don't know, could be violent. I think her ex got wind of what was going on and got someone to scare her away. Did her a favor as far as I'm concerned."

"So you think we should just forget about all this and go back to work like nothing's happened?"

"That's exactly what I think. That kid, Mari - more than likely, she killed her own grandmother. It was in all the papers. Can you imagine what she would be capable of if she ever hits the streets? Would you really want to be responsible for that?"

"So what you found in the library convinced you that Mari is guilty of what they say she's done, and Cindy is best off far away from her?"

"That's what I think. I don't believe Cindy would ever have been happy at Tillsboro Hospital with Mari there. She would have been trying to convince people of her innocence, probably trying to take her home and bring her up with her own kids. Can you imagine how much of a problem that could create both for Cindy herself and for her kids? To say nothing of letting that kid loose on the community. We have no idea who her next victim could be. If she hadn't been scared away, I would have had to fire her anyway, just to protect her from her own emotional attachment to that kid."

Ray looks at her strangely. She still hasn't made eye contact with him.

"Well, if that's what you think, I guess I'd have to agree that it would be a lot less trouble for us if we just dropped this thing and got back to our own lives."

"That's what I think, Ray. I've got to go home now. I definitely need to get some sleep. I'm glad we looked into this; it puts my mind at ease to go the extra mile. I feel like we did the right thing."

"Uh - OK then." Ray goes over and opens the door for her. "I'll walk you out to your car." He casually and gently puts his arm around her waist as if to lead her out. *He feels the wires around her middle.* Ray opens the car door for her and she settles inside, turns on the key, closes the door, and drives away.

"Damn, what now?" Ray mutters into the silent afternoon air.

Chapter 41

"We need to know if your friend, Ray, is involved in any of these shenanigans," they had told her. That's why she had agreed to wear the wire. The detective she had spoken to at the police station had been so hell bent on convincing her that Mari had indeed done in her grandmother.

"Too hell-bent," she figured. He's got some stake in this himself, I'm sure of it."

"And your friend, the male nurse," the detective all but snickered. "Just how convinced is he that the kid should be released from the hospital, that she's innocent?"

Jean decides it's time to let go of the rope, so to speak. Let the detective think he's won her over and see where that takes her.

"I don't know. I'll have a talk with him; explain what you've told me."

"Well, this is an ongoing investigation. We need to be certain he won't be doing any interfering in it from now on, or we'll have to take drastic measures with him, maybe bring him in for questioning," he sneers, "if you get my drift."

Jean gets his drift, all right.

"Unless, of course, you manage to convince him to stay out of police business. We'd have to be certain of it, of course."

"Well, you've convinced me. What would make you certain I had convinced him?"

"How about you pay him a visit wearing a wire. We'd listen in and go from there as far as what action we'd take."

"No problem," Jean told them.

So here she was, driving away from Ray's house, hoping that she had convinced the detective that there was no need to hassle Ray any further. How long she was going to have to wear the wire was another matter. She guessed that would depend on how long it would take before he was convinced that she and Ray weren't up to anything, and things had returned to 'normal' at the hospital.

She pulls into her driveway. The neighbor across the street is eyeing her. Usually, she's kept her distance from them, but something is obviously going on here today that the neighbor thinks she should know about. She heads over to talk to her.

"Hi, I'm Jean from across the street. You haven't seen anybody at my house today, have you? I've been expecting a visitor and he doesn't seem to have shown up yet."

"As a matter of fact, you did have some visitors. One of them came over to talk to me but, before him, there was another guy here - big guy - he tried your door and walked around back. I was afraid he was trying to break in and was just about to call the police when he seemed to change his mind and left. It was odd to see them at your house."

Jean knows she's referring to the fact that people rarely, if ever, visit her.

Jean describes Ray to them, including his car. "Could he be one of the people you saw?"

"Yes, that was definitely the second guy."

"So there was more than one? I was only expecting the guy I described to you."

"No, there was another guy who came before him. He was big, kind of burly, you know, stocky, short brown hair. Kind of looked like a professional boxer or something like that."

"Well, I don't know anybody who fits that description. I hope that it wasn't someone trying to get in my house when I'm not home. More likely, he just mistook my place for someone else's. Seems like I've had a lot of company today, even though I wasn't home to enjoy it. I really appreciate you looking out for the place when I'm not here. Thanks a lot." Jean starts back over to her side of the street, then stops and turns back to the neighbor. "You know, just to be on the safe side, if anyone who looks like the boxer guy shows up here again, could you do me a favor and give me a call? Here's my phone number."

Jean gives her one of her cards from work.

"I'll write my cell number on the back of this card in case you need to reach me when I'm not at work."

"No problem. I'll be happy to keep an eye out for you."

"I'm sure you will," Jean thinks to herself. Out loud, she says, "It's so nice to know someone cares enough to keep their eye on things in the neighborhood. Thank you so much, and if you ever need me to check on your place when you're away, just let me know. I'd be happy to do it for you."

"No problem."

The neighbor is more than happy to be able to have a hand in keeping riffraff off her street and out of her neighborhood.

Jean heads back across the street and opens her front door. Her telephone rings almost immediately. A gruff voice on the other end of the phone tells her.

"Good job, nurse Balcolm. You can take the wire off now. Just remember to put it back on when you head out for work tonight."

"So that's it," thinks Jean. "They must have my telephone tapped and be watching the house to make sure Ray doesn't make any surprise visits. Either that, or they're watching him. I guess that would make more sense."

She decides to make a few phone calls. She calls her sister in Oregon who she hasn't spoken to for at least a year. They're not close but for some reason, Jean feels the need to chat with her awhile. The conversation is a bit stilted, but it's a start towards improving their relationship. She calls her brother. He's not home so she leaves a message. Won't he be surprised! She even calls a neighbor she used to chat with a bit, but who moved away a couple of months ago. The neighbor left a new phone number in case Jean wanted to contact her and she had never bothered. For some reason, she feels like connecting with people today. It takes her mind off the craziness that's going on around her. She's hoping it also indicates to anyone who's listening in on her conversations that her life is relatively normal, that she's got nothing to hide. She apologizes to the neighbor for not calling sooner, but tells her that she would like to keep a relationship with her and that she values their friendship. It's a nice phone call. It leaves her feeling good about herself, like she's doing a small part in contributing to peace and goodwill in the world.

She hangs up. What next? Jean gets out a piece of paper and jots down all that's gone on today with regards to Mari's case - the papers in the library, the visit to the police station, the wire that the detective insisted she wear. Ray is probably wondering about the wire. She knows he felt it on her when he walked her out to the car.

Writing the details of the day's happenings leaves her feeling a bit panicky. So many questions with no answers. That's not the way she likes to run her life. She likes order, everything in its proper place. This whole situation with Mari and Cindy and Ray - it's anything but orderly. She breathes deeply and tries to relax while she gets ready for work.

"All will be answered in the proper time."

Jean is beginning to get used to such word/thoughts coming to her when she needs them, and she welcomes the calming effect this one has on her.

Ray is already at work when she arrives. He has done all the paperwork that has to be completed and he's looked after the patients' immediate needs. The chaos of the ward has subsided a bit and she's grateful to him for being so efficient.

Ray looks directly at her as she walks over to the front desk and she deliberately looks away.

"So, she's still wearing the wire," he thinks. He nods, and they head down the corridor to the window where Mari sits and waits for them. As they approach, Jean feels a calmness come over her, and a certain knowing that things are moving in the right direction despite all they've been through. Mari silently acknowledges their presence by taking each of their hands in hers. Softly, she tells them,

"You want to know what happened to Grandmother. I love her very much - to me, she is love. Long ago, men came and hurt her. When I thought she was gone, love left my heart, left my life. But when I went home, Grandmother came to me again. She told me that nothing can make love leave. It is always here, all around us. We simply choose it."

Ray feels such peace, it flows over him and into him, and he knows that she is right. This, right now, is all that matters.

Chapter 42

Ray has no idea how long the three of them remain there like that. Eventually, the din of the evening starts to intrude and become more insistent. They get back to the tasks at hand. The peace and calm that they take from their encounter with Mari flows from them through the ward and the evening passes gently and quietly. Ray is amazed at how their attitudes and actions affect everyone and everything around them.

The clock chimes ten. Jean approaches. She has finished what needs to be done with the patients, and it's time to work on the problem of finding out what happened to Mari. They know for certain now that she doesn't belong here.

It's also clear to them both that the reason she's in the hospital is because whoever killed her grandmother simply found her an easy target to pin the murder on so no one would ever know what happened. It must have been quite a shock for them when Cindy started to take such an interest in the kid after three years; that she would go through the trouble to do some investigating on her own. Thank God there are people like Cindy in the world who will try to right wrongs, even if it's not in their job description.

Well, at least they've answered the question. 'Why is Mari here?' Now they need to find out who put her here? It had to be someone in authority, someone who could pull strings. Why would anyone want to harm an old lady? From what they've read, everyone in town seemed to like her. She didn't have any obvious enemies. This is definitely not going to be easy, but it has to be done. They're all in too far to back out now.

"Someone who is closely involved with the hospital must have had something to do with it," Ray thinks. "How else would they have known so quickly when Cindy disturbed the records in the basement? They have got to be right here among us."

A chill creeps up Ray's spine. He looks around him. All he sees are patients. Is there a possibility one of them is spying on the staff? Impossible. Most of them are medicated and too far gone to even think of such a thing. So, that would leave the rest of the staff.

"Now, let's see. Who else was here when Cindy went down to the basement?" They'll have to check. Jean can do that. She's efficient. No doubt she can put her hands on copies of the back work records.

Jean opens a file and shows Ray its contents. It's her writings regarding what happened to her today. He's amazed. He had never expected the cops to go so far as to wire up Jean to make sure she convinces him to stop digging. And here he had thought they were just lazy and couldn't be bothered reopening a case they thought had closed three years ago. It's certainly more than laziness causing this kind of a response.

He addresses Jean loud enough to be picked up by her wire, "You know, things are pretty calm here tonight. Why don't you go home and try to get a good night's sleep for a change. Now that we know that Cindy and the kids are OK and on their way to a better life, you should be able to relax. I can look after things here until shift change."

"Thanks, Ray. That would be great." Jean leaves the file with him. As she walks away, she sees him rapidly scribbling in it. She puts on her coat and starts out the door, taking the file from him on the way. She puts it under her coat and heads to her car. It isn't until she is safely inside her own home that she opens it and reads what he's written.

"The cops are definitely in on this. Someone from the hospital is also; they just knew too much about Cindy's exploration in the basement. Any ideas who it might be? Any connections between the two? Who else was on staff that night?"

Oh, yeah, she's going to sleep tonight, all right.

Jean truly is exhausted. She lies on her bed with her clothes on and turns on the TV just to get her mind off the problems at work for awhile. She hasn't had time to relax for days and it feels good just to lie here. Before long, she has dozed off into a restless sleep. Over and over in her mind, the question keeps haunting her.

"Who, who would it benefit to keep Mari locked up in a mental hospital?"

Mari herself enters her dreams. There are no words, only images and visions.

Golden light surrounds her and fills up the room. "Look Jean, look to yourself. You'll find the answers only in yourself." And Jean sees herself seated at her desk in the hospital. She's busy, so busy. She's a very important person – the hospital needs her, couldn't function without her. She needs to control, to control everything in it, control everything around her. And Jean sees the black cloud that surrounds her and flows from her to fill the corners and crevices of the hospital, polluting everything in its path. The cloud is filled with overwhelming, terrifying fear.

Nausea and horror grip her and she bolts upright, jarred out of her sleep. These nightmares - does this mean that she will never be able to rest until she and Ray figure out this mystery and do right by this kid? She falls back against her pillows, haunted and exhausted and damp with sweat. She turns off the TV. She wants no distractions. Over and over, the nightmare replays itself in her mind. Control and fear, fear and control. That seems to be the message. Whether from Mari, or her own inner self, someone is trying to let her know that, if she looks hard enough, she will find that all this is due to someone who fears them. Someone fears what they can uncover and thinks that controlling them - herself, Ray and Cindy - will get rid of the fear.

Big help this is. Jean feels angry and self righteous. All she wants to know is who is doing this, and what she's getting is more mumbo jumbo. It's almost more than a practical person like herself can tolerate.

Suddenly, she laughs. "Well, here I go again," she thinks. "I'm like a two-year-old, throwing a tantrum because I can't have everything my way."

This sudden revelation about herself surprises her. If this thing is ever going to be solved, she knows, she has got to let go and stop trying to do it her way. This is much, much bigger than anything she has ever attempted before. She needs to listen to every voice - even the voice of her own unconscious, if that is what's speaking to her. She needs to take in every clue and every cue that she's handed. She needs to trust in a benevolent universe that's on her side and wants good to triumph over evil. This whole thing is so much bigger than her and her own small efforts to control her own life and the lives of others.

Jean looks back over her life. She has no friends because she didn't want anyone messing up her carefully controlled life, no family to speak of because they wouldn't live life like she thought they should. Work was about the only thing that made sense to her, gave her life some meaning, and even that she kept tightly controlled, under wraps. No wonder whoever had done this to Mari was able to be so successful in keeping her locked away and their secret safely hidden. They knew that Jean would brook no nonsense at her hospital. No underlings who checked back files for patients, no spending time attempting to communicate with patients who appeared non-cooperative, nothing but making sure all the papers were correctly filed, the ward was appropriately clean, and the patients were properly medicated so that they wouldn't give the staff any trouble.

All this carefully controlled environment needed to bring it to complete chaos was for one simple nurse to care, to take a special interest in a patient. How ironic.

She had hated Cindy for the longest time, hadn't wanted to hire her, but had no choice. No one else had applied for the job. She knew now that the reason she didn't want to hire Cindy was because she was afraid of her. There was just something about her. Even though she was a woman who had been trodden upon and who had gone through many hard knocks, Jean had recognized immediately that Cindy couldn't be controlled. Her strong spirit and her caring concern for others couldn't be kept under wraps forever. They were bound to come out, and they were bound to create chaos when they came into contact with Jean's tightly controlled world. It was only a matter of time.

Jean thought back to when she, herself, was hired. She had made it clear that the reason she had left her last job was because she couldn't run the ward as tightly as she had wanted. The director had insisted that the patients not be medicated unless it was absolutely necessary. Several doctors worked closely with the rest of the staff to try to bring the patients along and help them get back to a relatively normal life as soon as possible. She didn't like that. The patients weren't helped by people in authority refusing to admit that they were beyond help and that all they really needed was a clean, well-run facility. Structure and discipline were the words she used most often during the interview. She found it extremely irritating to constantly be in what she considered a state of chaos with new fangled therapies and approaches. She had been hired immediately.

"Well, how interesting life becomes when you're not afraid to search for the truth," Jean thinks. "How very interesting."

"Now, if I could only remember the name of the person who interviewed me. That guy was so impressed that I wanted to control everything on my ward. I must have played right into his hands."

She searches back, back into the recesses of her memory. Nothing. It's been at least two and a half years ago. She remembers it was a man. He was one of the board members who ran the hospital, if she wasn't mistaken. Was he also a doctor? She thinks so. She remembers it as odd that a doctor was on the board of directors for the hospital, yet didn't practice there. He had said he was retired.

Jean is nothing if not efficient. She has got to have the paperwork from the time she was hired around here somewhere. She knows that she will recognize his name if she comes across it.

The search is on. It was before she had moved into the house - she only moved to Tillsboro after she was sure she had gotten the job. So the papers have to be with all the moving stuff.

She discovers them in a corner of the attic under the papers that had been given to her at the closing for her house. The box where they were stored was dated and labeled.

"Wonderful. I guess being a control freak pays off sometimes. At least I know where to find things."

Jean opens the folders and checks to see if she has any information on the person who had interviewed her for the job. No name on anything. She checks her own notes on the interview and there it is -'Dr. Simon'. She hadn't wanted to forget him in case she came across him again. After all, they had gotten along so well. They had agreed on just about every aspect of running a hospital ward.

Jean wants to call Ray immediately and share what she's found out, but she has to wait, just in case someone is still listening and watching. Whoever is involved in this cover-up has powerful friends in the police department and, obviously, on the hospital board as well. Maybe this Dr. Simon is more than just a doctor.

What Jean still can't figure out is why it would be so important to anyone that Mari be blamed for her grandmother's murder. If what Jean believes is true, that the grandmother was murdered by one or both escaped mental patients, who cares? Shit happens - bad shit. Why all the cover-up? Why blame it on a kid?

This is what she wants to talk over with Ray. Somehow, they have got to be able to put their heads together and figure this out.

Chapter 43

Ever since Ray told Jean to go home and get some rest, he has been more than restless himself. He has got to figure out some way for them both to get together and discuss what they know without anyone else listening or interfering.

"Divide and conquer," he thinks. "If they can divide us for long enough . . .well, .maybe we can lull them into believing that we're no longer interested in Mari. But do we have time?" He thinks not. Things are moving too fast.

Something is going on that's beyond just their own curiosity and desire to solve this mystery, something that both he and Jean have a hard time understanding. They have each felt a certain unspoken, unnamed *other* that's pushing them to get this resolved. His dreams, his waking visions involving Mari, his unusual friendship with Jean, even his drive to help Cindy - everything in his life seems to have converged. Everything hinges on solving this mystery. He needs to speak with Jean; he needs to find out if she's having the same reaction to all of this.

It seems to him, if he's not mistaken, that this whole mystery of Mari has cut through all their lives. Whoever is following them around is trying to get them to stop searching. His life is now divided into a time before Mari, when he did his job and went home to an empty house to work and play on his computer, and now, when he feels alive and useful and full of energy. Now there are people who care about him and mean the world to him. He's taking the risk of caring again, and it feels right - but it feels scary also.

"I guess that's what life is all about," he thinks, "going forward through the fear. Anyway, that's all I can do right now. There's no going back now."

How this all happened, he doesn't know. He does know that it has everything to do with Mari and the bright, positive energy that she is bringing into their lives. Did the people who put her here have any idea what would happen, what would become of her? Surely they meant for her to waste away, medicated and controlled, until she no longer was the vibrant, living being she once had been. It seems to him that just the opposite has happened. How very frustrating for them. What they didn't know, what Cindy knew automatically, and Ray and Jean came to know, was that spirit is so much stronger than anything that can be done to a physical body. Truly, Mari is more spirit than body. Even before they had become so involved with her, they had sensed that.

Ray finds it difficult to believe his own thoughts. They seem to come to him unbidden. But he knows they're true, and he knows also that there is no doubt that this mystery will be solved.

He and Jean simply have to put all the pieces together.

But first of all, they have to get together. His shift is over - it's three in the morning. All is quiet - the patients long since asleep. One more time, he does rounds, checking that everyone is safely in bed and asleep before he's relieved by whoever Jean has set up to come on duty after him.

Three thirty and no one has shown up yet. Ray checks the schedule. Great! She's forgotten to fill it in. He has no idea who is supposed to relieve him. He'll have to call her.

"Jean, sorry to wake you. It's Ray. Did you forget to schedule anyone to take over from me? It's three-thirty and no one has shown up yet."

A groggy voice answers from the other end of the phone. "Damn, Ray, I must have slept right through my alarm. I'm taking the shift after you. I was going to do a double. We're really short-handed since Cindy's been gone. I'll be right there. Sorry."

"It's OK. Take your time. I'll wait."

It occurs to Ray that this could be the best thing that's happened. Now he and Jean will have another chance to consult on the evening's events. "Here's hoping she's not still wearing that damn wire," he thinks.

Ray has gotten used to the lack of sleep by this time. He dozes a bit at his desk, but comes fully awake when he hears the big front doors whoosh open.

He looks up expectantly. It couldn't be anyone but Jean at this time of the night.Or could it?

Chapter 44

Ray can scarcely believe his eyes. "Maybe I'm still dreaming" is his first thought. Standing at the front desk with Jean, looking for all the world like some kind of vision, is Cindy.

But what on earth is she doing here, and who is looking after the kids? All they need right now is for something to happen to those kids again.

"Don't worry, Ray." She sees the look on his face and reads his mind. "The kids are perfectly safe. They're being looked after by some people that I trust completely and no one can get to them or hurt them."

"Oh my God, Cindy, it's good to see you." Ray jumps up and gives her a hug. He can scarcely contain himself. "But where did you find someone to look after the kids up there? You don't know anyone . . . ."

Cindy silences him with a look. "Trust me, Ray. You know I'd never leave if I didn't think they were OK."

From the corner of his eye, he sees the smile on Jean's face.

"She just showed up at my place, Ray." Jean tells him.

"I don't believe it, Cindy. You have no idea how good it is to see you. But . . . the kids?"

"I ran into an old friend while I was shopping for groceries. I had no idea she was even in the area. We started talking and I told her why I was up there and she offered to help. The kids are a lot safer with her and her husband than they were with me."

"I don't believe it." Ray says again. A special feeling, like a warm current, flows through his body. Despite all they've been through, despite all they have yet to accomplish, he is so thrilled to see her.

It's Jean who interrupts the reunion.

"OK then, let's get down to it, shall we? We have got to figure out what makes sense, what's happening here."

"How do we begin?" asks Ray.

"Why don't we each tell what we know about Mari, how she got here, and our hypothesis about the why and the who. Maybe we'll be able to come to some kind of conclusion. Jean, you didn't remember to put the wire on, did you?"

"What are you talking about, Ray?" Cindy can't believe her ears.

"The cops wired her so they could check on what we were talking about. They told her that if she refused to wear it, I would be taken in for questioning on the grounds that I was interfering with an ongoing investigation into a murder. I believe they intimated that the questioning wouldn't be gentle, if you get my drift."

"I get your drift all right. They have got to have something to do with all that's been happening to us. I just wonder how much."

"Oh, they're in it all right. Up to their eyeballs. We're both sure of that," Jean tells her.

"OK Jean, everything was pretty routine tonight". Ray quickly fills her in on any changes in the patients since he's been here. It's been quiet, thank goodness. All they would need right now is for something else to go haywire.

"So, now that we're all here, let's try to put some pieces of this puzzle together."

Ray is standing with his back to the window, facing the front door. He sees Cindy's eyes widen, hears the sound of sirens coming from outside the building. He knows immediately what's happening. Soon, patients are awake and milling out into the hallways, frightened and confused.

The front doors swing open to the sight of about half a dozen uniformed men with guns drawn.

Jean, to give her credit, steps forward and confronts them head on.

"Doesn't matter who you are, don't piss off the head nurse," Ray mutters to himself.

"What's going on?" she demands. "What are you doing in this hospital with drawn guns?"

"Ma'am, could you identify yourself, please?"

"I'm Jean Balcolm, the head nurse and supervisor here."

"Well, ma'am, a call came into the police station about five minutes ago stating that you were in the middle of a riot and needed help."

"Does this look like a riot to you?" Jean gestures to the confused and sleepy patients milling around in the corridors. "The only problem we have here is that you people just woke all of our patients, and it's going to take us the rest of the night to get them settled down again. Do you realize what the sound of sirens does to these people?"

"Ma'am, we always feel it's best to err on the side of safety in these cases."

"Fine. Now would you just leave and let us get these patients back to bed."

"Yes, ma'am. We've been requested to bring Ray LeBrun back to headquarters with us for questioning. Sir, please come with us." Handcuffs are slipped on Ray's wrists and he is quickly led away. The rest of the uniformed men follow suit and leave the hospital as quickly as they had arrived. Cindy and Jean stare after them, stunned and shocked. They can't believe what has just happened.

Jean turns to Cindy, realization dawning on them. How did they know who Ray was?

So this is why they were here. It had nothing to do with anyone reporting a riot. They wanted Ray.

* * * *

Ray is not surprised when he isn't taken to any police station. He isn't even all that surprised when he is driven to an empty parking lot on the other side of town and beaten to within an inch of his life. He is surprised when he comes back to consciousness several hours later in a pool of his own blood, astonished that he can feel such pain - but mostly, he's astonished that he's still alive.

Ray stays still on the ground for awhile, checking for any sign of movement around him. He's afraid they are still there; ready to pounce on him again. Finally, realizing that he's alone, he tries to drag himself up on his knees. He has no idea where he is. Broken pavement, weeds, dirty and broken glass, and garbage surround him. Not the best place to wake up when every inch of your body screams in agony.

His ribs feel like they're broken. Somehow, he has to get out of here and get medical attention. He tries once again to get up. Both legs splay out at right angles from his knees, bones showing through his pants.

"This is it, then. He knows from his injuries and his medical expertise that it would have been merciful of them to kill him outright. "I can't walk. Broken ribs. Blood everywhere. The place is deserted. I'm a dead man."

But soft voices speak to him through the fog of his pain. "Do not give up. Too many depend on you now. Let thoughts of them guide you through this. Let us help. Know that you are loved."

Ray feels a strength he never knew he had; it fills him with hope. Slowly, slowly and painfully, he uses his arms and shoulders to drag himself, an inch at a time, across the filthy parking lot and through the shrubs and trees and garbage that surround it. He comes to rest hours later in front of a still-closed diner.

"Won't I be a surprise for whoever comes to open up," he thinks.

All that matters to him now is that he survive. This game they're playing - he doesn't even know the rules - but he is determined now that he's not letting them win, not as long as he's breathing.

Weak from pain and loss of blood, Ray passes out on the stairs of the diner.

The owner does a brisk business with the early crowd who appreciate his cheap breakfasts and the space to read the paper and have a cup of coffee. That damn old warehouse across the street is an eyesore, and he'd rather the town get rid of it - tear it down or make it into something presentable. But it doesn't seem to hurt his business any. He's in a hurry, anxious to get everything ready before the first customers start arriving. He pulls into the parking lot, opens the back door and starts the grill."Got to get it good and hot so it will cook things nice and fast."

Finally, with everything in order, he unlocks and opens the front door, anticipating his first customers of the morning.

He's a bit put off when he notices an obvious trail that leads out of the trees across the street, like something has been dragged. His eyes follow the trail right up to the front of his place.

"What the heck? It looks like a dead dog or a deer or something."

His first reaction is one of anger. "If anyone thinks . . . . this is some sort of sick joke. . . ."

He feels a wave of nausea rise from the pit of his stomach as he realizes it's a person. He turns the body over - the guy is still breathing.

He races inside and calls an ambulance. They arrive within five minutes at the most and find him cleaning blood off his front stairs, his customers milling around, curious, waiting - waiting for what? To find out what's going on, he guesses.

Finally, the body is removed and the ambulance disappears around a corner. He heads inside to start the day - his customers want their breakfast. The police arrive and cordon off the front entrance, so he lets his customers use the back. After all, everyone still needs to eat.

Chapter 45

As soon as the uniformed men leave with Ray, Cindy flies to the telephone. *Detective Larone* - thank God she kept his number. She digs it out of her purse and calls. No answer. She hangs up and calls again. A groggy voice on the other end picks up.

"What's up? Who is this?"

"Detective Larone, this is Cindy Murphy. You probably don't remember me, but I spoke to you at the station about a week ago regarding a body I'd found in the river."

"Mrs. Murphy, do you have any idea what time it is?"

Cindy knows she sounds frantic, but she can't help herself.

"I realize that it's the middle of the night, and I wouldn't be calling you except - I think this is an emergency. I'm a nurse at Tillsboro Mental Hospital. Some armed men just came in and took one of our staff away. They said they were police officers and that they were taking him to the station for questioning, but I don't think they were. We think he's in danger. I couldn't call the police because maybe one of them is mixed up in this. Please, help us."

To her surprise, all evidence of sleep immediately disappears from the detective's voice. He is alert and he is hearing what she is saying.

"What makes you think these people were not police officers? What happened?"

As calmly as she can, Cindy tells him.

"Some men dressed as police officers came to the hospital. They said they had been called because of a riot here. None of us called them. We would never call them. Nothing like that has ever happened here. I mean, there's never been anything even close to a riot here . . . . When they left, they took one of our nurses with them. They said they wanted to question him. We're afraid . . . he might be in danger."

Cindy hesitates. Is he still listening to her? Is she making any sense to him? To her surprise, he asks, "Is there anyone there with you who can look after the patients?"

"Yes, the head nurse is here."

"You need to come down to the police station immediately. Do you know where it is?"

"Yes."

"I'll be there in about fifteen minutes. Park in front, but don't go in until you see me. If I'm there first, I'll wait for you in the parking lot."

"I'll be there." She hangs up and turns to Jean. "I'm going to the police station. We've got to get help for Ray. That detective I spoke to - his name is Larone - I met him when I found the body in the river. He seems OK, like we can trust him, I mean. We don't have much choice. Ray's life is in danger, I know it. I'll call you when I find out what's going on."

Cindy doesn't wait for Jean to answer. She grabs her coat and purse and tears out the door.

Jean stands up from the desk and turns around.

"This is my fault," she tells herself. "If I had worn that damn wire to work tonight like they told me to, they wouldn't have barged in here to take Ray away. Why the hell did I think I could get away with it?"

Her eyes focus on the window behind her desk. She strains to see out, but the iron bars that criss-cross it impede her view of Cindy's dash across the parking lot and of the large black car that pulls out of the dark shadows, following her.

"First Ray, and now Cindy is in danger," she mutters "Who did Cindy call? Detective Larone. He's meeting her down at the station. Why didn't he just come here to speak with her?"

She picks up the phone to call the police station, then puts it back. He won't be there yet, she realizes. And we're certain that the police are involved in all this. I'd better not call.

Frustrated that there's nothing she can do to help Cindy, she lets go of the matter and turns her attention to what's at hand.

Jean does not see, but instantly knows that something is happening right here that needs her attention. She turns inward, towards her patients, toward the comfortable, toward what she knows.

"I'm here", she thinks, "and I need to look after what's here. I'm just going to trust - I have to trust - that the power that's obviously working in our lives will look after Cindy and Ray."

Immediately, she feels calm, and senses that she's doing the right thing.

Chapter 46

Jean moves down the wide corridor to the place where Mari usually sits. She feels the strong and loving energy that she needs now.

She stands beside the windowsill.

Slowly, steadily, Jean feels herself lifted up... It's not an unpleasant feeling, just unexpected. The Universe wants her attention. It lets her know that she's moving in the right direction and that it approves. Jean has no idea how she knows this, she just does. It is as clear to her as if someone were standing right in front of her and speaking to her.

And then Jean continues on her rounds. When she comes to Mari's room, she hesitates. The door is closed. She pushes it open. The bed is empty. Somehow, she knows, this is what she expected. She knew, deep in her heart, that Mari was not in her bed. Mari's nocturnal wanderings were no longer in question. The only question is,

"Where does she go when she isn't in her room? And how does she get there?"

Something has happened over the course of the past few months. Mari had been a child afraid - especially terrified of the nighttime. She had never wanted to go to bed. As a matter of fact, they had had to fight her to get her to bed and then out of bed in the mornings. They had to fight her to take her medicine. None of that is happening anymore. If they give her medicine, if they didn't give her medicine, it makes no difference to her now. She appears in the mornings of her own accord, refreshed, gently loving to all, and having a positive impact on each and every person and thing that she touches.

Jean quietly closes the door to Mari's room and continues to check on the other patients. Everything and everyone else seems the same - all are sleeping in the right beds, charts are properly filled out, the ward clean and quiet, as all should be in the nighttime. She doesn't need to control a thing. Jean feels a hush over the building, a blessing that's unspoken. Goodness and impending goodness are waiting, just waiting to be called upon.

"How do I know this?" She wonders. "Why do I know this?"

"Is this where Mari spends her nights? Does her spirit hover over this building that's brought such distress to so many, blessing it, turning things around, making them right?"

A horn suddenly begins to blare outside in the parking lot, dragging her attention away from her thoughts, forcing her attention elsewhere.

She realizes that, no matter how changed are the feelings in the building, outside, things are still a mess. What is happening to Cindy and Ray, those people she now cares for? Their lives are in grave danger. And here she is, helpless, unable to do a damned thing.

A sudden anger floods her.

That's what she hates about becoming involved with others, caring for them, loving them. You always get hurt; somehow or other, you always get hurt. And she's set herself up again.

"So you've made the decision to join the rest of humanity and leave yourself vulnerable to hurt and pain. Let it go, Jean, feel it all, the good and the bad. Let it go and welcome to my world."

A surprisingly gentle voice goads her, lovingly, determinedly.

Jean's anger dissipates as quickly as it arrived. She laughs out loud at herself and her foolishness. She knows that she's in it now; there is no choice. She's in it up to her eyeballs. And she's happy; finally, she's truly happy. She has joined the rest of the world, the world of hurt and pain, the world of love and happiness. No more going back. No more living in the shadows of life. The joy she feels is something she has never before experienced.

"Even in the middle of this worry, even in the middle of all the pain, I feel joy. This is unbelievable. I think I'll stay here."

Jean finishes her rounds, checking the charts on the doors of the patient's rooms as she passes, making sure each person is OK and sleeping soundly. Silently, she blesses each as she passes. From deep inside of her, something that she had come across in her readings a very long ago enters her mind, something she had thought to be foolishness at the time.

I make my rounds and I check my charts.
I awaken.
I make my rounds and I check my charts.

Chapter 47

A car sits in the parking lot outside the police station, its engine idling. Cindy parks beside it and looks carefully at the face through the window.

"Make damn sure it's him," she tells herself.

Jim Larone turns off his ignition, steps out of the car, and approaches. She does the same. He motions towards the station house. Silently, they approach the building and go through the metal door into a large room.

It's empty except for an officer at a small, cluttered desk.

Jim sits at a desk towards the back. It's significantly uncluttered compared to the other guy. Then Cindy remembers that Jim Larone is new here. He's probably not had the time or the paperwork to clutter anything yet.

"At least," she thinks, "he's got his own desk now. It would be a bit disconcerting to be putting Ray's life into the hands of someone who was so new to police work that he didn't even have his own desk yet."

So far, neither of them has spoken. He starts.

"Mrs. Malone, I know you told me what happened at the hospital over the phone, but would you mind repeating yourself so I can make sure I've got it straight." He takes out a pen and paper.

"He's taking a report," thinks Cindy. "I don't need someone to take a report. I need someone to do something to help Ray"

Out loud, she says. "It's Cindy Murphy, detective."

"Yes, Mrs. Murphy, sorry. I need you to tell me everything you know. Please don't leave anything out."

Cindy begins. She tries her best to be very calm and very explicit. Panic, she knows, will be of no help in finding Ray.

Finally, she finishes her story - men dressed in police uniforms stormed into the hospital claiming someone had reported a riot. When the supervisor told them there was no riot, nothing even of the sort, they left, taking Ray with them.

"Did they say why they were taking him?"

"They said it was for questioning, that they were taking him here. At least, I assume it was here. They said they were taking him 'to the station'." Cindy feels panic start to creep into her voice.

Jim Larone gets up from the desk and goes over and speaks to the officer who's been on duty all night. Cindy assumes he's asking if there has been any sign of Ray, if he has any idea what might have happened.

He returns. Mrs. Murphy, whatever happened at your hospital or to your colleague, he's not here. Have you told me everything? Do you know of any reason someone may have taken him?"

Cindy hears the word 'taken'. A light suddenly goes on. Her kids were 'taken'. Now Ray's been 'taken'. There's got to be some connection.

Her face contorts, remembering the pain, remembering how good Ray was during the time her kids were God knows where. She has got to help him. She forces herself to calm down.

The detective notices the change in her.

"Good," he thinks. "Now maybe we'll get somewhere."

She begins at the beginning. As succinctly as she can, she tells him about Mari and the hospitalization of a twelve-year-old for a murder she couldn't possibly have done. She also explains how she tried to get information on it, and that someone seems to have known of her search for the truth in the files and the library. She tells him about her children's kidnapping and the police refusing to help. And she tells him how the kidnappers told her to leave town and Ray helped her move so that she could get her kids back. "Now," she tells him, "Ray is missing and possibly in danger."

She takes a deep breath.

"Well, seems like you've had a pretty busy couple of days."

"Yes."

"And aren't you the lady who found the body in the river not too long ago?"

"Yes, I am. Why?"

Cindy can feel the desperation creeping back into her voice and under her skin. "Oh my God", she thinks, "what if he doesn't believe me? What if he thinks I'm a kook? What if he thinks he's dealing with a nutcase, and that he will have a great story to tell his fellow officers tomorrow morning?"

As if he's reading her thoughts, Jim Larone tells her. "You know, I believe you."

To himself, he thinks "Wow. Who on earth could make something like this up? She's got to be telling the truth. And if she is, this is a lot more serious than we'd believed. She and I and everyone else who knows about it - we're all in serious danger."

Cindy feels like she could collapse from relief. He believes her. He'll help them find Ray before something awful happens to him.

But she doesn't expect what he says next,

"You have to go back to the hospital," the detective tells her. "I need you there while I try to find out what's happened to your friend. I can't do anything with you here." Jim is concerned. He doesn't know how safe she is here in the police station. "Now, I'm going to walk you to your car and make sure you're safely in it. You go back to the hospital. I'll call them to tell them you're on the way. Who should I speak with?"

"You can speak with Jean Balcolm, the Supervisor. She'll probably answer the phone."

"OK, let's go."

Jim walks her out to her car.

"I don't want you to stop for anyone, just go directly to the hospital. Do you have a cell phone in case of an emergency?"

"Yes, it's right here."

"Good. Now remember, don't stop for anyone or anything. Just go straight back to work. I hope that whoever is doing all this doesn't realize you're back in town yet, but be careful just the same. Call me at this number when you get there." Jim hands her a piece of paper with a number on it.

"Thank you."

Thank heavens someone is finally listening. Maybe now they can get some help, not just for Ray, but for Mari, and for herself too. Maybe things can finally return to normal and her kids can come home and go back to their own school, she can get back to work, and things can be like they were before all this foolishness. She had never appreciated how precious simple things were, like being able to sleep in your own bed and have her kids go to their own school. She'll never take her life for granted again.

But her sense of relief is short-lived. As she rounds a corner leading up the drive to the hospital, a large black car pulls out from the shadows, blocking her from going any farther. Two burly characters step from the interior. Her fingers find a button on her cell phone, as she thinks, "What good will it do? How can he possibly help me now?"

Oddly, she feels no panic. As a matter of fact, she's exceptionally calm.

"Let's just see where this takes me," she thinks. She gets out of her car to meet the intruders.

Chapter 48

Jim Larone watches as Cindy leaves the parking lot.

A few months ago, someone from inside the department cued one of the big boys that something nasty was going on in Tillsboro. No matter how rotten the department, you could always count on a couple of good cops to try and set things straight. He got the assignment to find out exactly what was going on. So he was transferred here. Whoever is in charge of this mess is cagey, though. Jim has been here a couple of months and can't find anything out of the ordinary. As a matter of fact, it's a little too ordinary, as far as he's concerned. Aside from the usual few obnoxious idiots you find on every force, it's ordinary to the point of boring. He had been just about to pack it in and go back and tell his supervisor that someone had been making a big fuss over nothing.

But what a story he had just heard! It's a good one, if it's true. And it seems like it is just the tip of a nasty iceberg. Find out what's going on here and he will find out more about this town than you could imagine. He's got a secure line in his car. He heads over to makes a call.

"Hello, Marcus. Yeah, it's Jim. Listen, I think I'm finally on to something. I think these guys roughed up a nurse who works at Tillsboro Mental Hospital. He picked up on something they screwed up a few years back that they want to keep under wraps. They tried to get him to back off and he wouldn't, so they went right in to the hospital and took him. Talk about balls. Someone here is so used to getting their own way with no consequences that they're just being stupid."

"So what do you need from us?"

"Find that nurse. I don't care if he's dead or alive, I want him found."

"Will do. We'll need his name and anything else you got."

Jim proceeds to fill him in as quickly as possible. He's trying to be outside for as little time as possible so as not to arouse any suspicions.

"Make sure you keep this line open, Marcus. And be careful. Whoever's running this mess around here is not only dangerous, he's clever too, and that's a bad combination. Who knows what's been going on or what they will do to keep it secret."

"Sure, Jim, we'll let you know when we've found him."

Jim hangs up the phone and heads back inside. He wants to go over his notes, see if he can get a clue as to what's happening here.

"What the hell . . . .?"

The notes are gone. Did he put them somewhere? The only other guy here is still at his desk, but who else could it be? He crosses the room.

"I had some notes on my desk that I took from the lady who was just in here. They're gone. I want them back."

"Haven't seen any notes."

Jim grabs the guy - what's his name - Brown - by the shirt and yanks him up by the collar. Before he knows what's happened, there's a gun in his neck.

"Put him down, Larone."

Jim drops him. He falls in a heap on the floor.

"Now," says gun-in-neck guy softly, "what the hell is going on here?"

Jim is surprised. He had thought he and Brown were alone in the station. This guy - Morgan - he's too high up on the ladder to lower himself to covering the night shift. What's he doing here?

"I just took a report from a lady, left the notes on my desk to walk her out to her car, came back in and they're gone. This jerk is the only one who's been around here. I was just asking him where they were."

"You know anything about his notes, Brown?"

Brown scrambles to his feet.

"I didn't take nothing off his desk. What the hell would I want with his f***ing notes?"

Jim has no option. He goes back to his desk. He's certain those papers were sitting right on top and that Brown, lummox that he is, did something with them. Whoever is in on this did a pretty poor job of picking compatriots. Brown is a bully and stupid besides.

He should have taken the notes with him. Brown isn't the only stupid one around here tonight. As a matter of fact, Brown is probably the smarter of the two of them. Here he's gone and screwed up by leaving his notes around for any idiot to steal.

Jim only wishes that the nurses had brought him in on the story when it first started happening, when they first noticed something was wrong. He could probably have prevented this poor guy, Ray, from getting hurt and possibly even killed. Who knew how far these people would go to protect their secrets. He has no idea what the secrets are yet, although he has his suspicions. This whole thing could probably have been resolved if they hadn't tried to do something about it themselves. But then, who could blame them? They had no idea who they could trust or what they were up against. How could they? It was sheer, dumb luck that the nurse had spoken to him when she had found the body in the river, and it was luck that she had felt she could trust him. At least, it looked like luck. Could be just about anything, as far as he was concerned, as long as it helped him clean up this mess.

His cell phone vibrates. He doesn't want to answer it in here. Doesn't want to act as if anything's wrong other than that he suspects Brown screwed with his notes.

Jim heads out the door. He feels something pass between Brown and gun-in-neck guy. Brown smiles and picks up the phone on his desk. Who is he calling?

Jim's skin begins to crawl. He can feel this situation getting more and more dangerous by the minute.

Chapter 49

Cindy watches the men approach her. The darkness that surrounds and flows from them is thick and murky. Its fingers reach for her, making the hair on the back of her neck and down her arms stand straight up on end. Black fear grips her heart and clamps its icy claws on her throat, freezing her tongue and mouth.

They grab her arms, one on each side, and roughly drag/walk/carry her back to the large black car. No screams escape her frozen lips. . . . There's no point. Only a prayer pierces the terrible darkness -

"Her children. Please God they're not orphans before this night is over".

She's thrown into the back seat. One of them leans over and ties a dirty, dark cloth over her eyes and most of her face. The air is thick and difficult to draw in. She struggles to breathe.

A rough voice spits out at her. "Shut up with the gasping. You should be happy. We're taking you to see your friend."

Cindy's shocked. Just for a moment, she considers the possibility that Ray is OK.

She tries to remain calm, breathe without noise, without disturbing them. It seems like forever before the car stops.

The men get out. They're arguing. She manages to make out the words, "gone - how - where?"

Was Ray here? Is he gone? Maybe someone has come along and helped him.

One of them opens the car door, grabs her by the neck, and pulls her out. He yanks off the blindfold and shoves her face down, down - stopping a few inches above a piece of dirty, cracked pavement.

There's blood, fresh blood. She's close enough to smell it. And what looks like skin, pieces of flesh. Ray's flesh?

"See what's left of your friend? That's what happens to nosy people."

"Left of Ray?" she thinks. "My God, what did they do to him?"

In a matter of seconds, she's yanked to her feet. Her blindfold is back on and she's thrown back into the car. This time, though, it's not the back seat. A lid closes over her. She's in the trunk.

Every inch of her body screams in disbelief, "No! No! This can't be happening!"

But it is. It is happening. Overwhelming panic takes over.

Deliberately, forcefully, she shifts her mind. Survival - she needs to survive - for her children. They need her. For Mari. They have unfinished work. And for Ray - is there any possibility he could still be alive after what she's seen?

"Help me, someone please help me," she begs to anyone who might be listening.

With her asking, peace and calm once again replace fear and panic. She marvels at the change and she knows, it's OK - she'll be OK.

Her breath begins to return to normal. There has to be a way out of here. She can barely move with all the crap that's in here with her. They haven't tied her hands, probably thinking she would never be able to do anything – she is in the trunk, after all. She manages to pull her arms up and remove her blindfold.

The car is moving fast. She needs to do something before they arrive at their destination. She feels around as best she can.

There's no inside latch to release the trunk.

She might as well still have the blindfold on, considering she can't see a thing anyway. She feels some wires and yanks on them. "Maybe the taillights will go out and we'll be stopped", she thinks. "Of course, I could also electrocute myself. Doesn't matter, it would probably be better than what they have planned for me." She yanks harder and feels them come loose.

She feels the beginnings of panic again and deliberately calms herself. She's been in situations before, maybe not quite as bad as this, but certainly bad, nonetheless. She's gotten out of them, and she will get out of this.

"Now think," she tells herself. "There's got to be a way."

The wail of a siren pierces her ears - louder and louder. The car pulls over and stops.

"Oh my god, it worked," she thinks. "I can't believe it worked."

She can hear voices outside, but no one comes to let her out. What are they telling the police? Why is the trunk not opening? Shouldn't that be the first thing they check? She bangs as hard as she can, screaming.

"Let me out. I'm in the trunk. Let me out."

There is no answer. The trunk stays closed. Doors slam. She hears the squeal of tires. The car pulls back on the road and continues on its way.

Despair - she can't give in to it. If she does, she's as good as dead already.

And through the darkness and despair, evil and fear, Cindy feels something else in the trunk with her. A presence here, with her.

"This too will pass," it tells Cindy, "This evil, too, will pass and all things will work together for good again."

"Pray for these men". Cindy hears the faintest of whispers. "By saving them, you save yourself."

And with this strange message, the presence leaves. Cindy is alone again but no longer desperate or frightened.

The men who drive her to her death, or worse, she knows, are in much greater danger than she is.

Chapter 50

Jim jumps into his car. He checks his cell phone. It's probably Cindy calling to let him know that she is back at the hospital.

He calls the number on the phone. No one picks up. Strange. He doesn't have the number for the hospital, so he calls the operator and asks her to ring it for him. She's got to be there by now. Someone picks up and he asks for Cindy. She's not there. He asks to speak to the floor supervisor. It seems like it takes forever for her to come to the phone.

"Hello, this is detective Jim Larone. I interviewed your employee, Cindy Murphy this evening. She left the police station heading back to the hospital about half an hour ago. She should be there by now. I'm just checking to make sure that she made it back safely."

"No, she didn't. She's not here."

"Can you think of any place else she might have gone?"

"No. Do you have her cell phone number?"

"I did. She's not picking up."

"Then I'd say she's missing - and probably in danger."

"Yes, I'd say so."

From the conversation, Jim realizes that this lady knows what's going on.

"I'm coming to the hospital," he tells her. "I'll need any information you have, no matter how trivial, about both your missing nurses. I'll be there in about ten minutes. Don't leave. Don't go anywhere. If you hear from Cindy, call me. He gives her his cell phone number."

"Yes, OK."

He calls Marcus. "Marcus, we've got a situation here. I'm afraid some people are in serious danger. Have you tracked down the missing nurse yet?"

"Yeah, I think we found him in a hospital in Derry. This guy has no ID, but he fits the description you gave me. He's pretty badly messed up. We can't talk to him yet. We may not be able to talk to him ever. He could be brain damaged too badly. Big chunks of his skull, and lots of the rest of him were left behind where he was beaten up. Apparently, he was left in a vacant lot and managed to somehow drag himself far enough so someone noticed him and called an ambulance. I doubt if whoever did him expected him to survive, let alone get help. They probably don't know that he's still alive."

"Sounds like he'd be better off if he weren't."

"Maybe. What we can't figure out is why they didn't just get rid of him altogether. Why leave him there? Why take a chance on someone finding him?"

"Don't know, unless they got called away for another job that they had to do right away and were intending to get rid of the body after they took care of it."

"Cindy. They had to pick up Cindy".

"Who's Cindy?"

Jim tells him about the other nurse, about how he let her go back to the hospital and how she's gone now too.

"That's probably it, all right. I'll bet they figured they would grab her and just get rid of both of them together. Must have been a heck of a surprise for them to come back from picking her up and find their body gone."

"Listen, Marcus, I'm just pulling into the hospital now. I've got to talk to their supervisor. I don't know if whoever these guys are know about her being in on it, but if they do, she's in danger too. We need a guard for this hospital until we get it straightened out and find out who's involved and why."

"Don't worry, Jim. Someone will be right there."

"Marcus, be careful. We don't know how dangerous these guys are, but I think they've got nothing to lose now except their own skin. Whatever they're hiding, they are desperate to keep it hidden."

"Yeah, I know."

Jim hangs up. Damn. Why did he let Cindy go back to the hospital alone? Why didn't he tail her or something? He was too involved with that asshole, Brown. At least now he knows how involved he is in all this. Jim is sure that Brown is the one who made the call and had his boys pick up Cindy. And he did it right under Jim's nose.

Jim gets out of his car and heads into the hospital. A tall, lean nurse with a stern look on her face comes towards him.

"Hello. Are you Detective Jim Larone? I'm Jean Balcomb, the supervisor here. We just spoke. Is there anything I can do to help? Do you have any idea where my nurses are?"

"No, I'm sorry, I don't, Ms. Balcomb. I was hoping you might help us with that. Could you tell me what you know about what's gone on here recently? I understand this all began when Mrs. Murphy started to take an interest in a young patient you have on this floor."

"Yes, that seems to be where it all began." Jean repeats a story that's almost verbatim to the one he heard from Cindy.

Jim asks. "So you guys think that this kid didn't kill her grandmother, and that whoever did kill her found out that you were messing around with files and newspaper clippings and getting the drift of what really went on?

"I don't know. Yes, that's what I think. It's the only thing that makes any sense. There's got to be something about Mari - that's the girl who supposedly killed her grandmother - that someone doesn't want us to find out. I almost wish we'd left it all alone. No matter what happened to Mari, she's safe now with us. And it's not worth losing Cindy and Ray to find out what really happened to her grandmother and why she's here."

"Well, someone was willing to sacrifice her so that they could keep a secret. Now someone is willing to sacrifice your nurses' lives in order to keep it. I'd say it's got to be something pretty important, wouldn't you agree?"

"I guess so. Anyway, that's about all I can tell you. We - Ray, Cindy and myself - surmised that whatever happened to Mari's grandmother, the child didn't do it. Someone else did. And that someone else is pretty determined that we not find out who he is."

"That's a pretty good assumption for amateurs. I'm thinking you're probably right, considering the circumstances. It certainly looks like someone doesn't want you guys digging into anything to do with the kid. They were happy to leave her here to rot. And just as long as no one asked any questions about why she was still here, their secret was safe."

Just for a second, Jean takes offence at the crack about someone rotting on her ward, but she lets it go. Instead, she agrees with Jim.

"That's about what we thought."

"Yeah, now there's another possibility that has to be considered. Would anyone else benefit from having the kid left in here? Does she have any other relatives - anyone who might be getting something from her being in here? Did the grandmother leave anything of value that the kid couldn't get her hands on as long as she's considered incompetent?"

"We hadn't thought of that. As far as we could figure out, there were no other relatives. The grandmother was all she had."

"Is the kid around? Could I talk to her?"

"She's here, just down the hall there. That's her at the window. I doubt if you'll be able to get anything out of her, though. She doesn't speak."

"She doesn't speak?"

"Hasn't since the day she arrived, as far as I know. She seems to communicate without speaking, sometimes, though."

"How does she do that?"

"I couldn't really describe it. It's just that when she wants you to know something, you do. She's quite an unusual child. When you're in her presence, you feel something special. Come on, I'll introduce you to her and you can see for yourself."

Detective and nurse head down the long corridor to the window where Mari sits by herself. She turns towards them as they approach and smiles.

Jim comes closer. He's amazed! What is it about this child, this feeling? He could stay here forever.

"Of course she doesn't speak," he thinks, "words aren't necessary."

Jim knows just by being in her presence that it's all he'll ever want, only to stay in the presence of this child forever.

"Go. You must go. But remember me." She tells him.

As if awakening from a vivid dream, Jim goes. Back down the long corridor and out into the night. Jean watches. She knows the effect that Mari has on people, she's felt it herself.

Marcus must be here by now. Jim heads for his car and his phone.

"Marcus, where are you?"

"Hi Jim. We're just down the driveway, across the street from the hospital. We've got the road pretty well blocked off so we can check on anyone or anything coming or going."

"OK. I'm coming down. I think I'll head over to the hospital in Derry and check on that nurse that got so badly beaten up. Anything on the other one - the woman who was taken tonight?"

"No, we haven't been able to locate her. We did find her car, though - in the bushes right beside where we set up our roadblock. Someone must have grabbed her. We're checking it out right now."

"Right. Listen, Marcus, I know for sure that a guy at the station - his name is Brown - tipped someone off that the nurse was back in town and asked them to get rid of her. I'm sure he knows what's happened to her."

"We can't just accuse him without proof, Jim. I'd hate to play our hand before we get any evidence on these guys and lose it all."

"Marcus, this may be our only chance to save that nurse. God knows what they'll do to her. Is there any way you can get to Brown and make him talk without the others finding out."

There's silence on the other end of the phone for a minute. Then Marcus tells him,

"How about if you go back there and find a way to get him outside where we'll be waiting for him. You can't do anything for the guy in the hospital, but if we can get someone to tell us where that nurse is, we may be able to save her from a similar fate."

"Will do. You're going to have to leave someone here, though."

"Right. I'll just ride with you. We'll leave Johnny here."

"So that's who's with him," thinks Jim. Johnny, our own personal Rambo. They must really want these guys if they sent Johnny & Company.

"Don't make a fuss", they had told him. "Don't let on to anyone. Just find out what's going on in that town and we'll take it from there! Right! Man, it was always like this. Every time he worked with these guys, he found himself in the middle of some mess. Oh well, it made life interesting.

And that kid - what is it about her? How does she do that to people? He wouldn't have met her if he hadn't been on this case. And he's very happy that he met her.

Chapter 51

Cindy feels the car stop again. She hears muffled voices, then nothing. It's quiet, too quiet.

They left. They left her in the trunk.

Her breathing quickens. She feels herself panic. "It's OK," she tells herself. "It's going to be OK. She moves around and makes some room. She really is a tiny woman and this trunk would be quite large if it weren't stuffed so full of all this junk. She feels around her. Her right hand stops on a handle or something of the sort. She pushes against it and feels something give a bit. It's the back seat of the car. She pushes harder and sees light coming from the top of the trunk where it meets the inside of the car. Cindy can't believe it. She needs to be careful - someone may still be around. But quick, she needs to be quick too, before they come back. It doesn't take much. Once she has some light, she notices a handle. She pulls down on it and pushes against the seat. It folds down nicely. She rolls herself into the back seat. Gingerly, she lifts her head up to look out the window. The car is parked in a clearing surrounded by trees and bushes. She was right. The men are gone. There's no one around.

Cindy opens the door, puts the seat back up, and slides herself out onto the grass, keeping close to the ground. Voices - she hears voices in the distance - coming closer......she dashes behind a clump of bushes and scootches down.

"Please.......please...... don't let them open the trunk......They can't know I'm gone..... They can't look for me.......too close......I'm too close."

Fortunately for her, they have no intention of opening the trunk. They arrive back at the car with their hands full. They are so close that she can smell the gasoline as it's being poured over the car. They move some distance away, light a large torch and throw it at the car. Flames leap into the air. Before long, the car is completely engulfed.

"Well," thinks Cindy, amazed at how calm she feels. "That wouldn't have been a very nice way to die."

She feels the heat on her face and arms and, for several moments, she fears that the small clump of bushes in which she's hiding will burst into flames along with the car.

The men watch as the roaring flames gradually subside. Then one of them takes a phone out of his pocket and makes a call. He clicks it shut, says something to his companion, and they leave.

"I'm alive!" Cindy whispers to herself. "I can't believe it! They're gone and I'm still alive!"

Chapter 52

Jim stops midway down the driveway that leads out of the hospital grounds. He feels a sense of security when he sees Johnny leaning against the car talking to Marcus. How many missions Jim has been on - whenever Johnny is there, things turn out. He sticks his head out the car window.

"Hi ya, Johnny. Just tickles the cockles of my heart to see you here."

"Yeah, glad to be here Jim. Anything to help - you know me."

Jim knows him, alright. If there's any chance of some action, from a fight in a bar room to a punch out with some bad guys, just put Johnny in the middle of it. Every department needs a guy like Johnny.

Marcus jumps in Jim's car and they head for the station. They drive in silence, both wondering how the hell they are going to get Brown out of the station so they can take him somewhere and question him.

It's got to be fast and it's got to be clean so they don't get hung up trying to explain themselves to anyone. Cindy Murphy's life depends on it.

Jim makes a quick decision. He pulls in to the station, parks the car just around the corner from the front door and makes a call.

What luck! Guess who picks up the phone.

"Brown here"

"Brown, we need you! Get over to the hospital - now!"

The phone slams down. Jim was afraid he would object to leaving the station unattended. Guess not. He picks up a green plastic garbage bag from the floor of the car and follows Marcus, who's already positioned himself to one side of the front door. Brown comes out. They grab him, stick the bag over his head, tighten it just short of cutting off his breathing, and drag him back to the car.

Jim throws the keys to Marcus. They're well away from the station and Jim's gun is in Brown's face when the bag comes off. The look on his face is worth any effort they had to go through to get him.

"Surprise, Brown! You're not dealing with civilians now, so shut up and listen. You made a call as I was leaving the station last time. I think you told someone that Mrs. Murphy was back in town and she was making trouble again. Who did you call and where did they take her? And remember, your answer is important. It may save your life."

Brown is obviously terrified, but not of him. Jim needs to change that. He speaks softly and clearly, his mouth just inches from the man's ear.

"I know it was you set her up, Brown. If anyone harms her, the guys I work for will make sure you end up in prison for a long, long time. You know what they do to crooked cops in prison, Brown?"

No answer.

"Don't screw with us Brown. You have no idea who you're dealing with."

"I don't know where they took her. I just made a call like I was told to do and reported what had gone down. I was only doing my job. Morgan never liked you right from the beginning. Thought you wouldn't play by the rules like he wanted. Told me if I found out anything about you so he could fire you he would give me that promotion I'd been wanting."

"Morgan. This is getting better and better" he tells Marcus "Morgan's the Chief".

"This mess in Tillsboro does go pretty high up. The boss was right, then."

"I'd say he probably was right, yeah."

"Who are you guys? What the hell are you talking about?"

"Well, Brown, let's just say we're talking about complaints coming in about the way you guys are running things here in Tillsboro. Now, just who do you think is doing the complaining, and who do you think would get the complaints?"

"You're the Feds?"

"Close, Brown, only we don't have as many rules as the Feds. Let's just say that we're a unit that's specially designed to investigate and take down dirty cops."

"I don't know nothing. I only know that they told me if I was to keep my job, I needed to do what I was told and shut up about it. I got kids - I need that job."

Brown is telling the truth. Jim can feel it. He's actually starting to feel kind of sorry for the guy.

"Ok, Brown, let's see if you can help us then. Do you remember what number you called to tell Morgan about my report?"

"It's back at the station. If you take me back there, I'll get it for you."

"Is the guy who stuck the gun in my neck still there?"

"No, no one's there now"

"Don't know if I trust you Brown. You haven't really done much to peak my confidence in you."

"You know what I think. I think you guys blamed this poor kid for her grandmother's death and put her in a mental hospital when in reality someone you know and love did the dirty deed. Then, when an honest nurse tried to find out what happened, you and your friends were afraid that her inspection of the records would blow the lid off everything. I also think that there's a very good possibility that a lot of other people in that hospital are there because they made the mistake of going against some of the bigwigs in Tillsboro. Really convenient having a mental hospital in the town isn't it."

Brown is looking at him strangely.

"I don't know what the hell you're talking about. All I was told was that you had been transferred here because you were trouble and we should get rid of you if we could because we don't need trouble here. I swear that's all I was told."

How much of that is the truth, Jim has no way of telling.

"Yeah, it's amazing how much you miss when you're only looking out for your own ass."

"I didn't know. I'll help you guys. What d'ya want. What can I do?"

Well, the worm - or should he say snake - has turned. This guy is ready to give anyone or anything up as long as it saves his own skin. He could be useful.

They're back at the hospital. Marcus turns up the driveway. He stops midway to ask Johnny.

"Anything happening?"

"Nope, nothing yet."

"There will be. Keep your eyes open."

"Who ya got there?"

"Some guy from the station. His name's Brown. He's the one who called the enforcers on that nurse we're looking for. We thought he might have some information on where she is."

Brown takes one look at Johnny and tries to shrivel into the back seat of the car. Jim and Marcus drag him out and leave him sitting in the dirt, gagged and with his hands tied behind his back. Johnny won't touch him. He's got something against roughing up anyone who's stupid or scared. That's one of the things Jim likes so much about Johnny - no violence unless it's necessary. But Brown doesn't know that. Let him just sit there and wonder what they've got planned for him.

For now, their main goal is finding Cindy Murphy alive.

Chapter 53

Cindy watches the embers of what was once a car dwindle down. Then, figuring enough time has passed, she reaches in her pocket to find her phone. It's gone. She probably dropped it while they were putting her in the car.

She wonders if it's safe to come out of hiding and risk someone seeing her. Deciding she's got no other option - she can't stay in the woods all night - she follows the tracks of the car tires out to the main road. Her legs don't work quite right after being cooped up in the trunk, so it's rough going. It seems a lifetime until she spots a car coming her way. She steps right out in front of it, waving her arms. There's no way she is going to let it pass her.

The car stops. A kid - she looks to be still in her teens or early twenties - is driving. She hesitates before unlocking the car door. Cindy knows she probably looks like some vagabond. She begs.

"I'm desperate....... please .... I had a fight with my husband and he dumped me here. I've got to get back to town."

The car doors unlock. "OK, I'll help you."

"I got dumped here. I need to let someone know so they can come and get me. Where am I?"

"I'm heading for Derry. We're about midway between there and Tillsboro. Do you want to use my cell phone and call someone? Or I can give you a ride in to Derry if you want."

"Thank you. Yes, I'd like to make a phone call. Do you know what road we're on? How far are we from Tillsboro?"

"It's Route 22, about twenty miles from Tillsboro."

"Thanks." She doesn't have Jim's number on her, so she calls the hospital. Thank God it's Jean who picks up.

"Jean, it's Cindy."

Jean doesn't mince words. "Where are you?"

"I'm on Route 22, about twenty miles outside of Tillsboro heading towards Derry."

"OK, stay right there."

"I'm on the side of the road."

The line goes silent for a couple of seconds. Jean is thinking.

"Find something, something noticeable, so you'll be easy to find. Have you got something you could use? I don't want the guys to miss you, and I don't want you stopping anyone you don't know."

Cindy sees a red scarf inside the car.

"Could I borrow that scarf?" she asks the girl.

"Sure, if it will help."

"OK, Jean. There will be a red scarf on the right hand side of the road."

"All right. I'll let them know."

Cindy gives the phone back to the girl, who hands her the red scarf.

"Thank you so much. You know, you've probably saved my life."

"Are you sure I can't give you a ride somewhere?"

"No, I'll be all right. My friends will be here soon. By the way, what's your name? I'll need to return your scarf. Where should I send it?"

"Don't worry about it. You can keep the scarf. Good luck. Bye now."

Cindy moves to the side of the road and watches the tail lights of the car as it heads off in the distance. The thought flashes into her mind. "Maybe I should have taken the ride and just kept on going until I'm out of this mess, picked up the kids and found a job somewhere else and started over."

But she can't - she can't just leave. Her concern for Mari has spilled over into her concern for all the rest of those who are involved in trying to figure out what's going on in the hospital and in the town. She cares too much to just up and leave. She would never be able to live a happy, normal life. She would always be thinking of those she had left behind to fend for themselves. If she wants peace in her life, she needs to see this through to the end. She puts the red scarf down on the side of the road, anchors it with a rock so it won't blow away, and, once again, heads over to watch and wait in some bushes.

Chapter 54

Marcus hears the ringing cell phone, watches as Jim picks it up and speaks into it. He snaps it shut.

"Looks like we've found your missing nurse. She's waiting for us on Rte. 22 about twenty miles outside of town. Let's go."

"Was that her?"

"No. It was her supervisor at the hospital. She just got a call. There'll be a red scarf on the side of the road where we're to pick her up."

"So she's alive. Why the red scarf?"

"I guess she doesn't want to stand by the side of the road waiting for us and waving down cars."

"Gee, I wonder why?"

"Seriously, I'm surprised she's still alive. I can't wait to hear her story."

"Yeah, I know. It should be interesting."

The rest of the ride is silent as both men are conscious of Cindy's peril. Their concentration is focused on finding a red scarf by the side of the road... Finally, about twenty miles out, they spot it. They slow the car and come to a stop several feet beyond it. Jim gets out to make sure it's the scarf.

Cindy recognizes Jim and comes slowly out of the bushes. She's dirty, her clothes are torn, and she's pretty bedraggled looking, but she's walking and she's in one piece.

"At least she's fared better than her friend," Jim thinks.

The two men bundle her into the car and turn around, heading back for Tillsboro.

"What happened? Looks like you could use some cleaning up," Marcus tells her."

She thinks about it for a minute. There's nothing left in her house, not even any soap to take a shower. She directs them to Ray's house. On the way there, she tells them what happened. They don't seem surprised.

"Did you get a look at them? Would you know them if you saw them again?" Jim asks.

"Where are we? This your house?" It's Marcus asking.

"No" it's Ray's. I can't go to my house. There's nothing left there. Remember, I told you how I had to move out to convince these guys to give me back my kids. Yes, I would know them if I saw them again."

"Ray's house? You mean the other nurse?"

"Yes, it's his house. He won't mind me using his shower. At least he'll have soap and towels and I can get cleaned up."

"How are you gonna get in?"

"I don't know. Maybe he's got an extra key somewhere. I don't know."

Jim's gets out of the car with her.

"I'll get you in. Marcus, you stay here in case we get company."

Jim walks her to the door and manages to open it with very little effort.

"How did you do that?"

Jim shrugs. "Trick of the trade, I guess. You want me to come in and check the place out, make sure no one's here?"

"I'll be OK. They think I was burned in the trunk of that car. I doubt they think they will ever see me again."

"Yeah. You're kind of like the cat with nine lives. You keep coming back."

"Yeah," Cindy forces a laugh. "I guess I'm not that easy to get rid of. I'll tell you, some people are gonna be surprised to see me again."

She heads inside. She feels herself relax. It seems like home.

"It just feels so much like Ray," she thinks, tears welling in her eyes.

She heads for the bathroom and steps into the shower. It feels so good to let the water run over her. Finally finished, she wraps one of Ray's big white towels around herself and heads out to the kitchen to get something to eat. She stares out the window. She hadn't expected the two men who brought her here to still be sitting in the driveway. Cindy goes into Ray's bedroom closet. She puts on a pair of his pants, tying them with the belt from the housecoat. Then she finds a white nurse's shirt and tops off her outfit with it. She checks the mirror. She looks like someone wearing her big sister's clothes, but who cares. There's no way she can stand to put on her own stained and ripped ones. She heads out to tell the men to leave. She'll be all right for the night. No one knows she's here. They think she's dead.

Jim looks at her as if she's gone completely crazy.

"Yeah, right, lady. We're not leaving you anywhere."

"I need some sleep guys. I'll be OK here."

"You'll be OK nowhere until we get these guys and put them behind bars, Cindy. Now you're coming with us."

Cindy has no idea how she will manage to keep herself together without any sleep after all she's been through, but she does as she's told. She locks up Ray's house and goes with the men. They head for the hospital.

Halfway up Hospital Drive, the car stops. Jim gets out and seems to be addressing the bushes. Finally, Cindy sees the outline of another person, someone large. Jim is talking with him. He finishes and comes back to the car.

"Take her up to the hospital and leave her there," he tells the driver who's named Marcus. "I'll stay here with Johnny in case he needs me. Make sure everything is OK up there. This is the only way a car can get up, but someone might have come in through the woods or something. You never know with these guys."

"OK, I'll check it out. Be right back."

"Why don't you stay up there just in case?"

"Will do."

And just like that, Cindy arrives back at the hospital that she had left in such a hurry this afternoon.

"All that effort with so little to show for it," she thinks. "Here I am right back where I started, only exhausted and dressed in someone else's clothes. I don't even know where Ray is, and whether or not he's still alive. Not much progress here."

There is progress. There is always progress when you discover more about yourself, about how far you're willing to go because of your caring concern for others.

Cindy feels Mari's presence. She looks down the hallway, but there's no one sitting at the window in Mari's usual place.

"She must be asleep. Odd how I hear her and feel her with me even when she's not here."

Jean sees Cindy standing there in clothes that look to be falling off her body.

"What's happened to you? Are you all right?"

Cindy explains some of her night's adventures. She ends by telling Jean about her trip to Ray's house to shower and her hopes of getting some rest there, but the men didn't think it would be safe enough for her to stay.

"Well, you can find a place here to lie down. I'm sure it's easier for them to look after things if we're in one place."

"That's probably it."

Cindy wanders off down the hallway looking for an empty bed so she can get some rest. She finally finds one and lies down on it, but her mind won't let go. Something is bothering her, but it's staying just under the surface of her consciousness, not letting her rest, but not letting her address it either. Finally, she finds herself in that world between waking and sleeping, the in-between world.

You need to help those you care about, but remember also those who despise you.

She's shaking, someone is shaking her awake. It's Jean.

"Cindy, wake up. Shift's over. We need to head for Derry and visit Ray at the hospital there, see how he's doing."

"Ray? Visit Ray? You mean they've found him. He's alive?"

"He's alive, so far at least. I think he needs us to visit him. Even if he's not conscious, it will do him good just to know we're there for him."

Jean surprises herself with these words. She's always been such a practical nurse. If you can't see the healing, it's not taking place. Slowly, surely, in the past few days, she's moved from seeing everything on the physical plane to seeing things from an entirely new perspective.

"There is more to life than meets the eye", she thinks. "Much more than I had ever imagined."

"Let's go." She takes a good look at Cindy. "You look like an unmade bed."

Cindy laughs. "Hey, Ray's alive. I don't care what I look like after news like that."

Jean pulls something out of one of the desk drawers. Leave it to Jean to have an extra set of clothes on hand - heaven forbid she ever look messy.

"Here. It might be a good idea to change into a pair of my slacks before we go. The ones you're wearing could end up down around your ankles if that belt comes undone."

She's got a point. Cindy heads for one of the bathrooms to change. She turns to check herself out in the mirror. Her hair needs combing and her .... she stops, hand in mid-air.

There's a noise in one of the stalls - a small animal? One of the patients? ...... or .... she slowly pushes open the door of the only closed stall......

"You........what're you doing ....?" she manages to get out, before she's hit over the head and slides down in a pile on the floor and into oblivion.

She enters a long, black tunnel and heads towards the bright, all-encompassing Light. A voice speaks to her, *"Go back, Cindy. You need to go back. Your work is not yet done."*

She feels hands pushing her back and .... pain - oh my god, the pain .... her head ....she manages to open her eyes .... she's on the floor of the bathroom. She drags herself to the door, slumps against the cold hardness, and waits .... waits for someone or something to help her .... to let her know what she needs to do now.

Chapter 55

Jean, meanwhile, is waiting for her to come out of the bathroom wearing something decent so that they can go to the hospital in Derry and visit Ray. She doesn't want people thinking she has brought one of the mental patients with her. Even they look better than Cindy did, but that's because Jean has always been fussy about her ward and its appearance. She's always insisted that the patients look decent and, if they don't have any of their own clothes that look clean and presentable, she makes certain that there are hospital clothes they can wear. She herself checks on the linens and things that the laundry sends back to make sure they are doing a good job and all the patients have nicely laundered towels and sheets. She's still proud of herself for that. Her problem, she realizes, is that she was too focused on the outward appearance of the ward, and not nearly so interested in the other needs of the patients. It was almost as if she thought that keeping them clean outside made up for everything else. Cindy has been the one who has done the real caring, and she'd despised her for it.

"Well, that's certainly changed," thinks Jean.

"If we can ever get this place back to some semblance of normalcy, I'll be quick to show my respect for her and her talents. I'll bet we can do one heck of a job when we're both on the same track. Ray has always been a kind and caring person too. He'll be able to help us. That is, if he's ever capable of working again after what he's been through."

Jean is surprised at herself, at her ability to see through the fog of all that's swirling around them now. She is looking forward to a time where she and Cindy will be able to work together again, only this time with cooperation and respect for each other and for their patients.

"Maybe I'm dreaming, hoping that we can get this place back to normal, but what good is life without dreams," she thinks.

"What the heck is keeping her? How long does it take someone to change their pants?"

Jean is standing at the front door, waiting for Cindy to come out of the bathroom and join her. It suddenly occurs to her that maybe Cindy is still feeling some aftereffects from her wild night, maybe she needs help. Jean heads for the bathroom. She can't get the door open. She pushes, and realizes that something is blocking it. She calls to one of the orderlies to help her and together, they push the door open. Cindy's prone body is lying across the floor, unconscious, blocking the door.

Jean stifles the scream that rises in her throat. It wouldn't do to have the staff hear her lose it. She had never dreamed that anyone could have been waiting in the bathroom to harm Cindy. How did someone get in there? Why didn't she see anyone come out?

"Three strikes and you're out, Cindy .... three strikes and you're out." Jean mumbles to herself. "This is it. No more fooling around. You're going back up north with your kids and never coming back here until Jim and the good guys find out who's doing this and why."

"Quickly," Jean tells an orderly, "call Jim." Jean gives him the number and he quickly connects them. Jean tells Jim what happened and, almost before she can hang up, Marcus is ringing the front door buzzer. She sends the orderly to open it.

"What the hell happened?" he demands when he sees Cindy on the floor. Her eyes open and she seems to recognize them.

"I heard a noise in one of the stalls. I went to check, and he hit me over the head."

"Who hit you? Who was it?"

Marcus is incredulous. There's no way anyone got past him and his guys. There's simply no way into the building except through the front door, which he had his eyes on all night. Every other door leading into the building from the outside is firmly locked. The windows are barred. He checked everything himself earlier in the evening. Whoever did this had to have been in the building when he arrived, and is probably still here.

Cindy tells him, "I didn't recognize him. That's why I was so surprised - because I know everyone here."

"Come on," Marcus motions to Jean. "Let's have a look around. You'd know anyone who doesn't belong here, right?"

They leave Cindy in the hands of the orderly. She doesn't need stitches; it's just a bad bump. Marcus makes a call to Jim to send someone else up to watch the front door of the building while he and Jean check out the floor, opening closets and bathroom stalls, checking each patient, looking into closets. They find no stranger, no agitated patients, nothing out of place.

Marcus is still mumbling. "How could anyone get in and out of this building without being seen?"

"I have no idea."

"I don't think he was after Cindy in particular. He had no way of knowing she'd go into the bathroom to change."

"That's true." Actually, that thought had already occurred to Jean.

"So, why was he hiding in there?"

"Could be just a garden variety pervert. And of course, Cindy was in the wrong place at the wrong time. Just her luck. But how did he get in here? I've got to find out so it doesn't happen again."

"We'll figure it out, Jean; there has got to be an explanation."

The two of them head back down the corridor. Cindy is on her feet now, holding a cloth to her head.

"I'm beginning to think someone is trying to get rid of me." she tells them sheepishly.

"It certainly must have been a shock to open the stall and find a stranger standing there, and then to get hit over the head," Marcus replies.

"He was standing on the toilet"

"On the toilet?"

"Yes, that's why I didn't realize he was in there until he made a noise. I thought it was just a mouse or a squirrel had gotten into the building ...."

"....... and you were going to try and catch him and put him outside before one of the staff caught him and killed him," Jean finishes her sentence.

"You know me"......Cindy grins. "I almost get myself killed to save a chipmunk."

"Don't worry about it Cindy. It's a good thing. It's that soft heart of yours that's gotten us all into this mess in the first place." Jean smiles. Then unexpectedly, from the corner of her consciousness, she hears,

All messes look their worse when they're taken out of the shadows Jean, but they have to be exposed to the light in order to clean them up.

Jean feels herself surrounded in light. "Yes," she thinks, "that's right. "This has something to do with everything that's gone on here lately. This wasn't some random act. It's all part of the mystery here, and we've got to understand what happened before we can clean it up."

Turning to Marcus, she tells him, "The way I see it, there are two possibilities. Either this guy came in as a visitor during visiting hours and didn't leave when he was supposed to, or he was let in by the staff."

"I can't figure that one of your staff would let anyone in. He must have come in during visiting hours. Tell me, is that bathroom used a lot?"

"Actually, it's rarely used. The bathroom on the other side is larger and more convenient, so we use that one. I don't know why Cindy even went in there," Jean tells him.

"Well, this whole case is just full of crap like that, isn't it?"

Marcus sees the look on Jean's face.

"What, what is it?" He asks, "You're remembering something, aren't you?"

"Let's just go check. . . ." Jean heads down the corridor to the door that leads outside to the recreation area. She unlocks it and pushes it open.

"This happens a lot. Someone turned off the alarm so that the patients could go outside for awhile, to smoke or for exercise. Most times, they lock it after them, but forget to put the alarm back on. This is the only door that someone could have gone out without the alarm sounding."

"Yes, but the door was locked. If someone wanted to go out here, he would have to have a key."

"Only the staff have keys."

"Then how did he get out?"

Jean looks out into the courtyard of the hospital. It's empty, the high walls impossible to scale.

"If he did, someone would have had to help him."

"I don't know, Marcus. I can't imagine anyone letting him out and then someone helping him over the wall. Too much could go wrong with that scenario. There's got to be a better explanation of what went on here tonight."

"Well, if you've got one, I can't wait to hear it."

"I don't. I just don't think this one is feasible. There's got to be some other way that he got out."

"Well, I'm heading outside to check the perimeter and see if any of my men have information on this." With that, Marcus heads out the front door and down the long walkway towards the woods.

"He's downstairs. He's in the basement."

Who told her that? Jean whirls around to find Cindy standing beside her.

"How do you know that?" she asks her

Cindy looks at her strangely.

"Know what?"

Suddenly, both women turn in the direction of the door that leads to the basement.

"He's still here. He never left the hospital." Jean mutters under her breath.

Cindy nods her head slowly.

"Yes," She whispers, desperately trying to still her trembling insides. "He's still here."

Section 2: The Challenge
Chapter 56

The pale moon glistens in the starless sky as Mari rises from her bed and moves slowly out into the hallway. Colors swirl – green and blue, yellow and pink interspersed with shades of brown – dark and light and many shades in between. Feelings – feelings – the desperate tension between the darkness and the light – it's everywhere. And yet – from the tension comes salvation.

The time has come for the darkness to transform into Light. She's the only one who seems to know the difference, to absolutely feel and understand that they are simply two parts of the one reality. The darkness is necessary for the light to shine.

Mari looks around at the raging swirl of emotions. Fear of the unknown, caring concern for each other, guilt over the past, trust in the power of love - all of them mixing and gyrating in a crazy dance. Her strength is in her love for all of them and her absolute, undiminished belief that each one has a role to play in a special creation for which she's been called to be the catalyst.

She knows that Grandmother's love pours through her, surrounding her, filling her, flowing outward from her like a river, and filling the corridors, the nooks and crannies of the hospital blessing all that she touches.

Mari looks out through the barred window. The dark grey pall that hangs over the landscape stands in stark contrast to the warm, rosy glow that surrounds her, following her out into the corridor, moving outwards to enfold all she sees in its embrace.

It's time!

She turns towards the nurses at the end of the hallway, staring at the door to the basement. How they have changed since she first met them! Their beautiful pink/gold hue reaches outward, keeping the blackness that threatens to envelop them from harming them. Mari joins her own spirit with theirs and feels their strength increase.

"Come," she tells them "it's time to go downstairs. We have to go down."

The two women turn towards Mari. They are surprised at the sound of her voice, which echoes through the corridors like velvet. It seems to fill the space between them with an unusual softness, warmth and confidence.

Their fear folds into the golden mist and evaporates. Together, they move forward towards the closed doors of the basement.

It's time!

Chapter 57

Deep, deep down inside the bowels of his prison, he waits. The door to the basement opens, and the women's footsteps come haltingly down the stairs. They will find him; it's only a matter of time. Fear, hatred, anger flood his veins, a black and red liquid volcano.

Through the cobwebs and into the corners he slinks. Like a cornered rat, he will fight to the death. Too bad it has to happen like this, but now he has no choice. Stupid of him to allow himself to be caught in the bathroom like that.

The soft murmur of the women's voices reaches him through the darkness and surrounds him. He enfolds himself in a blanket of ice: hell freezing over - murder - only murder on his mind. He's done it before, he'll do it again. Survival, his very survival is at stake.

He's been warned. Let them find you, they told him. Let them find you and you will suffer, in worse ways than you can ever imagine, in worse ways than you've suffered before. And he had suffered before, terrible sufferings, sufferings a normal person could barely imagine.

They had come for him in the night, the long, cold fingers of hell reaching out from the darkness, piercing his brain, probing, probing. The pain was unimaginable. His screams mingling with the sound of blood gushing through his veins and out through his pores, his heart pounding, pounding, pounding. Wanting to live - wanting to die to escape the pain. How he survived he will never know. All he knows is that it can't happen again. He needs to make sure it never happens again. . . . . at any cost . . . . . .

The women's soft steps on the stairs come to an end and he draws further back into the recesses of his prison. He's been comfortable here. It's a good place - it suits him. Dark and warm and cozy, he could live here for many more years, watching. No one came until the lady who was looking at the papers; then another came. He couldn't let that happen. They might find him. They have to be stopped.

So he told them, the ones who feed him and make his life here possible. His life depends on them. They are the gods that supply his needs. They let him live so he can guard this place for them. No one is to come here. He needs to tell them if anyone comes here. But his gods don't stop them, these women looking, looking at the papers. They will find out, find out about him and his sins - his horrible, terrible sins.

He needs to stop them.

Deep, deep he presses into the corner - into the deepest darkest corner he can find. Surely, now he will be safe from prying eyes and probing fingers.

And now they're here - closer, closer, closer they come. He raises his weapon, raises it above his head. Let them come. Let them come near. He'll get them first, before they harm him - before they harm him and his home down here in the darkness.

It's them - the two women who came before. He knows. He can feel them, the ones who were here before. He feels their energy. Before, they came one at a time. They're together now, and stronger. And something else - someone else. What is it? Who is it?

Danger!! Danger!!

Her light - it shines. It hurts his eyes. Soon, it will discover him in his corner in the darkness. He lifts his weapon.

The women approach. His weapon feels hot in his hands and heavy for his arms. He's ready - waiting, waiting, waiting until they get close enough . . . .

One of them turns towards him. Her eyes pierce the darkness. She knows him. She's met him in the darkness in the before time. He is she - fearful, angry, hating . . . . . before - before grandmother's light reached through the darkness and touched her, before her heart transformed from the darkness into the light.

Powerful, overwhelming fear. Mari feels his fear, his anger, his darkness.

"Come," she tells him, *"come out of the darkness and into the light. Come, it's safe. You're safe with me."*

He pulls back . . . . back . . . . back . . . until he melds into, becomes one with the wall itself.

The fear is so powerful.

Tremble, his body trembles, inside and out. Closer . . . . . closer still she comes, until there is no space left between them.

The blackness screams inside his head.

"Kill her - use your weapon - kill her - use it".

Chapter 58

There's danger. Mari feels it. She looks straight at the man who stands there, brandishing a weapon at her. She has seen him before. He's one of them. He came through her yard on that awful day, killing anything that stood in his way. He lived in her home while she was outside in the corn. This man is darkness.

"It doesn't matter," Grandmother interrupts her thoughts. *"Compassion - love - these are all that matter. Let it flow through you to him."*

Mari feels herself go out to the man who raises his weapon against her.

"I won't hurt you," she tells him softly. *"Don't be afraid."*

Jean and Cindy watch. The events taking place before their eyes seem to move in slow motion. Their first inclination is to scream and run, but they can't leave this child down here with a man who's obviously deranged. Jean starts to step forward to pull Mari out of the way, to do something. Cindy takes hold of her hand and keeps her back. She will never reach Mari before the weapon strikes.

"Wait, wait a minute," she whispers.

She's terrified for Mari, at taking this chance, but this is the only chance they have. She knows that one false move on their part could cause Mari to be a crumpled pile on the floor of the basement. She also knows the power that can come through this child.

She's hoping against hope for redemption once again.

His lips move, even as the weapon he holds descends. His shriek pierces the wall of dingy, brown muck that flows from him and surrounds him. It sends chills up the spines of the two women who stare, transfixed at the scene being played out before them.

"**Who are you?**" he screams. "**Go away . . . . Go away. . . . Go away.**"

In an instant, just as the weapon is about to strike, it is deflected as if by some invisible hand. It jerks to the side, barely missing Mari's head and falls with a 'clump' to the floor.

Jean moves forward once again. Cindy keeps a hand on her arm, holding her back. Mari is still in danger from this large, hairy, unkempt, obviously unstable man, but Cindy knows that it is important that this scene play out.

They watch as the blackness that emanates from the man mingles with and tries to dissolve the golden hue that surrounds Mari. They see the struggle as it moves outwards from him.

And they recognize that these powers have met before.

Suddenly, Cindy knows that the power that controls this man fears Mari, and she knows that this is the person who was responsible for the death of Mari's grandmother.

She looks at Jean, and Jean returns her look.

"Does she know what's happening?" Cindy wonders. "Does she realize what it is that's being played out right before our eyes?"

The scene seems almost unreal. If she weren't witnessing it herself, she would never have believed it.

This delicate, ethereal child stands opposite the dark, hulking mass of a man. Her golden hue in stark contrast to his dark, dangerous, threatening one. Its pounding pulse beats against her, against her light. Colors ebb and flow, surrounding them and, with the colors, feelings of warmth, love and caring concern, of hate and despair and death.

And suddenly, darkness, ever darkness overwhelms them. Deepest darkness - impossible darkness - darkness with an edge that chills the bones, thickens the blood, and freezes thoughts on everything horrible that's ever happened to them. Downward they spiral, falling, falling - deeper and deeper into a darkness that brings them to the edge of hell and invites them in. Nothing remains for them but their sins and the sins of those who have sinned against them. Jealousy - yellow, slithery, slimy jealousy, and anger, red and hot hatred, black, brown, bruised hatred. All is evil. Nothing exists but evil.

Cindy's before life passes through her mind's eye. Everything she has experienced, every evil done to her, every person who's maligned her, every fear she's had, every hatred felt . . . .

"You were right, they were wrong, many great injustices have been done to you." The darkness tells her. "Dwell on them, feed them. Feel how good it is to feed them."

Just for a moment, she hesitates.

"Help me," she prays. "Help me."

As waves of darkness threaten to overwhelm, her knowledge that the Light of love, compassion and caring concern for her and for all is here with her, fills her with strength and a power that she's never felt before.

And the darkness reminds Jean of a childhood spent lonely and destroyed by a father whose only attention came in the form of sexual advances. Her past consisted of burying feelings, of coping with feelings of worthlessness, pain and bitterness by controlling all that goes on around her. Up, up through the layers of denial and anger they come. Fear clenches its bitter fingertips around her throat. The fear that lives in the darkness and the darkness feeds on the fear and will not let it go. Choking and gasping, Jean falls to the floor, but she will not be undone.

Only their *knowledge* of the light keeps them from completely losing their minds, from becoming raving maniacs who turn on each other and rip each other's throats out and feast on the blood that drains from wretched, ripped bodies.

Murky - dense - the air becomes thicker and thicker until they struggle to breathe through something that feels like molasses, choking the very life out of them. Gasping, they draw labored breaths.

Tighter and tighter the darkness presses in on them, drawing visions to them of torturous death, of horrible peril. The weight presses in, surely the end is not far behind. Perhaps the end is better than this anguish.

Throughout their struggle, it asks but one thing of them, "Will you agree to work with me?"

And from both women, the answer comes in the form of a single thought.

"No."

And, with their answer, the pressure increases, but into their line of vision comes a pinpoint of light - and seeing it, they hold on -

Again evil speaks, "Work with me. Work with me and I will release you."

"No," they whisper through tortured lips.

And the pinpoint of light increases.

"Focus on me." It tells them. "You become stronger as I become stronger. You are Children of the Light. You can push back this darkness."

The darkness recedes, then strengthens again. Like a wave that moves backwards to gain momentum, it rushes forward and slams against them once more, its dark, probing talons tearing and clawing at places in them that they didn't even know existed.

And the light too is here, washing over them, transforming the evil, reminding them of who they are.

They feel Mari's presence.

"Focus on the Light," she tells them. *"Know who you are."*

And in the presence of the Light - and their answer, Cindy and Jean feel their strength increase. In increments, then stronger, ever stronger, they feel themselves joined to Mari and her strength. That strength flows through her and ever outward, and the three become as one and fight against the darkness and all its promises. The darkness begins to recede.

For eternity, the battle rages . . . .
and then it's over . . . . . just like that . . . . . it's over. The Light shines through the darkness . . . . The darkness, transformed by the Light, is no more.

The man who cowers in the corner, uncertain and still frightened by what he is seeing has no knowledge of such feelings of Light. He has known only the deep, despairing grasp of the darkness. Mari reaches out to him. Meekly and gently, he takes her hand.

Up from his basement dungeon they come. Up, up from his home of darkness. Up through the shadows and the fog and the mist. Slowly, ever so slowly they climb. It's been such a long time since a human touch didn't mean pain for him, such a long time since there was light in his life.

Was there ever such Light as this in his life?

Chapter 59

Cindy and Jean watch what's happening between Mari and the man from the basement, then follow both of them up the stairs. "What is he doing here? How long has he been here?" Cindy wonders.

"How long has he been living in the shadows and the corners of this dark and dingy basement, far away from any light, terrified and alone? If not for Mari, he probably would have died down there, could have died in so many, many ways. What was the possibility of them finding him like this?"

Cindy's awareness moves to her own inner self. It's amazing how her whole outlook on the man changes as she herself changes. Her fear is gone and she feels only compassion for him.

She reaches the top of the stairs and glances down the corridor at the clock behind the large front desk. The hands have barely moved since they went down into the basement. She looks around. Everything seems to be in order. She walks swiftly down the hall to check on patients. No one is stirring. Everything is peaceful. A hush has fallen over the floor.

Jean remains still, watching her, unable to bring herself back into focus right away.

"Is everything alright?" she asks when Cindy returns.

"Fine, everything's fine."

Cindy stands close to her side, watching, waiting.

"For what", she wonders. "Why are we waiting?"

All around them the corridors pulse with a kind of glowing, golden light energy. Cindy has a feeling that it's been there all along. They just weren't aware of it. The walls and other objects appear to flow, like they are no longer solid.

She wonders if Jean sees what she's seeing.

Suddenly, Jean shudders and a large sigh escapes her lips. Yes, Cindy realizes, she sees it all. She softly asks -

"What do you make of this? What's happening?"

"I think," Jean answers, "that this is what truly exists. What we were seeing before is life through eyes that were clouded. What we're seeing now is what really is."

"What do you mean?"

Cindy actually does have some idea of what it is Jean is trying to say, but she wants someone else to say it. That way she can be certain it's real.

"I think," Jean quietly answers her, "that you know what I'm trying to tell you. I can't explain exactly what it is that I'm experiencing because it can't be put into words, but I'm quite sure you know what I mean because you've been with me right through this."

"You're right. I'm sorry. I do know what you mean. I guess it's just that it's so different from anything I've ever experienced before . . . . . it's - it's wonderful."

"Wonderful, magical, mystical - however you want to describe it. All good."

"Yes, it's all good."

"Mari seems to have disappeared. Where did she go with the man from the basement?"

Strangely, neither of them are all that concerned. They know now that Mari was never in any danger. Someone looks after her. Someone whose love and compassion for all of them is bringing about huge changes in their lives.

"I'll just pop down the corridor and see if I can find her," Cindy replies.

She finds Mari safely tucked away in her bed, sleeping soundly.

"Now, where did the man go?" she asks herself.

Her question is soon answered as Marcus enters the large front doors. He is leading the man back inside. "He told me he came from here," Marcus explains. "Said he had a story to tell and was looking for someone to help him. Who is he? Is he the one who conked Cindy over the head a while ago?"

"Yes," Jean tells him. "We think he was just scared and didn't mean to hurt her. He's apparently been living in our basement. Someone has been feeding him and he's probably been coming up at night when it's quiet and we're on rounds to use that bathroom. It's rarely used, out of sight of the front desk and close to the basement door. He never expected Cindy to go in there."

"Quite a surprise for him, I'd say. Is there somewhere we could go to talk? I really don't want to have to put him in a patrol car and take him down to the police station right now. Who knows what's going on there. Anyway, he looks like he's been through enough for now."

"Come right over here." Jean leads the way to her office. "You'll be able to talk to him without interruption in here."

Gently placing his hand on the man's back, Marcus slowly and quietly leads him down the corridor to Jean's office. They enter and Marcus closes the door behind them.

"This should be interesting," Jean tells Cindy. "I can't wait to hear this story."

Each minute seems like hours as the two women go about their evening's work while they await the outcome of Marcus' interview with the man. Finally, the door to the office opens, and he motions to them to come inside.

What a tale! And he has no doubt that the man is telling him the truth. He's going to need the nurses to fill in some of the details of the story. It won't be long before he and the men with whom he works are able to bring peace to this institution and order to the town. This time it will be for everyone, not just the privileged few who run things now. They've got quite a job in front of them, but he's confident now that they will be able to clean things up and make this place a decent place for everyone to live.

Section3: Questions
Chapter 60

Mari wakes up, refreshed and relaxed. She looks around. The early morning sunshine makes light patterns on the floor and walls and across the bed. The golden rays warm her inside and out, and she takes some time to reconnect with her inner self, consciously allowing the Light to flow through her once more. This will help her, she knows, when she connects to the people who come into her life. It's particularly important today, since the time has come to figure out what's been happening here and decide how to balance things, to set things right. She opens the door to her room and makes her way toward the nurses' station.

They have been waiting for her. Their pleasure at seeing her increases as she softly glides down the corridor towards them. She feels the currents; the silver strings that connect the three of them become fuller and stronger as she makes her way closer and closer to them.

It's good that she's here!

Chapter 61

Marcus, too, has been waiting for Mari to wake up. The nurses wouldn't let him wake her, even though he's anxious to get to the bottom of everything that's gone on here. They insist that she sleep. They know that she needs to refill her energy and it's important to go with the flow, rather than to force things to happen. If there's one thing they have learned for certain these past few days, it's how important it is to allow events to unfold of their own accord, especially when it comes to dealings with Mari.

Marcus is intrigued with the way she moves. She almost seems to glide above the earth, as if she's being pulled by invisible threads, rather than walk towards the two women. They seem unfazed by this, as if it's a completely natural occurrence for them.

He watches as they form a semi-circle, watches as a glow that seems to come from within each of them becomes stronger, more vivid. They pull closer, ever closer.

It seems almost sacrilegious to interrupt them, but he needs to find all the pieces to the puzzle if he is to figure out what is going on here. He approaches.

They turn towards him. They have been expecting him. They welcome him into their midst.

Cindy smiles.

"Where did you leave the man from the basement?" She asks.

"He's still in the office. I don't quite know what to do with him. Maybe you can help me."

"We'll do whatever we can. How can we help?"

Marcus' voice softens. These women - what is it about them?

"Maybe," he says, "you can just help me put some of the pieces of this puzzle together. I need to figure out exactly what's going on in this hospital - and in this town, before I call in the troops to set things right again."

"OK. Why don't you tell us this man's story, and we'll see what we can do to help make sense of it all for you."

"Yes, well, from what he's been telling me, awhile ago, well, this guy, Bradford and another guy named Grant escaped from here and made it to a cottage in the woods about an hour's walk from here. They went inside, snuck up on an old lady who was in bed sleeping. Grant wacked her over the head with a club of some kind that they found by the door. She never knew what hit her."

"Yes," says Mari softly "that was my grandmother. I was frightened and I hid outside in the corn so they couldn't find me."

Marcus turns towards her. "Good thing they didn't. This guy, Grant, sounds like one real nasty character."

"That would probably have been around three years ago," Cindy tells him. "Jean looked it up in the newspapers in the library and found out that two guys escaped from here about that long ago. They were never recaptured. That also corresponds to the length of time Mari has been here."

She turns to Mari. "And so how did you end up here?"

"I don't know. I can't remember very much about it. It's all kind of a blur after I found Grandmother like that. The next thing I remember is being angry - very, very angry. I was like that until I felt Grandmother's presence again. She let me know that she was with me even though her body was no longer here. I think the fact that Cindy was kind to me had something to do with it. It helped me remember kindness and love and what it feels like to have someone care for me. It helped me remember the before times and bring what I learned then into the now."

Tears threaten to run down Jean's face.

"I'm so sorry, Mari. I was hurting so much myself that I couldn't get out of my own way to look after you properly. I thought that if I kept everything clean and calm around here, that was the best I could do for you and all the rest of the patients. It never occurred to me that what you needed most of all was just someone who cared."

"I forgive you for that." Mari puts her arms around Jean. Jean feels the warmth flow from Mari into her and knows how truly forgiven she is.

Marcus' own edges soften. Calmly and quietly, he continues.

"So, it looks like these guys escaped from here, killed Mari's grandmother and, when the authorities found her in the house living with her dead grandmother, she was taken here to be evaluated. The escapees were never recaptured, no one made the connection between their escape and the death of Mari's grandmother or, if they did, no one said or did anything about it."

"They blamed the grandmother's death on Mari," Cindy tells him.

"Of course they did. That was the easiest thing to do. That's why they were able to leave her here for so long."

"OK." Jean is calm again. "So, we know who killed Mari's grandmother, we know why they stuck Mari in here. But why was someone - why is someone going to such great lengths to intimidate Cindy and keep her from finding out anything about Mari? Who would care so much that Mari stay here?

"There's more. Let me finish," Marcus interrupts her. "After they killed Mari's grandmother, Bradford got scared. He wanted to go back to the hospital, but Grant wouldn't let him. Said he had a lot to do before he went back. He was already in a mental hospital, so it didn't matter now who he killed. If they caught him, all they could do to him was put him back in the hospital, so he intended to even a few scores while he was out. And he didn't mind killing Bradford too, if he didn't help him."

"Sounds like a real charmer."

"Yeah. He shouldn't have been in here, in this hospital in the first place; he needed to be in a more secure facility."

"So why was he here?"

"My question exactly" Marcus replies. "Bradford - you know, the guy from the basement," he says when Jean looks at him as if she doesn't understand what he's talking about. "He told me that they left the old lady's house when she started to smell. I'd say that was after about three or four days. He was scared and pissed off at Grant who was ordering him around, so he managed to lose him and hike back to the hospital. He tried to get over the fence and in through the back door again, but couldn't - the door was locked. So he went around to the front door. Someone was waiting for him. The front door opened, and he was smashed in the face with something and given a good once over. For a few minutes, Bradford thought that Grant had followed him and was about to make good on his promise to kill him. When he was dragged down to the basement and told to stay there or there'd be dire consequences, he realized that it wasn't Grant's voice he was hearing. Someone, probably the same person or persons, has been feeding him ever since. What I want to know is why? What's the point of all this?"

"Good question," Jean replies. "I get the feeling if we knew the answer to it, we would know what's actually going on here."

"Well, that's about all he was able to tell me. Is there anything else I should know that you guys have found out that might help me here?"

"We don't know much more." Cindy tells him. "Just when I started trying to help Mari, my own life started to spin out of control. First, my ex shows up unexpectedly complaining that I'm leaving the kids alone at night to work. First time he's ever taken any interest in them. As a matter of fact, he left me because he couldn't handle the responsibility of bringing up kids. Then, when he couldn't get me away from the hospital, my kids were kidnapped and I was ordered out of town in order to get them back. Now Ray has been beaten practically to death. I assume it was for trying to help me out."

"And we have to figure out how all this fits together."

"Just our interest in Mari and trying to help her, as far as we can tell."

"It's got to be a lot more than that," Marcus replies. "Bradford tells me that he and this guy Grant didn't escape by themselves three years ago. They had help. Someone left the back door open for them and arranged to meet them out at the road, but they decided to leave earlier than planned that night. Grant didn't trust the guy who was supposed to help them. He had the idea of using the open door to escape earlier, and then taking off on their own."

"It would be interesting to know who left the door open for them, and why. I would have to agree with you, Marcus, that these guys were probably here to be evaluated, and they would probably have been sent to a more secure facility." Jean adds. "Any chance that we could get some last names? Maybe we can get more information on them from the files downstairs, why they were here and what their prognosis was . . . . . why would someone help them escape?"

"I doubt very much that you would get anything – I'll bet their files have been removed or destroyed."

"You're probably right, but it wouldn't hurt to check."

"You can try if you want. I think it's a waste of time."

Jean looks over at him.

"Marcus, what's on your mind? Are you able to piece any of this together yet?

"It's starting to get a bit clearer. Let me go talk to Jim. Maybe he can help us answer some of the remaining questions."

The women watch as he leaves the hospital through the large front doors. All three see the glow of silver thread that follows behind him.

Chapter 62

It's dark, no stars in the sky - looks like a storm is brewing. Marcus leaves the relative safety of the hospital and crosses the parking lot. His eyes are peeled for his men hidden in the bushes, guarding it, watching that everything is all right. He needs to speak to Jim, and these guys will know where he is. But where are they?

A flash from among the trees on the other side of the lot draws his attention and he moves towards it. There they are.

But it's not his men who watch Marcus' big frame as he moves across the parking lot towards the trees.

It's a tough job, but the money - wow - this could set him up for good. No more petty criminal jobs, no more struggling to make a buck to eat. He has to see this job through to the end. Get rid of this interloper who has no right being here anyway.

All he has been told is that the job is to get rid of the two nurses who are in the hospital tonight. Then go to room 18b and get rid of the girl. She should be asleep, he's been told. Simple, he's been told. Although getting into the place might be difficult. What they hadn't told him was that it would be guarded like Fort Knox.

Moving on his belly, dressed all in black, with even his face blackened, he has managed to slip and slide his way through the web of security. He hadn't spent all that time in the woods for nothing. That's how he got so sneaky, why he calls himself Coyote. Why the heck are they guarding the place like this, anyway? Are they expecting him? Is this a trap?

"Keep focused," he tells himself. "You've got to stay focused and get this job done. There's no way they can screw you after this. You're protected. Even if you're caught, you're protected. Look who sent you out here. You can't miss. And, after this, you'll be set for life."

That's his mantra "set for life". That's what he needs to keep telling himself.

Coyote watches as the large man heads towards him, closer and closer to his hiding place.

"Must have been the flashlight. I should never have had it on. Can't make noise or all the rest of them will arrive and then it is game over for me."

He flattens himself against the tree. "There's no way he can see me here," he tells himself. "Closer, come closer now . . . ."

A blinding flash of light, followed by intense pain, followed by blackness is all Marcus knows as he crumples to the ground in a large lump. The blow would surely have killed a lesser man.

It's still dark when he comes to. He fights the nausea and the pain which threaten to overwhelm him again, and drags himself to his feet, painfully forcing himself to open his eyes. He looks towards the building. Everything seems still and normal except for one small item. The front door seems just ever so slightly ajar, like it hasn't quite closed behind someone. There's trouble!

Because of his carelessness, these people he's supposed to be protecting are in serious trouble, maybe even dead already. Whoever did this to him wasn't fooling around - he's out for murder. Marcus knows it! It's probably already done! How the hell did anyone get through his men, anyway? He's got to find Jim and the men. How long has he been out? He checks his watch. About half an hour - more than enough time for whoever did this to him to have taken care of business inside too.

Chapter 63

Coyote enters the building and an eerie feeling comes over him. Damn! What the hell is wrong? He's tempted to just give up and get the hell out of here. But it's the money, all that money he's been promised, and he keeps going. There's no one at the big front desk, no one to stop him from heading straight towards the room where the girl is supposed to be, the one he's been sent to murder. Then he'll look for the nurses.

* * * *

Mari floats, high, high above her bed - watching - watching. Her friend, her new friend is on the ground in the woods. "Wake up! Wake up!" She calls him out of his unconsciousness.

Outside, a light grows in the dark night air and surrounds her friend and carries him to a place of healing. Inside, evil stalks the hallways and corridors of the hospital, despite the incandescence of the lit bulbs and lamps that try to keep away the darkness.

Someone is here now. Someone who cares only for himself and his own survival. Someone who thinks that his survival depends upon killing, upon murder, upon mayhem and destruction. He doesn't know that, as he kills others, he himself is killed, the part of him that's truly alive. He doesn't know.

Compassion for the man who stalks the corridors overwhelms her. The lessons are so difficult sometimes.

He enters her room. She watches as he moves towards her bed where she should be sleeping. He doesn't notice that she's not there. He slams his weapon against the bedclothes again and again. Foolish man. Suddenly, as if hit by a bolt of lightning, his arm seizes above his head and fear contorts his face into a mask of terror. What's happening to him? She wonders if his lessons will be sooner than she'd expected.

He seems frozen in space, unable to move. Slowly, slowly, she feels her body come to rest again on top of her bed, no longer floating. Is this what he sees that terrorizes him so? A minute ago, Mari knows, he was willing to send her to her death. Is he so frightened of the sight of her now?

Chapter 64

It should have been so simple!

But even all that money won't keep him here now. He's never seen anything like this.

A ghost, maybe?

Terror overwhelms him!

As if this place wasn't horrifying enough, now spirits come to haunt him for all his evil deeds.

His fear lifts a bit and, as soon as he's able to move, he slowly begins backing out of the room. If he can just make it to the front door, nobody - not the people who sent him here, not the people who guard the place, and certainly no one from inside here - will ever see him again. A guy like him can slither and slip through the cracks of society, into the dark holes of its underbelly, and never be seen, never be noticed, never be caught. He will never need to tell anybody what happened to him tonight. Just let him get the hell out of here.

He tries to open the door. His fingers freeze on the knob. It won't open!

He feels himself sliding down, down - towards the floor - till he lays there, a blubbering heap on its slippery surface. He looks over toward the bed, at the air above it where the spirit seemed to appear.

Now, all that falls into his line of vision is a small girl, a child really, lying on top of the bedclothes, dressed in white. A light glows around her. He's very sure that this is the spirit, the one who terrified him. She doesn't seem terrifying now.

"As a matter of fact," the thought crosses his mind, "as a matter of fact, she'd be an easy target for me now."

But he can't move. He is frozen to this spot, lying on the floor with his arm and hand extended up over his head, his fingers still touching the doorknob. He's like a fly caught in a Venus fly trap. Like a fly he'd been enticed by the lure of the sweet nectar of money and all it could offer him, and like the fly, he had been caught . . . . .

"Enough of this stupidity. This isn't the way things work." He yanks at his hand and his fingers. "What's going on? Why won't they come loose?"

It's something, he knows, to do with the girl who lies on the bed. She's the one who's keeping him here, unable to escape.

"Please, let me go," he begs her. "Let me go and I'll leave and never bother you again."

"No", she answers. Her soft voice piercing the darkness that surrounds him. "No, that's not what I want from you."

Now frightened again, he pleads. "What do you want? Let me go and I'll do what you want."

"No, you won't." She rises from her bed and goes slowly past him, straight out the door. It opens and closes behind her without ever disturbing him or moving him out of the way.

He is no longer confused.

He knows now that he is in the presence of something that he simply has no way of understanding.

Chapter 65

Marcus is a sight. Still warm blood covers his head and his face as he hobbles quickly toward the hospital. God only knows what he will find inside. With every agonizing step, the realization hits him more fully. He should have been more careful. He had thought that just because he had some men guarding the place, it would be safe. Little did he realize how far someone would go to still the voices inside. In his impetuousness and foolishness, he has failed them all.

He pushes open the heavy doors. Mari comes slowly down the hallway, heading towards him. She smiles. She's been expecting him.

"Are you all right?" he asks as she approaches. "I got hit over the head by someone waiting in the trees on the other side of the parking lot when I went looking for Jim. Then I noticed that the doors to the hospital were open, so I thought I'd better come back and check on all of you. Where are the other nurses?"

"There's a man in my room. I think he's probably the one who hit you. You might want to ask him what he's doing here. You will probably get more answers from him than you can from Jim."

Mari's calm, gentle voice takes Marcus by surprise once again. When she speaks, it eases any tension in him.

He hurries down the corridor toward Mari's room, opens the door, and finds a large, unkempt man lying still on the floor. His wild, dark eyes, framed by black, bushy eyebrows speak of a strange, untold fear and a terrible desperation.

"Please, please help me. Make her let me go. I'll leave here. You'll never see me again. Just let me go."

"Like hell I will. Get on your feet. What's the matter with you? Why can't you stand up?" Marcus grabs an arm and drags him roughly to his feet. He slaps some handcuffs on him. "Now, do you wanna tell me what you're doing here?"

The man seems shocked. Marcus has no doubt that his meeting with Mari has been quite an experience for him. Obviously, he had intended quite a different scenario.

"Come on," he half drags, half leads the man to Jean's office, expecting to find Bradford still there. He intends to put this new guy and Bradford together, hoping that maybe they will recognize each other. Maybe they're in this together. That would give him some clue as to what's happening here, what's been happening - what all this is about.

He opens the door to the office and finds Jean sitting at her desk talking quietly with Bradford.

"Marcus, what are you doing here? I thought you were going to find Jim."

"That was my intention. But when I left here, I thought I saw one of my men in the woods on the other side of the parking lot. I went over to talk to him and got pistol whipped by this guy. When I came to, I saw the door to the hospital still open and figured that whoever hit me had come in here. Fortunately, he doesn't seem to have had a chance to harm anybody yet."

"But Marcus, you've been gone a good half hour. What do you mean, he hasn't been able to harm anyone yet? If his intent was to hurt someone, wouldn't he have done it by this time?"

"I don't know. I found him in Mari's room."

"In Mari's room? Is she all right?"

"She's fine. She met me in the hallway and told me where to find him. He was on the floor and didn't seem able to get up."

Jean takes a good look at Marcus' prisoner. He looks like he's in shock, trembling and on the verge of tears.

"What happened to you?"

"I don't know." His voice is quiet and subdued, not at all what she expected.

"Will you tell us what you're doing here?" she gently asks him.

"They told me to come here and kill the girl and the two nurses who were working here tonight."

"Who told you to do that?" Jean asks quietly.

Marcus interrupts, "How did you get in here? I've got men guarding every inch of the place."

"I had to camouflage myself and crawl on my belly."

"Who sent you here?" Jean asks again. She shoots a look at Marcus letting him know he's not to interrupt again.

The man's face remains expressionless, only a slight twinge of his dark eyebrows show that he's thinking about it. He's coming back to reality, and considering the wisdom of telling anyone about the person who sent him. He's caught now, and they're everywhere. How will he be able to hide from them now?

"Damn," Marcus thinks. "I've done it again. If I had just left her alone with the questioning, she would probably have been able to get it out of him. But I had to go and interrupt."

Jean is speaking again. "Marcus, maybe you had better find Cindy and let her take a look at your head. You look like you were hit pretty hard."

He's aware again of the throbbing in his head.

"That's probably a good idea." He hesitates. He doesn't want to leave her alone in here with these two.

As if reading his thoughts, she tells him, "Go on, I'll be all right."

Of course she will. For some reason, these women seem more able to look after themselves amid all this violence and craziness than he is with all his weapons, experience and reinforcements.

He leaves the room to find Cindy. His head is hurting like a bugger and he needs to get it tended to.

He finds her sitting at the front desk talking to Mari. When she looks up and sees him, her face registers shock and surprise.

"I can only imagine what I must look like," he mumbles.

"Like you lost one hell of a fight," Cindy tells him.

She leads him into one of the nursing rooms and tells him to sit on a chair while she takes a look at his head.

"It's not too bad, but you should probably have an X-ray, just in case. Did you lose consciousness?"

"Does it look bad?"

"Yes. Were you out? Did you lose consciousness?"

"Yes."

"For how long?"

"A bit."

"That's enough."

"Just patch me up, will you, and I'll tend to the X-rays a little later."

"All right. Hold still. This will hurt a bit."

A few minutes later, he's cleaned and ready for business again.

"At least you look better now," Cindy tells him. "And make sure you have that X-ray. You could have some serious damage there."

"And what then? Maybe I should stay home and keep quiet for a few weeks?"

Cindy looks him straight in the eye. Gently and sincerely, she tells him, "You need to look after yourself Marcus. We would miss you if you weren't around."

Marcus looks at her. She means what she's saying. It's been a long, long time since anyone has spoken to him like this.

Chapter 66

Jim is tired. The stars are still out, but pink rays of dawn are just beginning to show in the morning sky. It's five a.m. He had expected to hear from Marcus by now, but he guesses that he's been busy inside the hospital trying to figure out what's going on. He hopes that nurse who was hit over the head is all right. Must have been a patient who got out of hand. Surely, it wouldn't be the first time a patient hurt one of the staff.

It's time to check in. Jim rifles through his pockets for the number, then picks up his cell and calls the front desk. There's no answer. He hangs up and calls again. This time, a recorded voice tells him that all the staff are busy but to leave a message and someone will get back to him as soon as possible. It also instructs him that in an emergency, he can call the hospital in Derry, or he can call 911 for an ambulance. Damn, why doesn't Marcus carry a phone with him? Now he will have to go up there himself if he wants to talk to him.

Jim puts down his phone and picks up his walkie-talkie. He needs to let the men know what's going on or he's liable to be tackled or something worse, maybe even shot, when he approaches the hospital. He will head up there on foot. There's no need to take a car for such a short distance.

Despite the cold morning air, Jim is lathered in sweat by the time he reaches the large front doors. He rings the buzzer and a strange voice, one he doesn't recognize, bids him come in to the front desk.

There's a buzz, and he pushes the heavy doors opens, then makes sure they close tightly behind him.

He is surprised to see Mari behind the desk. She looks at him as if she has been expecting him. She is dressed all in white, her long hair draped over her shoulders and down her back like a shawl. Her green eyes scan his face. He knows that even his very thoughts are no secret to her.

"Come," she says softly. "Come closer."

He approaches the desk.

"Marcus was hurt tonight, but he will be all right soon." she quietly tells him. "Cindy is fixing him up. They're in that room over there if you would like to see him."

Jim finds it difficult to leave Mari's presence. Slowly, he moves towards the room that she has indicated. Inside, he finds Cindy and Marcus. They look up when he opens the door.

"Oh, hi Jim."

"Hi, Jim. I was just patching Marcus up. He got quite a knock on his head."

"I can see that. What happened?"

"Actually, it happened as I was coming to see you. I didn't want to telephone, thought I'd just mosey on down and talk to you. It was pitch black out and, of course, I had no idea where the men were stationed, so when I saw a flash of light across the parking lot, I just assumed it was one of our guys, and I headed over. Before I knew what happened, someone hit me over the head and I was out for about a half hour.

Cindy interrupts, "You were out for half an hour?"

"Yes. When I came to, I noticed the front door to the hospital was ajar, so I assumed that whoever had hit me had come in here to do some damage. And I was right. Fortunately, he didn't get very far. There was no one at the front desk, so he went straight to Mari's room. I don't know what she did to him, but he was pretty scared when I got there."

"So, he knew which room was hers?" Jim asks.

"Apparently."

"And where is this guy now?"

"Jean has him in a room down the hall. Whatever happened, he's pretty traumatized and he's talking. He told us that someone hired him to come here and murder Mari and the two nurses."

"Jean is the other nurse, right?" They both nod yes. Jim is quiet for a bit. Then he asks, "And he hasn't said who it was that hired him?"

"No. At least, not that we know of."

"OK then. Can you show me which room they are in?"

"Come on, I'll show you, but there's more you need to know."

"How much more can there be?"

"Well, you know how you sent me in here to make sure everyone was OK when Cindy got hurt?"

"Right"

"Well, we did a little investigating, and it turns out there's been a guy living in the basement here, using the bathroom on the other side of the nurse's station that no one ever goes in. Cindy caught him in there and it scared him. That's why he hit her. And get this - he's one of the guys who murdered Mari's grandmother. He and another guy escaped from here about three years ago. He came back to the hospital because the guy was giving him a hard time, threatening him. He got scared, and this was the only place he knew that he could get some help. He never made it. Someone was waiting for him. He was beat up, then dragged down to the basement here and told to stay, or there would be dire consequences. Someone, we don't know who, has been feeding him ever since. He was probably pretty disturbed to begin with. I'd say he is a lot more so now."

"So where is this other guy now?"

"He's with Jean also."

Jim looks at him as if he's lost his mind.

"You mean you left two men, one of them - probably both of them - disturbed and dangerous, in a room with one of the nurses?"

He's right. What the hell was he thinking? That knock on the head must have affected him more than he thought.

Without another word, they both turn and rush down the corridor. Cindy watches.

Marcus' mind races ahead of him, dreading what they will find.

"I can't believe I left her alone with them. Oh my God, how could I have been so stupid?"

They reach the end of the corridor, fling open the door, and stare inside with amazement. A large desk is pushed back against the wall and three chairs sit neatly in the center of the room, as if occupied by some invisible guests. There's no mess, no chaos, no evidence of any struggle. But the room is empty.

Marcus hears his heart thump - thump - thumping in his chest. He's speechless. He looks back down the corridor. Cindy's not there. Once again, a familiar feeling of being out of control, of not knowing what's going on, takes over, gripping his bowels and stomach tightly in a horrible knot.

His eyes move to the front desk, searching.

Mari sits quietly, her eyes following their every move. "She knows," he whispers to himself. "She knows where they are and what's going on here."

"Come with me." he tells Jim.

Quickly, they head back down the long corridor towards the front desk. Once again, Mari's eyes draw them in as they approach, speaking to them, challenging them to understand.

"She knows us," he thinks. "She knows everything about us. And yet, we have no idea who she is."

Chapter 67

Mari feels her energy flow outward toward the two men as they approach, calming and welcoming them. Her serenity surrounds the space around the desk, and the closer they get, the more conscious they are of its presence. Drawing nearer, they are folded into feelings of peace, joy and unity with her and with each other.

A thought comes to Jim.

"I don't have to die to go to heaven. This is it - right here, right now."

It seems almost sacrilegious to speak, so they stand there beside the desk, each man a silent monument to the power of the unseen. Mari reaches out her hands, and they feel the energy that flows from her become stronger in them. All is good. All is calm. All is right.

They know they are becoming stronger, stronger in body, stronger in mind, stronger in spirit. Nothing can harm them now. Free from fear for the first time in their lives, their minds take on an unexpected awareness. They know that all things will work out as they need to, as they should, and that all will be well. What a difference knowing Mari makes in their lives – this one small person, one small life.

Mari slowly removes her hands. She smiles softly. "We still have a lot to do," she tells them, "But yes, all will be well."

Chapter 68

Jim looks around. Cindy is now standing at the desk with them.

She sees his look and answers his unspoken question. "I just popped back into the room where I checked your head so that I could clean it up, Marcus. No need to worry."

Marcus thinks, "If I hadn't been in such a panicked state, I'd have realized that's where she was. Interesting how fear clamps down on us, makes us so much less able to solve problems, to be productive. No fear. What could we do with our lives if we had no fear?"

A slight smile plays at the corners of Mari's lips. He smiles back at her, thinking,

"She knows."

Out loud, he asks, "Mari, do you have any idea what's happened to Jean and the two men? Is she all right?"

"She's fine. They'll be back soon. Don't worry."

"Do you know where she is? Are the men with her?

"It's all right. She'll be fine."

Jim wants to believe her, but all his instincts tell him otherwise. How could Jean be all right when she is with those dangerous men? It doesn't make any sense. But then, nothing that's happening here today makes much sense according to his experiences. It almost seems like they have entered another world, a world where anything is possible.

"How much longer before they're back?" he asks her.

Mari doesn't answer. Instead, she tells him firmly, "Jim, there's nothing you can do that will help her or anyone else right now. Look after yourself."

Now what on earth does she mean by that?

Jim leaves her and Marcus and Cindy, and wanders slowly off down the corridor. He carries with him a remembrance of their presence and the feelings they evoke in him.

His memory carries him back further still, back to a time when his life was filled with light, a natural light that was always with him. And then, there had been a father who left, a mother who couldn't protect him from life's bullies. Day by day, the light dimmed, and it grew darker and darker, until there was no light left at all in his life. The light just went out.

All his life experiences, he now knows, have been attempts to recapture the light. And now he's found it again. In Mari - in these people - in this hospital. Or rather, he recognizes it again. Jim realizes now that it had never really left him. He had felt betrayed by the light, and so had built a life with no room for it, until he no longer remembered that it even existed. He turns his head and looks back at the three people still standing quietly and calmly at the desk. Clearly, he sees the beautiful silver threads that connect him to them, glittering and glowing and spinning, themselves made from the Light. Never again, he knows, will he be able to lose sight of them now that he's found himself, now that he knows that he himself is part of the Light, now that he knows himself once again.

He walks back to the desk, each step deliberate, and asks,

"OK, now. What can I do to help?"

As if in answer, the phone rings.

Chapter 69

It's six a.m. when Ray finally wakes up from his coma. No one is around to welcome him back to this world. He keeps his eyes closed as he listens to the whirring and ringing noises that surround him.

What happened? Where is he?

His eyelids flutter.

Slowly . . . . . slowly, he opens them and begins to take in his surroundings. He realizes that he is in a hospital.

The machines that he is hearing are attached to his own body, breathing for him, pouring liquid into him, relieving his kidneys of fluid. He begins to flex some of his muscles. He can tell that they haven't been used for awhile. They aren't responding well, and they hurt. What happened?

Flashes of memory come back to him. He was taken from work and mauled by two large men. Why? How could something like this happen to him? He tries to think back over the last few months. He struggles to remember.

A woman named Cindy comes to mind. Why? He's in love with her. He tried to help her. That's why he is here. She has children. Bits and pieces of memory come back. He fell in love and tried to help her and her children. Someone objected. Someone important and filled with rage objected.

Footsteps . . . . the door of the room opens . . . . Ray sees a sudden, swift movement through partially closed lids . . . . **overwhelming terror** . . . . the door closes. He struggles for breath. His last thought is of Cindy.

Chapter 70

"It's Ray. He's dead," Cindy whispers before anyone picks up the ringing phone.

The men look over at her, shocked. Not at the fact that Ray could be dead, they have known that was a distinct possibility since hearing about his horrible condition. What shocks them is the certainty in Cindy's voice.

Marcus answers it. He listens. Then he replaces the receiver.

"Ray, the guy who was taken out of here by the police and ended up in the hospital?"

"Yes."

"You were right. His respirator came unplugged sometime last night. It was a busy night. No one noticed. He's dead."

A feeling of sadness comes over Cindy. Ray was in love with her. Now she will never get the chance to tell him how she feels about him, how grateful she is for all he had done for her.

"He knows, Cindy," Mari tells her gently. "He knows how you feel about him. He's always known."

Sadness settles over the small company for awhile. It's difficult to get beyond Ray's death. Once more, Cindy feels her heart ripped out of her chest and broken in two. It's a familiar feeling, one that almost seems natural to her. She tries to remember the good parts of their relationship, but it's difficult.

"It's OK Cindy," Mari tells her. "It's OK to feel sad. You love him. It's good to mourn Ray. But know that it never ends, the love. He will always be with you now, even if you can't see him. That's the way love works."

But the comfort of Mari's arms around her speaks more to Cindy than any words. They stay like that for awhile until it feels like her broken heart is back in her chest and she can walk and talk again.

The men leave them standing at the front desk, and go back down the hallway.

"We can't leave them here alone, but we've got to get over to that hospital and find out what happened."

"Yeah. We both know that wasn't an accident. Bells would have been ringing all over the place if a respirator was accidently unplugged. That guy's death was deliberate."

"This is our fault. We should have had someone guarding the guy."

"Yeah, well, I thought the reason we don't want anyone to find out we're here is because we don't want to give them the chance to cover up anything. Putting a guard on him would've blown it all. Anyone seeing that would have known we are onto them."

"You're right. I say we wait for a report to be filed, see who writes it up, and what they say about the cause of his death. It's gotta be done today."

"OK, I'm scheduled for duty tonight. Should be easy enough to get my hands on it. I don't know, though, this seems like such a mess. Maybe we should just call in the information we have before someone else gets hurt."

"Believe me, if we quit now, we might save our own necks and those of our friends here, but we'll never figure out who is behind all this. Whoever is making the mess, he's been doing it for a long time and he's covered his tracks thoroughly with underlings. We have just gotta keep digging until we know for certain what's happening and who is in control of it. That's the only way we're going to clean it all up for sure. It's like lancing a boil. You've got to get to the root of it or it will grow right back."

"Yeah, you're right. I guess we really have no choice. We have to keep going."

"That's what we do, Jim."

Jim's thoughts turn to Mari and Cindy and Jean. Where the hell *is* Jean, anyway?

The men reach the room where Jean was last seen with the two men. They open the door and go inside. The desk is now in its place in the front of the room and the two chairs are arranged neatly facing it.

Jean is sitting at the desk. She looks up.

"Hi Marcus, Jim. Have a seat." She points to the chairs.

Shocked, the two men approach the desk, but remain standing. Marcus speaks first.

"Jean - where were you? We thought something had happened to you. We were about to launch a search."

"I'm fine. I was getting them settled. I just finished the paperwork to admit them."

"You admitted them?" Marcus is astonished.

"Of course. I think it's fairly obvious that they are both in need of help."

"How about the fact that maybe I might want to press charges on the guy who wacked me on the head and damn near killed me?"

"You can do that later. You're the one who left him in my care. That's a responsibility I take seriously."

Jim cuts in, "Well, I'm glad you're all right."

"I'm more than all right, Jim. You will never believe what they told me."

Jim feels excitement building in the pit of his stomach.

"Well, go ahead. What did you find out?"

"It's amazing what people will tell you when you're treating them kindly and they think you are on their side. They were more than willing to help in any way they could."

Actually, Jean is astonished herself. In her earlier life, she'd have been happy to call the cops and let them look after these guys - lock them up and probably never get them the help they need. Her new approach has yielded results that surprise even her.

"OK guys, here's what they told me."

Marcus can hardly contain himself. This case has taken them in so many different directions. He can't wait for Jean to speak.

"Come with me." Jean tells them. "Cindy and Mari need to hear this too."

They leave the room and Jean carefully closes and locks the door behind them. It's important that her paperwork not be disturbed or read.

They head down the corridor toward the front desk where Mari and Cindy still stand, their heads close together as if supporting each other. The colors that surround them swirl and vibrate together, Mari's beautiful bright light intermingling with Cindy's more muted tones. And surrounding both of them, another light - bright, beautiful, perfect in its crystalline clarity – "Ray," Jean says softly.

She turns to Marcus and asks, "When did he pass over?"

Marcus isn't surprised that she knows about Ray's death. He is curious, however. "How did you know?" he asks her.

Jean nods her head in the direction of the front desk where Cindy and Mari are quietly talking.

"Do you see what I'm seeing?" She asks the men.

They turn in the direction she's pointing and stare at the scene before them.

"Yes" Jim replies. "I see it now."

Marcus nods. He sees it too.

There is no doubt in any of their minds that Ray is here with them. And there's no doubt of his love for Cindy. They approach the front desk and draw closer into a circle of caring concern and love for Cindy and empathy with her for the loss she's suffered with Ray's physical passing. The light is for them too, and their compassion and concern causes it to become stronger and brighter until it fills every crack and corner of the room. The room itself and everything in it seems alive - vibrating and pulsing and loving.

Strength - and no fear - no fear anywhere. Nothing can harm them now.

Section 4: Answers
Chapter 71

In another part of town

The first thing you notice about her is how thin she is. Not the distracted, gangly kind of thin one sees on a mother or a working woman who has no time to look after herself. No, this thinness is what a person wears when they pare down their diet and spend enough time at the gym so they are sure to be in the best physical condition possible. This is the thinness of someone who plans to live forever.

If one word could define her, that word would be entitled. Always, she has been entitled. Entitled to her father's money, entitled to all the goodies of life, entitled to always have her own way. Entitled.

The crazy brother was never an obstacle to her. As a matter of fact, he's been a wonderful counterpoint to her own brightness. And brilliant she is. She has always been a star. She has always been first in everything. First in sports, first in academics, first in looks, first in schmoozing her father's clients, and first in her father's love. Life only gives.

Daddy was thrilled with her. Daddy gave her everything he had. Then he became sick and feeble. Daddy was of no use to her anymore. Daddy was a liability. Daddy's gone now.

You don't want to depend on her or be in her power. Those who are not useful, she disposes of with disdain. She owns it all, as she owns the furniture, the gardens, the houses she lives in.

In the beginning, the family belonged to her and did her bidding. Mother and father made sure of that. The idiot brother was no problem. She used him as a servant for as long as she could, and then he was quickly dispatched. After that, it only stood to reason that her father's company needed to be hers. And so it was. Next, the town needed to be hers. There was no problem buying her election to town council and then to mayor. Hell, everyone in town owed their livelihood to her. What next? What next?

Like the beautiful cobra lily, her prey has no chance once caught in the sticky tentacles of her narcissism. Slowly, surely, it's consumed.

Never filled for long, always demanding more, she moves on to her next project. This time it will be the governorship of the state. This is her greatest challenge to date.

To insure that her next victory will be complete, she needs to make sure that no one stands in her way. With great precision, she executes her plan. Step by step, she maneuvers the players in her drama. Like a chessboard, when someone moves one way, she's right on top of it, delighting in the challenge to her power and her intellect.

First, there's the little obstacle of her crazy brother and his peccadillos. She had thought he was safely out of her way when she placed him in the town's mental institution. He was close enough for her to keep her eye on him, yet out of her hair so she could pursue her ambitions.

And things were under control, or so she thought. All those people in town whose paycheck included an extra little something to keep their eyes open for any trouble were reporting back to her that all was smooth sailing. She was safe to pursue her dreams.

"Just make sure to keep a lid on things," she told all of them. "Nothing can happen until the election."

Then that nosy nurse threatened to unravel all her hopes.

"Get rid of her," she tells them. "I don't care how. Get rid of her or your lucrative careers are over."

Stupid, stupid people. Do they want the goose that's laying the golden eggs to fly away? Many are the rotten smells she's taken care of in this town with her money and her influence and her schmoozing. There probably isn't a jail big enough to hold all the people who have their hands out for her money. If she goes down, they all go down.

Let there be fear, let there be distrust, let there be hatred, let there be division. Her insatiable appetite can be fed by only one thing now – more power.

Chapter 72

Looking back, she realizes that she should have just gotten rid of her crazy brother instead of planting him in the hospital. She had thought that having a mentally ill brother that she was looking after might garner some sympathy for her, maybe even enough sympathy to put the vote count over the top in her favor some day.

Then, all hell broke loose when he had escaped and murdered that old lady. Fortunately for all of them, there had been a convenient scapegoat; they had found that girl with the body. And then she had looked after that asshole who helped him escape and things had been nice and quiet for awhile. Too bad he had floated to the surface of the river after all this time. Couldn't anyone do anything right around here, for God's sake?

Thank heavens for Ed, her darling newspaper editor, the one person she kept closest to her. He reminded her so much of Daddy. He was so wonderfully useful. She promised him everything. And he was just so smitten by her that he did everything she asked. Ed had been able to sway public opinion in town so that there was not the slightest bit of objection when the girl was locked away. Trial by media - wonderful thing - so long as you control the media.

Later, Ed had kept ambitious reporters away from the body in the river. If someone had been able to find out that the body belonged to one of the guys who had escaped just before the old lady was murdered, they just might start putting two and two together, might start asking questions.

That's why it was so important to get rid of the nurse. She and her friends were getting too close, too nosy. What was wrong with those damn cops? Couldn't they follow a simple order? What the hell was the point of murdering the male nurse and leaving alive the one that was giving them all the trouble? Why was she still around, anyway? Because she had kids? Who cared?

Sentiment does nothing except hold you back. This world rewards the unsentimental, the strong, those who do what needs to be done. There is no room for sentiment in her life and ambitions. And she will brook no sentiment in those who are supposed to be doing what they're told, who she is paying big money to do what they're told. Sentiment will sink them all!

Finally, tonight, they tell her - tonight for sure she will be gone, with her nurse friend and the kid too. Yeah, right. They haven't been able to get rid of them yet and it's cost her how many thousands?

If she could, she would just blow up that damn hospital with all of the nuts and their caretakers in it. Just get rid of it all. Wouldn't that cause quite a sensation around here!

Actually, that really isn't such a bad idea. After the initial shock wears off, after she has offered some of her own funds in memory of her beloved brother, of course, to help rebuild it somewhere outside of town, maybe even out of the state - well, won't she just be Miss Popularity.

Why not blow the whole damn thing up, idiot brother and all? Make a few phone calls. Cover her tracks well enough. Great ambitions require bold measures. They're not for sissies or fools who don't know how to get things done. That's it! Sometimes you need an explosion to clear the road ahead and plow forward. Terrible accidents happen all the time. And, with a bunch of crazy people living under one roof, it's surprising something disastrous hasn't happened before now. Who knows what they're capable of?

She picks up the phone.

Soon, very soon, she's going to sleep in the governor's mansion.

Now who is in need of a little financial assistance at the gas company? Who has secrets that they need to keep hidden?

Chapter 73

Mari raises her head and looks around, her green eyes shining bright in the early morning light. She feels evil descend like a grey shroud and begin to unfold. Its tentacles are reaching, reaching, drawing around the outside of the building, trying to work their way in. The morning mist rises up from the grounds and drips back to the earth, its steady pat. . pat . . pat distinct and ominous.

It's time. Those who deliberately harm others must take responsibility for their actions. Their world is inside out. They don't understand that they can't still the demons inside by becoming demons themselves. While harming others, they harm themselves, and what they fear becomes reality. Only with justice comes peace, both within and without.

She turns towards Jean and quietly addresses her.

"Tell us what you know. What did you learn from the two men?"

They listen intently as she tells them the story.Bradford, the man they had found in the basement, once belonged to a very wealthy family. His sister had been the apple of their parent's eye. As disappointed as they had been when their only son proved to be simple and unable to cope with life, they were thrilled when their beautiful, talented, brilliant daughter emerged as the family star. He had watched as, with their fawning permission, she manipulated them and everyone around them. Finally, she managed to gain control, not only of her parents, but of all the family assets, including the factories that keep everyone in this town working and affluent.

Then, their parents passed away under mysterious circumstances; at least Bradford thought the circumstances strange. His mother died in a car accident and his grief-stricken father began to depend more and more on the daughter he adored. Shortly thereafter, he too passed away. Their deaths were never questioned, since sister held all the strings that kept everyone in town working, and, after she'd planted some gossip that her brother might have had something to do with their father's death, there were no objections except his own when she had him committed. Indeed, most people thought it a good and generous thing she did to save him from harming anyone else, including himself.

The rest they knew - how he had escaped with the help of another inmate named Grant, how he had become afraid of Grant and tried to make his way back to the hospital, only to be badly beaten and taken to the basement, where he had lived ever since. Bradford was terrified. He was sure his sister was behind the beating and his life in the basement where he couldn't give her any trouble. He was fed by someone once a day and was told to use the bathroom on the first floor which was always empty. His job from then on was to guard the files and, if anyone ever came down to the basement, to tell the person who brought his food.

Jim asks her . . . . . "So, I take it that you think the sister may have somehow been behind what's happening here?"

"Of course she is. There's no question she's behind it. Not only that, I think that this place may hold more than one patient who shouldn't be here, who was in someone's way."

"Yeah, a dumping ground for unwanteds. Wouldn't be the first time that's happened."

"And Bradford's sister is . . . . . ?

"Bradford's last name is Custard."

"You're kidding!"

"Yes, his sister is Lillian Custard. Our lovely lady mayor. The one who might be running for governor next term."

"Oh, my God. Cindy can't believe what she's hearing.

"So that's what this is all about. She doesn't want anyone to find out that her brother could be implicated in a murder. That would be a hell of a lot harder for her to explain than a brother who's mentally incompetent and who she's kindly looking after. I can see why she would want to keep it secret. And she's the only one in this town who would have all the resources to make possible what happened to me and to Ray, and to anyone else who got in her way. I suspect that it was really convenient for her to pin the murder on Mari and just keep it under wraps that her brother had escaped and was involved."

Jim adds, "You know, I wouldn't be surprised if the body that Cindy found in the river was the guy who helped Bradford escape. We need to check into that. Looks like things are starting to come together."

Mari shivers just as a loud buzz - buzz - buzz from the front door interrupts their conversation. They look at each other questioningly. Jean walks over to the desk and releases the lock and lets their visitor in.

Chapter 74

The mayor smiles. It's time to head to the office. She'll be there before anyone else arrives for the day. She needs to be prepared for her appointments and ahead of schedule. This will be a big day. Before long, all hell should break loose and she will get a very upsetting call. She practices her response to the tragedy before the mirror. Just the right amount of grief, not overwhelming, but appropriate.

It will be a relief to finally get this problem resolved. It's been going on far too long and she's sick and tired of it, not to mention the effect it could have on all her hard work. She's not going backwards now, not for anyone, and especially not for some stupid mistake made by her idiot brother. He won't be in her way anymore, nor will any of the meddlesome people from that hospital. It won't be long now.

Isn't this just the way it always is - if she wants something done right, she's got to take control and do it herself. She tried to get the police to help - what bumbling idiots they turned out to be. Trying to scare the nurse away - how stupid. All they did was cost her more time and more money. The nurse got attached to the kid, and then nothing could stop her. Figures. Emotions always seem to make people do dumb things. The nurse risks her own life to help that kid; how very valiant of her. And how very, very stupid. Well, all the stupid people should be out of her hair pretty soon and, with any luck, she will be able to turn the tragedy into a PR bonus for herself and her ambitions - and aren't her ambitions the only things that matter?

Well, time to get to the office and make sure her schedule isn't too busy today. She'll have enough on her plate.

Chapter 75

The man who enters the hospital through the front door is nice, very friendly.

He wears a uniform and carries a small bag.

"I understand you've been having a bit of trouble with your hot water heater," he says politely.

Jean nods. "Yes, I noticed it was leaking when I was down there. We store our files in the basement so I don't want it to burst. Could you just let me know if it can be fixed or if we need a new one?

She looks over at Jim, who is standing beside the desk.

"Jim, could you please show this man to the hot water heater? It's over by the far wall on the right."

"Sure, Jean." He addresses the man, "Come with me, please."

Mari watches as the man follows Jim towards the elevator. There's a strange feeling attached to the man. It's not good. She turns to Jean and asks,

"Do you know him?"

"No, but when I was down in the basement I noticed a leak. I certainly don't want to lose those files down there. Who knows what they may contain. It's about time they sent someone to fix it."

"Who did you report it to?"

"I called Manning; he's the head maintenance guy."

"Is he one of the people we see cleaning and helping around here?"

"No, he just coordinates everything. I doubt you've seen him. He's got an office somewhere downtown. Why?"

"I don't really know why. I just have a strange feeling about this guy. I'm wondering if he's been here before."

"Well, I guess you know we trust your feelings completely, Mari. That makes me nervous. Marcus, why don't you go check that Jim is OK - and be careful."

Just then, the basement door opens and Jim reappears. Cindy realizes she's been holding her breath since Mari spoke. She breathes a sigh of relief.

"Hi, Jim. Everything OK down there?"

"Yeah, seems to be. It does feel a little odd to be down there after what we went through just a while ago, but everything seems all right now, except for that water heater. You're right, Jean. It's really leaking."

Jim is OK, but Mari can't shake the feeling that something is wrong. The man downstairs - she could feel his emptiness, the coldness around him. She silently slips away, opens the basement door, and starts quietly down the stairs.

She feels his presence, turns to sees him adjust something on the wall. He is nowhere near the furnace or the hot water heater. She silently watches him put his tools away and head hurriedly towards the stairs. He is not taking the elevator. She smells just a faint hint of gas. What has he done? As he passes her on the stairs, she feels again that strange, cold emptiness.

She calls up the stairs, "Jim, Marcus - stop him!"

But there's no need. He stops, smiles, and calmly speaks to them as he passes.

"That young lady who was with you just a few moments ago is downstairs calling you. Maybe you had better go see what she wants."

Then he walks over to the large front door, opens it and disappears into the darkness. Time to go collect his paycheck. His job here is done.

Chapter 76

Mari hears a commotion at the top of the stairs and looks up to find Marcus staring down at her.

"Mari, what are you doing down here?"

"That man - did you stop him?"

"No, he just left. Is something wrong?"

"He didn't come to fix the hot water heater. He turned on the gas. Can you shut it off?"

"I smell it." He turns to yell up the stairs. "Jean, do you know where the shut off is to the main gas valve?"

Jean arrives on the run with Cindy. "What're you talking about? What's wrong? Oh my God, I smell gas."

"The guy that was here just turned on the main gas valve. We've got to get the patients out before something happens. Quick, call the gas company - call 911."

Jim dials the operator, trying desperately to keep the panic out of his voice. He tells her, "We've got an emergency at 5461 Tillsboro Drive. A main gas valve is pouring gas into our basement and we don't know where it's located to shut it off."

"Isn't that the hospital?" she asks him.

"Yes, it is."

Immediately, she connects him to the gas company.

"We'll send someone. Get everyone out of the building."

He hangs up the phone. "We've got to get everyone out now."

Already, Cindy and Jean are sending patients outside, as far away from the building as possible. The men surrounding the building appear out of the darkness. Cindy shouts to them, "We've got a leaking gas pipe. We've got to get everyone out. Help us!"

Marcus is in the basement with a rag over his mouth looking for the gas line/valve. "This is impossible." He thinks, "I'll never be able to do this!" He feels himself start to panic.

Suddenly, strangely, someone is beside him; a warm, reassuring presence. *"I'm not alone,"* he thinks, suddenly calm. *"Someone is helping me."*

From deep in the darkest corner of the basement, he hears a hissing sound, like a snake ready to strike. He heads directly for it.

Meanwhile, parked along the side of the road, a truck sits idling, waiting for just the right moment.

"I'll feel it," he thinks. "I'll feel when just the right time is at hand. Let them run around for a little while and, just when they think they're safe, when they've discovered where the gas is coming from and have it shut off, then I'll strike. Nothing can stop me. There will be enough gas in that basement so that one small spark will blow the whole thing up. It will be beautiful! Just a few more minutes. He feels so powerful. I wonder if they realize just how short their time is on this earth. I wonder if they know that, no matter what they do, they can't stop it. I am the master!"

A pleasurable thrill runs through him. How he loves it all!

And how much more wonderful is this - he's getting paid for it.

"I guess this is how you feel when you do your heart's desire for a living." He smiles. "I guess this is what they mean when they say you should 'follow your bliss'."

Chapter 77

"We should be hearing sirens by now," Marcus thinks as he tears up the stairs to help get the patients outside and away from the building. "Where the hell are the sirens? We need all the help we can get."

He sees Jim. "I found the main valve and shut it off," he tells him. "But the basement is still full of gas. We've got to get these people out of here until the gas company arrives and gives us the all clear."

"At least it's shut off. Thank God for that." Jim is directing, as the orderlies try to get the dazed patients out the door. "Where the hell are the police and fire trucks? We need help here."

Marcus can see that his men are trying their best to help, but there's no place to take the patients. It's early and it's cold outside. Most of them are still in their pajamas. They're milling around on the other side of the parking lot, confused and dazed. Some of them are trying to head back inside. It could be hours before they will be able to return to their own rooms.

"I've got to grab some blankets for them," he tells Jim. Then he sees Cindy and Jane heading outside with armloads of blankets. "Where did you get those?" He yells. "I'll get some more."

"We should be OK now. We have enough," Cindy tells him. "We're just going to need these until help arrives."

But no help arrives.

They wait. Ten, fifteen, twenty minutes. Still no one arrives to help them.

"What the hell is going on here?"

Chapter 78

Where's the noise? Where's the pandemonium? Where's the confusion?

On the other side of town, the name-brand side, she waits.

"That's strange. Surely I should have heard some kind of an explosion by this time. He said the whole town should hear it."

An ominous feeling begins to creep up her spine.

"Suppose something went wrong."

She tries to dismiss the thought.

"What could possibly go wrong?" How could fate fail her in this most important venture of her life?

But her pulse races and bile starts to rise from her stomach and into her throat. This is ridiculous. She can't stand this waiting. Where's the explosion?

Then she hears it! Not the thunderous bang that she had been expecting, but something more like a *whoosh* - and a crack - kind of like lightning - along with a great gust of wind.

Soon, very soon, her phone should start ringing.

She takes a deep breath.

She's ready.

Five, ten minutes go by - then fifteen. Where are they? Where's the call? She is the mayor. She should be called first. Why is her assistant not on the line calling to find out what happened? What she should do? What their response should be? Maybe she's still on her way to work; she's not usually in before nine. She should be here by now. Where's Ed? Why is he not calling her for her reaction to the disaster? She can't call. No one can know that she knows what happened. Was it really the hospital blowing up that she heard? Did she just expect it; want it, so much that she thought that's what she heard? She starts to sweat. How well did she know the man that she sent out to do the job? He should have been one of the best. She had done her research. She had promised him that he would never have to work again if he would take care of this problem for her. It was perfectly safe. She had made sure the cops didn't hassle him just in case something went wrong. He seemed so happy and grateful, a kindred soul. He got what he wanted when he gave her what she wanted. Then he would call her to get the money wired into his account and she'd never see him again.

Finally, the phone rings. It's not what she was expecting.

Her assistant tells her that she will be late for work since there's a traffic jam on Tillsboro Drive and she's stuck in the middle of it.

Calmly, she asks, "Is anything wrong?"

"Something at the hospital. I'm sure they will have it cleared up soon. I shouldn't be too long."

"Did you say there's a problem at the hospital?"

"Yes, it's something at the hospital, I think. I can't see what's going on."

"Well, if you see anything, call me and let me know. I hope everything is all right there."

"I don't think there's any need to worry. It seems to be clearing up now. I should be in shortly."

She hangs up. She has to find out what's going on.

She calls Ed at the newspaper; he's always in early.

"Hi, listen, Lucille just called. She's on her way in to work and is stuck in a traffic jam on Tillsboro Drive, just outside the hospital. Anything going on there that you've heard?"

"Nothing that I've heard of. I'll check into it and keep you posted, though."

"OK. Thanks Ed. Call me as soon as you hear anything. You know how I worry about that place, what with Bradford being in there and all."

Ed knows for a fact that she doesn't give a tinker's damn about Bradford. All she wants is to make sure he doesn't make any waves for her on her trip to the governor's mansion. But Ed doesn't care. He's going to the mansion with her.

Chapter 79

Back at the hospital, Jean breathes a sigh of relief. Looks like everyone is safely out and away from the building. The patients and staff, as well as the men who had been guarding them, are calm. Everyone is patiently waiting for the gas company to arrive and give the all clear for them to go back inside and continue their day's routine.

Where the heck is the gas company, anyway? Many of the patients haven't had their medications or their breakfast.

Despite that, no one is complaining. They actually seem to be enjoying the excitement - a little break in the day's schedule. Everyone is warm and comfy in the blankets that Cindy and Jean and the orderlies managed to get out of the building before they evacuated. They sit on the ground, quietly talking.

"Wow," thinks Jean. "This is good. Everyone is cooperating. Maybe we can even learn something from all this. The fresh air seems to have a nice effect on everyone. This is great."

Jim is busy talking to people and organizing things. Finally, he gets back to Jean and gives her an update.

"Marcus was able to shut off the gas, but it needs to be cleared before you can go back inside. I've been in touch with my supervisors and had them call the gas company to see what's holding them up. They're on their way now. Apparently, after we spoke to them, someone called and told them that there was no problem at the hospital, it had been a prank. The call came from the Tillsboro police station, so they thought it had to be legitimate."

"They know where it came from already?"

"Yes. They have a setup where they know who's calling in case of an emergency. A lot of times, people are so panicked that they forget to leave their address, so they're able to quickly track them down through their phone number. This one came from the police station. They are sure of it. That's the only way they would disregard our call."

"That seems odd." Jean is puzzled. "Why on earth would someone from the police station call the gas company and tell them to disregard our call?"

"You might also be interested to know that my men picked up a guy in a van who had parked down the road a bit, just a few hundred yards from here. He had a remote device with him for detonating explosives. There's probably something in your basement that he was going to set off. It wouldn't take much. One spark and you guys would have been toast."

Jean's puzzled look quickly dissolves into one of horror.

"And it would have looked like an accident. They could have blamed it on a gas leak."

"That's right. Although I don't know how they would have explained the call from the police station telling the gas company to stay away. My guess is that someone didn't coordinate things well enough. They thought that you wouldn't have time to call and, when you did, they panicked."

"How the heck would anyone know we called?"

"No doubt your phone lines are being monitored. You and this hospital are a huge threat to someone - someone with a lot of power and money in this town - lots of money - to pay for whatever they want. And I think we all know who that is now."

"This is unbelievable! They would actually blow us up?"

"They couldn't care less about you guys. You're in their way. That's all that matters."

"Jim, you really think Lillian Custard is behind all this? It's hard to believe . . . "

"Think about it Jean. Who controls everything in this town? Who would have the resources and the motive to make this much trouble for you?"

He is interrupted by the rumble of a large truck coming up the drive. It stops in front of the building and two men get out. Jim quickly checks to make sure that they actually are from the gas company. Then he heads inside with them.

Jean approaches Marcus.

"Marcus, please fill me in. What's going on?"

He speaks to her while keeping a careful eye on the comings and goings.

"Well, Jean, the reason my men and I are here in the first place is because of rumblings that have been going on for a long time. This town is dirty - at least the people who are running it are. There have been some pretty serious allegations of bribery, fraud, etc. – so, with the election coming up and all, we were sent here to find out exactly what was true and what wasn't."

"Who sent you?"

Marcus ignores her question, but continues on with his explanation.

"Jim was transferred to this police department a couple of months ago to try and get a grip on what's happening. He couldn't find much until Cindy's visit opened things up for him. That's when he realized that someone had something really important to cover up - and it all seemed to revolve around the hospital. When he started digging, he also found out that you can pretty much do or have whatever you want around here as long as you're on the mayor's good side. She owns all the major businesses. She's a powerful person in this town, but she wants more. She's running for governor in the next election. That's why we think she orchestrated all the nasty stuff that's been going on here."

"Why on earth would she want to get rid of all of us?"

"I think she's always been neurotic about someone finding out that her brother and his friend murdered Mari's grandmother. She just couldn't risk a trial and someone digging up any dirt on her, because there's a lot of it. And once she decided to cover that up, well - things just went from bad to worse. All it took was a little payoff each month for someone to keep her brother hidden, until Cindy started digging. That made her nervous and she decided she needed to get Cindy out of the way. Then – well, you know the rest . . . . . you lived it."

"When everyone she had hired to solve the problem didn't seem to be able to do the job - let me tell you, you guys aren't easy to scare - getting rid of all of you just seemed like a good idea. One big boom. She really doesn't care who she blows up. If you are in her way, you're going to get it. Besides, she could make gravy off the fact that this building blew up with her brother inside it. The sympathy vote might even mean the difference between her winning the governorship or not. It's kind of tight in the polls, so I hear."

"She would murder all of us for some votes? That's hard to believe."

"People have started wars for the same reason, Jean. Never dismiss the depravity of the human mind when someone feels entitled."

"How are you going to prove it's her? She employs practically everybody in this town. It's going to be a mess."

"Oh, not so much. There's no question of proving. The guy we found in the van on the road outside the hospital is singing like a canary. And just in case that's not enough, we've got that telephone call from the police station to the gas company. Whoever did that will crack when we get through with him. She will fight us with everything she's got, of course, but we're good. We've got enough to put her away."

"God, I hope so, Marcus. It will be good to feel safe again."

Marcus looks over at Mari.

"You were always safe, Jean," he tells her softly.

They see the men from the gas company exit the building with Jim. He walks them to their van and comes over to talk to them.

"You can take everyone back inside now," he tells Jean.

"Marcus, you and I have some work to do downtown. It's my understanding that our people are at the station now going over some files. There were only a few men on duty this morning when the call went in to the gas company, and they were more than happy to point fingers at each other. Everyone is denying everything and the place is in chaos. We've got quite a mess to clean up."

"Let's not forget that Ray was beaten to death by some guys who claimed to be policemen."

"Yes, I'm sure Cindy and Jean can identify them."

"And what about the cause of all this mess? What will happen to her?"

"Let's go. We're seeing a judge from out of town right now. Then we'll pay her a visit."

* * * *

The patients and their caretakers slowly climb the front stairs and head in through the large front doors. Cindy and Jean linger outside a bit with Mari. The two nurses turn towards her, and she tells them

"You go on ahead. I need to stay out here a bit longer."

Cindy takes Jean's arm. "And we need to look after things inside," she tells her.

Mari watches as they head back into the hospital. Before they enter, they once more turn towards her. She smiles.

"I'll be fine," she tells them.

* * * *

Mari feels the moist, brown earth under her feet, the cool morning mist on her skin, the first golden rays of the sun on her face. Once again, the earth dances for her, sings the praises and joy of being alive.

She looks over at the building. A warm glow fills the cracks and corners, and lights up the windows and doorways with the promise of love, kindness and caring concern for those inside.

This is why she came here. And this is why she came back.

Mari smiles and the earth feels her delight and smiles with her.

* * * *

Printed in the United States
142655LV00005B/26/P